A Bridge to Die On

Fayla Ott

Heritage House Publishing

To my husband and boys

You are the bridge God built beneath me when I
couldn't see the other side.
Thank you for steadying my steps and walking
with me, always.

When you pass through
the waters, I will be
with you; and through
the rivers, they shall
not overflow you: when
thou walkest through
the fire, thou shalt not
be burned; neither shall
the flame kindle upon
thee. [Isaiah 43:2, KJV]

Prologue

1878, Twenty miles north of Meridian, MS.

*S*tuckey *listened to the ramblings of the stranger who'd invited him to join him for supper and a spot for his bedroll near the warm fire, while the darkness perched on his shoulders, willing him to revisit the familiar deed he craved. But he'd vowed to start a moral path. There must be a reason he escaped justice when the rest of the Dalton gang fell into the hands of justice. It seemed God had spared him with another chance, even though he hadn't given much thought to a higher being serving any purpose in his life. He figured it wouldn't be too difficult a task to settle into a dignified occupation that didn't involve crime. Maybe he'd marry and start a family. The idea introduced the foreign concept of moral stability to his mind, which had embraced anything but. He shivered against the cold truth that this might not be as easy as he thought.*

"*The wind is slow tonight, but she cuts a fierce blow through the breeches all the same. Hot coffee takes the sting out, especially if you add a bit of assistance—if you know what I mean.*" The stranger winked, showing him a flask of whiskey before adding it to his tin cup. He took the coffee but declined the whiskey. He never cared for the way it dulled his senses, though he was happy the man drank it—his slurred words thickening with every sip. Soon, this fool would pass out, granting him both peace and quiet. It was the perfect chance to take everything he had, including that property deed he'd so readily boasted about moments ago. No, he couldn't. But the temptation clung to him, thick as the night air. Here sat an easy victim and his spoils, his for the taking if he dared to fall just once more.

"*Ne'er caught your name there,*" the stranger said, his eyelids drooping, matching the pace of his speech.

"I didn't give it." He didn't look up from his coffee but watched the black liquid swirl amidst the glowing reflection from the orange embers of fire.

The fool laughed, swaying as he brought the tin cup back to his lips. "*Fair enough. Ain't no need for introductions—whiskey don't need no names, and neither do we.*"

The stranger continued his ramblings. At least with the drunken slur, the dull speech became more tolerable. "*Been called Red since I was a boy. Ma and Pa died of diphtheria—God rest their souls—and my only brother died in the war. Friends, too. Never married. Didn't have much to my name, but then my cousin up and left me his place on the Chunky River. Won it in a card game, never even used it. Luckiest man alive—until he wasn't. Lost a load of cash in a bad hand right before he got himself shot trying to win it back. I hadn't seen him in years, but I suppose you don't forget your kin. Yes siree, it was a surprise getting that letter.*"

Never even heard of no Chunky River, but here I am on account of him. Shame, really, since he was my only kin left, I reckon. But I suppose it gave me a fresh start. Of all places, though—out in the middle of nowhere in Mississippi. Still, I hear tell Meridian's an upcoming town these days. Never been to the area, have you?"

The fire crackled low, embers pulsing like the dying heartbeat of a thing already condemned. He tightened his grip on the tin cup, but the warmth could not settle the chill stirring beneath his skin. This was hunger—not the kind that gnawed at the belly, but the kind that whispered in the marrow, in the place where violence lived. It had been too long since he last felt it. Too long since he had let the hunger win. One last time. One last kill. After all, this man had no one to care if he lived or died. It would also give him a way to start over. No one in Meridian knew what Red looked like, so it'd be so easy to assume a new identity. He'd use the man's real name on his property deed, though. Red wouldn't do for his image. The more he thought about it, the more excited his senses grew, and begged him to satiate his cravings. He'd better do it before Red passed out drunk, or he'd miss the light leaving the man's pupils, and if this had to be the last time, he wanted to savor each minute. Each glorious second.

It had to be the last time.

Stuckey reached inside his duster jacket and pulled his pistol from its holster. Pausing, he turned it over in his hands, his finger hovering over the trigger.

"Need to clean that gun, Mister? I got some bear grease in the wagon, and we can heat some wa—Ahhh!" Red fell to the ground, clutching his right arm as blood spewed from his shoulder. Eyes wide, he tried to rise, but screamed again as another bullet ripped his other shoulder.

"What are you doing to me?" Red crawled on his back, using his legs to thrust him away from the fire. His wails hushed the crickets, which only served to heighten the sensation of power in the act. Nature had to take notice.

He closed his eyes and breathed in the scent of gunfire and blood, preferring the man's wails to his endless chatter. He walked over to his victim, staring down into Red's terror-filled eyes.

"There's just something about a man's behavior just as he knows he's about to die. Only moments ago, you laughed in your drunken state, but it only covered your desperation and misery. No one ever appreciates the service I offer, allowing them to let it out once and for all, so they can finally acknowledge what they've been denying all along. Go on, scream. You now have an excuse to wail." He fired again, watching his victim crumple over his leg as it spilled red life onto the dirt in a trail that flowed toward the fire in a slow trickle, like ants marching to their purpose.

"Stop! I'll do anything! Take my horse and wagon. My satchel, too." The man's face wrinkled in fear and anguish as he lifted his hands to shield himself from more danger, but the gun fired again, hitting the other leg, and Red's breath labored as he spoke through his pain. "Why? Why would you do this to me? You don't even know me."

Stuckey adjusted his hat on his head, then ran his thumb along the velvet front of the wide brim. "See, that's the difference between me and other killers. Their motives are much simpler than mine. Fear, revenge, power, and greed—all simple motives for simple men. I could give you a motive, but you aren't likely to comprehend it."

"Please. Just tell me why."

Red's raspy voice thrilled him, and he smiled as he bent down next to the bloody ground, pressing the pistol against the man's forehead. Despite the life already draining out of him, his eyes bulged in fear.

"You're just like all the others—thinking if you only knew why this was happening, it'd somehow make it less painful."

"Just tell me why. Why do you want to kill me?"

He sighed, as if the question was a burden. Then he smiled—because it wasn't. He leaned in, his breath warm against the man's ear.

"Because I crave it. Because I need it. And because I like it."

Stuckey brought his gun up, but hesitated, then slid it back into its holster. His knife was better. It was intimate. Personal. He had always favored the knife. It gave him time to linger in the moment, to feel the pulse of life struggle beneath his blade.

In one quick motion, he retrieved his weapon of choice. The knife slid deep. Red jolted, his body shuddering against the blade, his eyes wide—frozen in shock, then in the stillness of death.

The crickets resumed their song, a fitting encore to his performance. He welcomed their applause, settling back by the fire. The coffee was nearly cold, but he drained it anyway, staring into Stuckey's vacant gaze.

He never forgot the eyes. Or the smell of red blood. Red's blood.

Funny how the victim's nickname suited his death.

He smiled. His own name suited him, too, since he preferred the knife. But no one else would call him Stuckey.

No one alive, anyway.

The large demon, Sonnellion, crossed his arms and smiled with wicked delight. "You'll stay with him, Belias. Remind him what this feels like and make it impossible for him to live out his moral intentions. Stupid man. He thinks God spared him, but it was us who rescued him. He owes Beelzebub for snatching him from the clutches of justice, and we're going to make him pay his dues."

Belias nearly snickered, his excitement fueled by a lust for authority, especially when the others glared at him. After being cast aside for so long, this mission belonged to him. He couldn't believe it, but he'd make sure he didn't fail.

What about me?" Verrier snarled, his envy spewing from his mouth, his breaths ragged with rage at being overlooked. He sneered, eyes flashing with malice as he turned toward Belias. "I'm twice the demon you are, yet here you are, licking at Sonnellion's feet like some obedient whelp. What makes you worthy of this mission? I've broken more souls in a week than you have in a century. No wonder Sonnellion keeps you on a leash."

Carreau joined in the protests, just as Belias lunged at Verrier, but Sonnellion blocked his attack with a sharp flick of his clawed hand.

"It's always you three, isn't it?" Sonnellion said, exhaling in frustration. "While I certainly enjoy the competition, I can't tolerate the bickering right now. After these pathetic humans fought their civil war, I hoped their defeat might destroy any faith they still held onto, but we see that didn't happen. More churches are being built, and a surge of Christianity is spreading the disease even more." He spat on the ground as if ridding himself of the foul idea.

Verrier straightened, still fuming. "Then why not take advantage of our strength here? Why send Belias while we—"

"Because your time is better spent elsewhere," Sonnellion interrupted, his voice as cold as the abyss. "You and Carreau have other matters to tend to. There are other strongholds in danger of falling to the enemy, and I won't risk losing ground to those wretched light warriors. You are needed elsewhere—go, before I question your usefulness."

Carreau sneered, but he knew better than to challenge the order. Verrier cast Belias a final look of hatred before he and Carreau disappeared into the shadows. The smaller demons lagged, hoping to gain a spot in Sonnellion's favored army.

Sonnellion exhaled and turned back to Belias. "Now, let's focus on the mission at hand."

"What does this murderer have to do with the church?"

"Belias, surely by now you know the answer to that question."

"He will bring fear and death."

Sonnellion waved a large, clawed talon in a flippant turn that matched his eyeroll. "Of course, he'll bring fear and death, but tell me why that matters."

Belias straightened, hoping to answer correctly. "Because fear and death distract the church."

"Exactly." Sonnellion slapped Belias on the back, forcing the smaller demon onto the ground next to the dead man, while the smaller demons laughed. He didn't dare frown at the humiliation. No matter how much he hated getting shoved down in front of the other demons, he knew they hated his superiority in this mission even more. He wanted to ask Sonnellion if another promotion lay in wake of success, but he learned long ago to let Sonnellion deliver rank at his discretion.

"I'll leave you to it, Belias. Summon your devils and assign their tasks at your command. And Belias?"

"Yes, Sonnellion."

"Don't fail." Sonnellion's breath swirled in front of Belias in a sulfuric smoke that singed his mouth.

He swallowed hard at the order, the threat behind it clear. No matter what, he couldn't fail this mission. Not if he wanted to avoid torture much like the dead man endured moments ago. No, worse. Demons couldn't die, so torture could be eternal if Beelzebub or Sonnellion decided that's how long they wanted it to be.

No, this man would kill again, and Belias would make sure of it.

———

Uriel crouched low on a tree branch, undetected by the demons, and wept at the sight of the fallen man. But he wept more at the destruction to come at the other man's hand, if Lucifer's plan unfolded as intended. The murderer's new moral compass had failed at the campsite because it wasn't rooted in repentance but in a different ambition with the same ego. His addiction to blood easily overpowered his false sense of morality.

He froze when Sonnellion turned in his direction, knowing that a lone angel might struggle to fight the group of demons—especially these stronger warriors as they banded together around the spirit and strength of the man's willful evil. He gripped his sword, ready to fight if he had to, but relaxed when Sonnellion turned his focus back to the demons under his charge, who squabbled over the mission again. Uriel released a heavy, quiet sigh, retreating into the shadows, waiting until Sonnellion left Belias with the murderer. The lone demon observed his new servant and whispered into the man's ear. Uriel flinched as the man stared at his latest victim and smiled.

It might be his latest victim, but it wouldn't be his last.

He'd seen smiles like that before, and smiles like that preceded death and deep sadness. There was only one way to fight such evil.

Uriel launched into the sky, eager to be free from the stench of sin and death, but also to gather others who could help him fight it. He'd need a team of light warriors for this one. And he'd need a team of prayer warriors, too. He just hoped they could find them in the town of Meridian, Mississippi.

A Welcomed Stranger

Stuckey, Early Autumn, 1878

He just might like this new town. Meridian pulsed with activity, its streets surging with merchants calling their wares, horses kicking up dust as their hooves thudded against the packed earth, and the ceaseless churn of progress. Newcomers poured into the hotels before staking their claims and building their homes. He sent a thanks to the poor ole sucker he killed to get the established little property on the river, with a cabin, well, outhouse, and barn already built on a swell above the riverbank. While modest, it included the proper amenities, and he could be comfortable living near Meridian, along the riverbank not far from town. He walked through the grass outside the cabin, listening to the sounds of solitude. The river below murmured in the evening air, swollen from recent rains, carrying with it the scent of damp earth and decay. Whoever built the structures on the property wisely chose the top of the slope for the foundations. If the water ever crested, it would take a deluge to reach his doorstep or his livestock. Who would ever think of looking for a member of the Dalton gang in the middle of Mississippi? And with so many transient people coming and going, he could blend in without stirring curiosity or too many questions. He'd learned over the years that people liked things to make sense. A man like him? He'd never make sense to them. So, he'd get them to trust him on their terms, even if it meant pretending. He hated pretending.

He pulled the property deed from his pocket and looked at the first and last name written in legal terms. He spoke the name aloud, slow and deliberate, letting it settle on his tongue. Over and over, until it felt natural. Until it belonged to him.

He imagined the faces of his old gang and laughed. They would never believe it. They had always thought he was the wild one, the unpredictable one. The one who took things too far. But he was the one still standing, wasn't he? The rope would take them soon enough. They'd swing in the wind, and he'd be here, warm and comfortable in his new home.

"Who's crazy now?" His laughter filled the empty house, bouncing off the walls. He kicked open the trunk the previous owner left behind, digging through its contents. A few moth-eaten shirts, a pair of boots with a worn sole. Useless. But that was fine. He knew how to get what he needed. And he would.

Dragging a chair closer to the fire, he stretched out, staring into the dancing flames. A gentleman. That's what they'd see. A well-dressed, respectable man—maybe even a businessman with a trade, someone who earned his place among them. He'd tip his hat, shake hands, flash that easy smile. They'd never suspect the truth.

Never suspect what he was.

What he would always be.

But first—he needed money. He could steal what he wanted. After all, the Dalton gang had taught him well. But theft never truly satisfied him. Stealing made a man weak. It forced him into shadows, made him hide, scurry like a rat with stolen crumbs. That wasn't him. That had never been him.

Hiding his identity, masking his nature—it irked something deep in him. The bold spirit within him screamed for position, for recognition. For power.

His gaze flicked back to the trunk, the flickering firelight casting jagged shadows across its lid. He'd passed a lone traveler along the river earlier, no more than a few miles from here. No one would miss him.

One more victim. One last kill.

After all, a fresh start requires more than a new home. It required capital. Travelers carried cash. Travelers disappeared all the time.

Stealing was necessary.

Killing was the reward.

Just one more time. That's all.

———

Catherine Porter stepped into White's General Store, hoping to find white sugar. She really wanted to bake a pie for Sunday after church, but the store hadn't had sugar in days.

"Miss Porter, how can I help you today?" Mr. White stood behind the counter, his crisp white apron tied neatly around his waist, a white hat pulled low over his pale forehead. He was rolling out a fine, white fabric, his pasty fingers smoothing it with precision, as if wrinkles were an offense he wouldn't tolerate.

The irony wasn't lost on her. Mr. White with all the white things. She worked hard to suppress a giggle as she asked, "Do you have any white sugar?"

The words had barely left her lips before the absurdity struck her. Mr. White. White sugar. The apron, the hat, the fabric. The thought tumbled out in a laugh before she could stop it.

His hand stilled. A single blink. Then, ever so carefully, he lifted a brow. "Would you like to share what's humorous, Miss Porter?"

Her mirth shrank under his gaze. "No, Mr. White. I'm just being silly."

She forced her mouth into a straight line. No, he probably wouldn't find it funny at all.

"We just got sugar in yesterday." Mr. White untied the cloth cover from the barrel and scooped the sugar with careful precision. He leveled it off with a steady hand, not a grain out of place, before pouring it into a crisp paper sack and folding the top into neat, symmetrical creases. "Anything else? If you need flour, you'll have to wait. We just can't seem to keep flour and sugar in stock these days. Getting lots of new settlers in the area. Hard to believe I've been here only two months, but I'm no longer a newcomer, thanks to all the newcomers pouring in every week. The railroad sure has caused a boom for this town."

"I noticed that. It's good to have a bustling community, though, don't you think? My pa says the south needs all the help it can get since the war tore our part of the country apart. We ought to be grateful the railroad is doing so much to boost our failed economy."

"Indeed, although the war is long past, and some might say its impact is overstated," Mr. White said, his eyes piercing hers with a steady gaze.

"I wouldn't say that, Mr. White. The war left a mark that hasn't yet faded from the south's memory."

"Well, it's been over a decade, so I propose we move ahead. Oh, that new man Sanderson is heading over here. Believe his first name is ...let's see...Matthew. That's right. Goes by Matt. Matt Sanderson. Interesting fellow." Mr. White stared behind her. She turned around and saw a handsome man coming through the storefront door. He immediately assessed her figure with his eyes, as men typically did. Funny, but she didn't feel repulsed by it this time.

"Mr. Sanderson, this is Miss Catherine Porter. Miss Porter, this is Mr. Matthew Sanderson."

"It's Matt. You can call me Matt, ma'am." He tipped his hat to her, flashing a bright smile.

She couldn't help but notice how his brown hair and brown eyes complemented his tan face. "It's a pleasure, I'm sure, Mr. Sand...uh...Matt, and you should come meet my father. He's at the livery. Our horse threw his shoe on the way to town."

"Yes, Mr. Porter runs the post office," Mr. White said. "Thanks to him, I can send out orders quickly and receive shipments from my suppliers without delay. He keeps everything in order, which is more than I can say for some postmasters. And his lovely daughter Catherine here is now a frequent customer, too, so it's a nice setup for me, I suppose."

Matt glanced at Mr. White, but ignored his statement and looked down at her again. "Why don't you let me purchase my dry goods here, then I'll escort you over to your father at the livery?"

She blushed. "That would be kind. Thank you."

Mr. Sanderson purchased a shovel and some coffee before taking her arm with his free hand. As they walked over to the livery across the street, Catherine stopped, then gasped. "Why, Mr. Sanderson, you're bleeding!"

He looked down at the bloodstains visible on his pants leg. "Blast!" At her gasp, he looked up and appeared sheepish. "I'm sorry, ma'am. Forgive my slip of the tongue. I'd hate to offend a lady like you. Please accept my sincere apologies."

She peered at his leg, frowning. "Yes, that's fine, but Mr. Sa-Matt, what on earth did you do to yourself? Do you need to see Dr. Vaughn?"

"Oh, no need. I'm afraid my dressings came off sometime during my walk here. I've been cutting some wood for a project on my land, and I must admit I acted without caution, so the saw blade nicked the front of my leg. It'll heal nicely, though, since I already applied a poultice."

"Well, alright, if you're sure." He put his hand on the small of her back when they crossed the street.

Horses pulling wagons clomped on the dusty road, while chatter, shouts, and whistles sounded all around the vicinity. Shoes on the sidewalks echoed louder than the horses in the streets, and she bristled at the noise.

"Not a city girl, eh?" He spoke at her side, and she flushed under his watchful gaze.

"I wouldn't say that, exactly. I just prefer calmer streets, although I'm glad for the bustling activity. It's good for Meridian to have so much commerce added to the area."

"Oh, I agree, but I'm not sure you did a moment ago."

"Don't be silly; I couldn't be more thrilled for our town."

His expression changed, but then he smiled. "Maybe you are, at that."

"What about you, Matt? Do you like busy towns?"

"I like towns with interesting people, busy or not, and I find this one isn't lacking." They reached the planked sidewalk, and he turned her to face him, with his hands on the sides of her arms. "Before I meet your father, might I know if you're courting anyone?"

Heat flooded her face, and she wished she hadn't left her fan at home. "Why, no, not at the moment, but..."

"Forgive me, Catherine, I know it's too soon, but can you do me a favor?"

"A favor?" She squinted, wondering what this handsome man might propose, and hoping he wouldn't be inappropriate. She found him almost irresistible, and it'd be a shame if she couldn't get to know him better, under the appropriate measures, of course, despite the inappropriate ways he looked at her since he'd met her in White's store.

"I'd like to ask that you not court anyone else."

At her shocked expression, he held up a hand and continued, "I know, it's quite forward of me, especially since I only met you moments ago, but I'd like time to get acquainted with you and your father, and when enough time has passed, I'd like to ask him to court you, if you're willing."

She tried to still her thumping heart because she wondered if he could hear it inside her chest, pounding as if it wanted to jump out. "I think that's an acceptable proposition, granted my father is okay with it."

"Okay with what?" Her pa, tall and broad-shouldered, with gray appearing at his temples, appeared before them, eyeing her new friend with interest and a measure of suspicion. His guarded assessment didn't surprise his daughter, who often tolerated his protectiveness since she knew the motive behind it.

"Pa, I'd like you to meet Mr. Matthew Sanderson. He's new in town, and he walked me over from Mr. White's store."

Matt stuck out his hand. "It's Matt, sir. Nice to meet you. How's your horse's hoof?"

Her pa shook Matt's hand and visibly relaxed. If a man cared for horses, her pa considered them a decent human being, even if his interest in his daughter might not be welcomed yet.

"She'll be fine. Blythe is fixing her up now, so she'll be good as new. What do you do for your livelihood, Matt?"

"I'm not sure yet, but I'm just settling in, so I'll get my bearings soon enough. Thinking about hunting and selling some game, maybe. Are there any merchants who need fresh game? Fish, deer, rabbit, maybe some frogs for frog legs and such?"

Catherine grimaced but the two men didn't notice. How could anyone eat frog legs? She'd tried them once as a child, and the idea of what sat on her plate churned her gut, so she didn't even take a bite. Years later, she tried them again, since her pa cooked them, and she figured she should see why so many considered them a delicacy of sorts, but once she did take a bite she proceeded to vomit right after swallowing.

"You might check with a few folks, but your best option is to set up shop yourself and get the word out."

"I thought about that, but I'm not sure I want a storefront just yet."

"Don't need one. Just hang your hat where folks can see it, or even know about it, and you'll get business soon enough. Treat people fair around here, and you'll be alright. Are you a good hunter or fisherman?"

"I'm good enough."

Her pa nodded in satisfaction. "Wouldn't work otherwise. You'll need to supply the demand, and with so many moving into the area right now, you'll have plenty of demand soon enough. Some folks ain't got time to hunt or fish, since most are working with the railroad or a business. Some stores do sell wild game, but it's not regular, and they often run out. I hear tell there's a gent opening a restaurant, so you might want to check with him, too. Name's Crane, and he's staying at the hotel with his wife and children."

"Looks like I got a possibility, then, don't I? I'd better see to my settling, since I still have much to do. It's nice to meet you, sir."

Her pa and Matt shook hands, and then he turned to her, tipping his hat. His eyes seemed to say something just for her, and for a moment, it frightened her, until he smiled and the corners of his eyes crinkled and his brown pupils dilated. She smiled back, allowing him to take her hand and kiss the top. Shivers crawled up her arm from his lips and she dropped her gaze in shyness as her pa watched. No one had ever kissed her hand before. She wouldn't have let them try, anyway, so why now? When Matt walked away from them, her pa didn't speak but looked at her with amusement shining in his eyes.

"What is it, Pa?"

"You've never let anyone kiss the top of your hand before, Cat."

When he used her nickname, she knew he teased her. "Pa, it's just a polite gesture of manners, and most men around here wouldn't know such manners if God smacked 'em in the face with them."

"Catherine..."

"Oh, alright, I admit he fascinates me, and maybe some of these men have manners, but..."

"But?"

"It didn't mean anything. I'm just being polite to the newcomer."

"You know what I think, Cat?"

"You're going to tell me anyway, aren't you, Pa?"

"Yes, I am. I think you're like my mare in there. You keep throwing a shoe when you need it most."

"Pa, you're not making any sense."

"What about Zeke?"

"What about him?"

"I know he'd kiss your hand if you'd let him."

"I hardly know him, Pa."

"Didn't you just meet Mr. Sanderson?"

She huffed. "It's not the same thing."

"Why not?"

"Because Zeke is odd. He's only been here three weeks, and he acts like he owns the town, strutting around like a king looking for his throne."

"There's nothing wrong with a bit of confidence, Catherine."

"A bit?"

"Like I said, throwing shoes. You like Zeke, maybe more than you admire Matt, but you're not ready to admit it just yet, are you? Yep, throwing shoes."

"If you weren't my pa, I'd throw a shoe at you." She picked up the bottom of her afternoon dress, where the skirt almost caught the bottom of her heels, and huffed as she stomped ahead of him, his laughter following her down the planked sidewalk.

An Unexpected Visitor

Reese, Present Day, Lauderdale County, MS.

Reese Hayden slammed the framed photo onto the hardwood floor, satisfaction curling through her chest as the glass shattered. The photo slipped free, revealing the glossy lie of his smile—the one she had believed for too many years. In that frozen moment, with his arm slung around her, the betrayal had already begun.

She ground her heel against the frame, glass crunching beneath her weight, distorting the perfect couple they had once pretended to be.

"That felt good," she murmured to the empty house.

Silence. It would take time to adjust to that.

Her new home, left to her by her uncle, wasn't anything special—outdated, in need of repairs—but it was hers. Not Dylan's. And for that reason alone, she loved it.

Her ex-husband was hours away now, in Springfield, Missouri. With her. Reese had needed a clean break, far from the home they once shared, where she had spent too many nights crying into a pillow, knowing he was just a few blocks over in another woman's bed. At least here, she wouldn't run the risk of seeing them together. Once had been enough.

She picked up another frame—her wedding photo—and lined it up next to the broken one. This time, she used a hammer.

For the next ten minutes, she destroyed every picture where his face appeared, relishing the splintering glass, the sharp crack of wood, the finality of it.

"Even better," she whispered.

Sliding the wedding ring off her finger, she studied it in the dim light. It had claimed her hand for over a decade, just as he had claimed her heart.

"Better sell it," she muttered. "Gonna need every penny to fix this place up."

She tossed the ring onto the counter and grabbed a broom to sweep up the remains of their life together. Under the sink, she shoved the broken frames into the garbage. The cabinet door popped open again, sagging on its loose hinge. She sighed, adding it to the long list of repairs.

Stepping onto the back deck, she inhaled the warm, humid air. The wooden railing needed a pressure wash, but it was solid. She'd make this place a home—eventually. Below, the river whispered against the rocks, the steady rush soothing the frayed edges of her nerves. She couldn't wait to set up some chairs out here, maybe a hammock.

A loud splash shattered the quiet.

Reese flinched, gripping the railing. The sound was deep, like something heavy had been dropped into the water. A fish. It had to be, right? But no ripples followed. No lingering disturbance, just the steady pulse of the river. She strained to see past the reflection of the porch light, her breath hitching as shadows rippled across the surface.

She exhaled a small laugh at her own nerves, but as her eyes drifted toward the bridge, her pulse ticked up again.

A rope swung from the beams, swaying gently.

Had that been there before?

She squinted, trying to make out the details in the fading light. The way it swayed felt... off. The frayed end suggested it had been cut. But how long ago? She hadn't noticed it earlier, but maybe she just wasn't paying attention.

Still, something about it itched in the back of her mind, like trying to recall a memory she couldn't quite grasp.

The air felt heavier now, thick and damp against her skin. The usual nighttime chorus of crickets and frogs had gone silent. She hadn't noticed the quiet until now, and somehow, that was worse. Only the river remained, murmuring its way down the bank.

A sharp gust of wind pushed against her, making the rope twist sharply.

She swallowed hard. *Move. Go inside.*

But she didn't. The rope stilled.

A knock at the front door sent a jolt through her, and she jumped.

"Reese, you really need to chill," she muttered, stepping over unpacked boxes as she went to answer it.

She swung open the door to find a woman fighting against the leash of an enormous black dog. The thing panted and yanked, its paws scraping against the porch as if it had somewhere better to be.

The woman herself was small—no taller than five foot two—with the kind of wiry frame that looked deceptively fragile. But there was nothing delicate about the way she yanked back on the leash with practiced determination. Short, spiky midnight-black hair poked in every direction, as if she had run her fingers through it one too many times. Square-framed glasses perched on her nose, slightly crooked, like she had forgotten they were there.

"You got an anchor in there, honey?" she huffed. "'Cause Cash here sure could use one."

"Cash?"

"As in Johnny," the woman said with a grin. "Man in black. Lab in black. Seemed to fit. Besides, Cash loves the music."

Before Reese could respond, the woman untied the leash and waltzed right past her into the house.

Reese blinked. Well, that's new. "Uh—can he get loose?"

"Nah." The woman waved a dismissive hand. "And if he does, he'll come back. The secret is bacon. Feed a dog bacon, and they'll be yours forever. Good rule for men, too."

Reese didn't bother mentioning that she'd fed her ex plenty of bacon, and he still ran straight into someone else's arms.

Instead, she peered at her guest. "Do you live around here?"

The woman clucked her tongue. "Right. Introductions. Folks are always telling me I need to do better at that. I live down the road a ways. Brick house on the hill with the fuchsia flowers up the drive. Name's Adeline, but I won't thank you for calling me that. Just call me Addie."

"Nice to meet you," Reese said slowly. "I'd offer you something, but I haven't been to the store yet."

Addie shrugged. "Better make sure you stock up on tea. And I mean real tea. None of that raspberry or peach-flavored nonsense. And don't get me started on coffee, with all the lattes and such. But I guess the younger crowd likes them, even here." She surveyed the room. "Where's your furniture?"

"It hasn't arrived yet. I ordered all new pieces. Should be here in a couple of days."

Addie lifted an eyebrow but didn't comment. She slid open the glass door to the deck and stepped outside.

"This place has always had the best view of the river," she mused. "Too bad Art didn't keep up the house all those years. You got someone to see to repairs? Are you married?"

"No, I'm-." Reese hesitated. "How come you haven't asked who I am?"

"No need. I know who you are. Art's only relative, niece, maybe?" At Reese's nod, she continued. "He told me once he had a relative that he'd leave the house to once he passed. I just put two and two together."

Reese's chest tightened at the mention of her uncle, the one she never really knew—and still didn't know why.

"So you're not married?"

Reese had heard about Southerners asking personal questions, but this was a bit much. "No, I'm not." Reese stared at her, daring her to ask more than she wanted to answer.

The spunky woman stared back, unwavering in her pursuit of information.

Reese found herself explaining. "I'm divorced."

"Oh? Is that why you have some broken picture frames on the floor?"

She thought she'd cleaned it all up. "Yep, but I'd rather not talk about that."

"Fair enough." She looked out the window again, staring at the bridge below.

"I guess you know all about Stuckey."

"Who?"

Addie turned, giving her a sharp look. "Land sakes, child. How can you move to this river without knowing about the legend of Stuckey?"

Reese frowned. "Should I?"

Addie didn't answer right away. Then she gave a slow, eerie smile.

"Well. If you don't know, you will soon enough. He makes it a point to meet anyone who dares to live on the river."

She laughed, but Reese didn't think it was a joke.

She shivered.

"Come over to the house for supper," Addie said. "Cooked up a mess of ham hocks and beans, cornbread, and, of course, sweet tea. It's usually just Cash and me, but my grandson's joining us tonight. He's been staying with me this summer. A little gruff these days, but he's harmless."

After meeting Addie, Reese could only imagine what the grandson might be like.

"I really need to unpack—"

"Unpacking can wait, girl. You need to eat. And you don't have groceries." Addie gave her a pointed look. "See you at seven."

Then, without another word, she stepped off the porch and untied Cash, leaving Reese standing there, stunned. So that was southern hospitality.

Outside, the bridge creaked.

Reese turned toward the glass doors, peering into the dusk, where light merged with darkness in the shadow of the trees. She couldn't see the rope anymore, but she imagined it, swaying over the water like one of the pendulums in Uncle Art's old wall clocks.

It was a warm spring night, but her arms prickled with cold.

Maybe she should get a dog. Not one like Cash, though. One that Cash would be afraid of.

She shut the door, but the uneasy feeling didn't leave. Even as she turned back to her boxes, she couldn't shake the sensation that someone watched her from the bridge.

An Angel Among Devils

Stuckey

*H*e *watched her talk to her pa. The lift of her chin set her shoulders in an arch over the curve of her back. She should be his choice to bear his children—but he'd rather take her life than her body. Should he?*

A cold sweat prickled along the back of his neck, dampening his collar. It wasn't fear—he hadn't felt that in years—but something more insidious. A hunger. A gnawing, clawing thing inside him that never slept, never ceased its demands.

He had thought, for a time, that he could tame it. That he could let the thrill of deception sustain him—the quiet victory of being a man they would never suspect. But hiding was tedious. And tedious things made a man restless.

Restless men made mistakes.

His fingers curled into a fist against his thigh, nails biting skin. No mistakes.

The girl would be off limits for a kill. She had too many ties to this town, as her father knew everyone, and everyone knew him. No, he couldn't follow that trail of temptation.

He pressed a thumb against the pulse in his wrist. Steady. Controlled. For now.

He knew they still looked for him, but the cover he worked out couldn't be any more brilliant. He didn't know how he'd keep from getting bored, though, not with life reduced to mundane details. Already his life had changed from thrilling adventure to those monotonous details, but maybe she could make things a bit more exciting. Not as exhilarating as a kill but thrilling in other ways. He must be patient, or he could mess things up with her.

Turning back to the tasks of his day, he ignored the stir in his gut to do something, anything, that brought back the sensations his last kill provided. Rubbing the back of his neck, he steeled himself against the thirst that begged him to quench it, and hoped he could fight it off the rest of his days. He took it back. There was one thing he feared. He rubbed the circumference of his neck and grimaced. He'd always feared the rope.

Belias and Sleim circled unseen, their forms like shadows without light to cast them, slithering between the gaps in Stuckey's thoughts. They didn't have to speak yet. They knew how to wait, how to let the silence work against him.

But Sleim was impatient. He always was. He sidled up to Stuckey's ear, but Belias pushed him aside. Belias knew better than to rush. He understood the weak spots of this man who basked in snuffing out life.

Sleim sidled up to the other side and whispered poisonous notions in the man's psyche, and Belias delighted in the effect they both had on their target. He whispered again, knowing just what to say to stir the pot of his lust for violence.

One more kill. That's all, Stuckey. Surely you can have just one more victim. Who's going to know? These are Mississippians, and just a bunch of ignorant river rats at that. You could kill all you want, and they'd never guess it's you who's doing the killing. Besides, I think you know the perfect way to find kills, don't you? Maybe you don't need to stop at all. You can kill whomever you want that way, can't you? After all, it worked last night.

They watched Stuckey squirm and close his fists tight against the mental thoughts, trying to ignore the overwhelming lust for death and power as it washed over his senses, but the sensation proved too much to bear, and he gave up on his tasks for the day.

The demons shrieked when light invaded the space, and they recoiled against the unwelcome intruder. Light warriors flanked a man, and the beings stood tall and powerful, full of strength. Belias hadn't seen such light in a long time, especially in these parts, so this man must be a prayer warrior. He wasn't the preacher. They'd already scouted that man's essence, and found it lacking in any spiritual strength, which only strengthened the devils assigned to him. No, this one was a regular man, but not a regular Christian. Belias motioned for Sleim to escape, and the two demons scurried away from the brightness and plunged toward a darker realm with relief. Just before he slipped through the black hole, Belias looked closely at the light warriors' faces, then gulped a hard swallow when he recognized the warrior who guarded the man's right. Fury replaced fear as he spoke the warrior's name, his hate rolling from his tongue like venom from a serpent's fangs, each syllable laced with the weight of old wounds and battles lost.

"Raphael."

———

They had been watching.

From the moment the murderer's hands first spilled blood at the outskirts of Meridian, the light warriors guarded their silent warrior—not only to protect him, but to encourage his exhausted spirit.

Raphael stood among them, sword unsheathed, its radiance held at bay for now. His expression was unreadable, though the other warriors around him shifted, uneasy.

"He isn't gone yet," one murmured, eyes trained on Stuckey's form below. "He still fights it."

"No," Raphael said, quiet but firm. "He only fights the fear of being caught."

The demon Belias pressed closer to Stuckey, whispering in his ear. Stuckey stiffened, jaw clenching. The angels felt the shift.

"It's happening," Uriel said. "His resolve is crumbling under the weight of his temptation."

Across the room, the man of prayer—the warrior whose prayers carried weight—paused. He felt it too. Those with the gift of discernment often could. Such a rare gift should be protected. Already, the devils itched for a vulnerable place in the man's defenses. They hovered just out of the realm, watching, drooling for a chance to attack.

Raphael's grip on his blade tightened.

The presence of darkness thickened around them, swirling through the air like a gathering storm. Shadows stretched unnaturally across the room, curling like smoke, reaching with intent. Belias whispered again, his voice a thread of poison weaving into Stuckey's thoughts.

"Just one more kill. No one will know. No one will miss them."

Stuckey's breath came in sharp bursts, his hands twitching at his sides. The battle waged within him, and the angels braced for the moment he would fall—or flee.

The man of prayer narrowed his eyes, before dropping his gaze to Stuckey's hands. He murmured a silent plea, and from the moment his lips moved, light broke through the thickening gloom. A single word, a single name, and the demons shrieked.

Raphael stepped forward, his presence flaring in strength. "Enough."

Belias snarled, recoiling from the sudden radiance. The dark forms quivered, their influence wavering against the onslaught of truth, of power beyond their reach. They slithered back, cursing, but they would not yet depart.

Stuckey staggered, eyes wild, breath shallow. He moved away from the man whose presence disturbed and alienated the evil around him. The demons followed, but they hissed at the light warriors with their slimy tongues flicking, spitting curses like sparks as they spewed their curses at the angels' feet.

Uriel exhaled, his gaze steady, and directed at the one they tormented. "He won't last long."

Raphael nodded. "No. But the one who prays... he will endure."

They remained steady in position as the man of prayer lifted his words again, unwavering. The battle was not over. But tonight, light had pushed back the darkness—for now. And now was the foothold, the ember that could ignite something greater. Now was the turning point.

Now changed everything.

The Storm Brings Devils

Reese

That was Addie's grandson?

Reese had expected a sullen teenager, resentful at being stuck with his grandmother in the middle of nowhere during spring break. But she had not expected him.

The man standing at the stove looked nothing like a bored, brooding teen. If anything, he had a rugged, almost classic handsomeness—like an old-school movie star who had spent too much time in the sun. Dark hair, sharp features, and a quiet intensity that was as unsettling as it was striking. And there he was, wearing an apron, stirring something thick and steaming in a cast-iron dutch oven.

"Reese, that there's my grandson, Jamie. Jamie, this is Reese, my new neighbor."

He turned, stepping toward her, his gaze sweeping over his grandmother before settling on Reese. His eyes locked onto hers with a quiet, assessing weight that made her pulse stutter. He extended a hand—polite, measured—but there was something else behind those eyes.

"It's James, actually," he said.

Reese took his hand, unable to look away. For a second, neither of them spoke.

The moment stretched just long enough to be uncomfortable.

Addie broke the silence. "Another way we differ. I prefer my nickname, and Jamie prefers his given name. Problem is, I can't get used to it. Been calling him Jamie since he was in diapers."

James—or Jamie—turned back to the stove without another word, a far cry from his grandmother's brand of hospitality.

Reese cleared her throat. "Could I see your view of the river?"

Cash nuzzled her hand, pressing his wet nose into her palm. She chuckled, scratching his ears, earning a sloppy lick across her fingers. She swiped them on her jeans.

"Looks like Cash approves," Addie said. "That says a lot. Sure, come on out this way."

She led Reese through a side door off the kitchen. The deck wrapped around to the back of the house, overlooking the water below. The river was wide here, its muddy current slipping along the tree-lined banks.

"That's the Chunky River, in all its murky glory."

"I think it's beautiful."

And she meant it. There was a raw, untamed beauty to it, the kind that had been left untouched by time. The trees loomed over the water, their long branches dipping low as if whispering secrets to the current. Fireflies blinked between the trunks, their golden sparks winking in and out of the gathering twilight. Crickets sang their evening serenade that echoed and bounced off the water.

"It is a nice view," Addie admitted. "But not as nice as yours. That house was abandoned for years until Art showed up about twenty years ago. I didn't even know it was for sale until he'd already moved in. Do you know why he settled here?"

Reese leaned against the railing. "No, I didn't know much about him. My dad left when I was young, and apparently I didn't see my dad's family much before that, anyway. I was just a baby when he left." She didn't know why, but she couldn't bring herself to tell Addie her father died, and to the other woman's credit, she didn't press about him. "Mom tried to keep in touch with Uncle Art, though. I think she sent him photos of me through the years."

Addie frowned. "I never saw any in his house the few times I visited."

Reese's stomach twisted. "I found some in his desk. My mom told me he didn't have any other siblings other than my dad, so I was his only family, but he wouldn't come to see us. He never tried, even after my dad left. I guess my mom made peace with it, but I could tell it disturbed her, though she wouldn't say much about it. She just said Art was a loner. A hermit."

"She wasn't wrong," Addie said. "But it's easy to keep to yourself out here if you're not careful. This river has a way of isolating a person. Sometimes that's good, sometimes not."

Reese could do with some isolation, and that's why she thought this place would be perfect for her.

"Gram, we're ready."

Reese turned at the voice. James stood in the doorway, watching her.

There was no welcome in his eyes.

Before stepping inside, Reese glanced toward the riverbank.

A shadowed figure stood beneath a cypress tree, half-hidden in the gloom.

Her breath caught. The shape was unmistakable—tall, human, unmoving, watching. A cold prickle crawled down her spine. Something about the way he stood, rigid and unnatural, sent a flicker of dread curling through her gut.

"Who's that man down there?"

Addie followed her gaze. "What man?"

Reese blinked. The figure was gone.

Her fingers curled around the doorframe. That wasn't possible. He had been right there, as real as the trees around him.

"You didn't see him?" Her own voice sounded too tight, too uncertain.

Addie let out a slow breath. "Sounds like Stuckey's in a hurry to meet you. Usually, he takes a bit longer."

Reese frowned. "What?"

James' voice cut through the thick air. "Gram, leave the ghost stories outside, and come in for supper."

Reese hesitated before sliding the door shut behind her. Her pulse was still uneven, her skin still tingling with the aftershock of seeing something—someone—standing there.

She cast one last look over her shoulder, scanning the trees.

Nothing.

And yet, the feeling remained, coiling deep in her chest.

That man had been real. Not some trick of the shadows. Not a ghost story waiting to be told.

A live, breathing man. And he had been watching her.

———

Reese decided dinner was dangerous in this county. Reese had eaten more carbs and butter in one meal than she had in days. She didn't even want to think about the sugar in Addie's peach cobbler, but it had been worth every bite.

James had hardly spoken during dinner, spending most of it texting. Addie shot him a withering glare. "Put that phone away, Jamie. We have company."

James sighed but obeyed, sliding it into his pocket. Even then, he barely spoke.

Until Addie took the dog outside.

"So," he said, voice even but unreadable. "You show up here after the house sat empty for a while. Art barely spoke about family, and now you're living in his place. Why now?"

Reese stiffened. There it was. The suspicion.

She knew that tone, that assessing stare. Dylan had mastered it. The way a man could make you feel like you had something to prove just by standing there, like you owed him an explanation for simply existing.

She forced her shoulders to relax. "I don't think that's any of your business."

His expression didn't shift. "Gram is my business."

Reese folded her arms. So that was it. He was protective of Addie, and she was the intruder. "What exactly are you implying?" she asked, irritation rising. "She invited me, not the other way around."

James' expression didn't shift. "That's Gram. She knocks even where she isn't wanted."

Reese bristled. "I didn't say she wasn't wanted. I just meant—"

James exhaled sharply, drumming his fingers on the table before stopping abruptly. His jaw clenched. "Never mind."

But Reese saw it—the brief flicker of something deeper. Not just suspicion, but something bruised underneath. She had the distinct feeling he wasn't just wary of her.

"Look," she said, trying not to let her irritation show. "I didn't come here to cause trouble. I came because this was my uncle's house, and I wanted a fresh start."

James didn't move. Didn't nod. Didn't accept her words at face value. Men like him never did.

She forced herself to hold his gaze, refusing to let him pick her apart.

"I guess we'll see," he said finally, before pushing away from the table with a dish in his hand, heading for the kitchen.

Reese exhaled, tension still coiled tight in her chest.

Judging by the look in his eyes, he didn't trust her.

Well, she didn't trust him, either. She didn't think she'd ever trust anyone again, not even Addie, who was probably one of the most straightforward women she'd met.

He re-entered the dining room, just as the screen door banged as Addie walked in, Cash padding beside her. "What'd I miss?"

James smirked. "Nothing."

Addie's eyes flicked between them. "Mmm-hmm. Right."

Reese pushed back her chair. "Thank you for dinner, but I'd better head back."

"Good thing you drove," Addie said. "Rain's coming. Just a drizzle now, but around here, it don't stay light for long."

Reese had considered walking, but the darkness was oppressive, the trees swallowing what little moonlight peeked through the clouds.

She hesitated at the door. "Addie... you never told me about Old Man Stuckey."

James let out a low chuckle, but Addie just shook her head.

"That's a story for another day."

Reese wasn't sure if that made her feel better… or worse.

By the time she reached home, the sky had cracked open. Wind howled around the house, whistling through the cracks in the siding. Rain lashed against the windows, and thunder rumbled low in the distance.

Reese unpacked another box, but her mind circled back to what Addie said. Who was Stuckey? And why had James reacted the way he had?

The lights flickered, then dimmed, then cut out completely.

Darkness swallowed the house.

Reese sighed. "Of course."

She groped her way to the kitchen, feeling for the plastic storage container that held flashlights. Finding one, she flipped the switch.

Nothing.

Her stomach knotted. "Seriously?" Her voice sounded hollow inside the empty house.

A gust of wind rattled the windows. A tree branch scraped against the deck, a slow, deliberate sound, like fingernails dragging across wood.

She rummaged for a candle, but froze when she heard it—

A footstep. On the deck.

Her breath hitched. Lightning slashed across the sky, illuminating the glass doors—

A figure stood outside. A man. The same one she'd seen on the riverbank. Then, the darkness swallowed him as her heart pounded.

She waited for it, frozen in place. Lightning struck again, and he still stood there, but this time, his face changed.

He was a different man, with a different face, and he smiled at her through the glass with red eyes.

A rope hung around his neck.

Reese's scream ripped through the storm.

Sanctuary and Scorn

Catherine

Catherine hesitated at the threshold of the little church, gripping her Bible in one hand and a folded fan in the other. The murmur of voices swelled around her as parishioners gathered, their greetings warm and full of familiarity. She watched as they clasped her pa's shoulder with jovial slaps, their laughter easy, their conversations effortless. He belonged here.

She did not.

It wasn't that people were unkind. She had met plenty of polite individuals since they'd arrived a year earlier. But polite did not mean welcoming, nor did it mean genuine. Polite people said their hellos, smiled in passing, and moved on—to speak with those they truly cared for, those whose presence mattered more than hers.

At first, she had made the effort, seeking out conversation, weaving herself into the seams of the congregation. She had offered warm smiles, helped with charitable work, and served alongside the other women in their community efforts. But the distance remained. Subtle. Unspoken. Averted gazes when she entered a room. Murmurs that hushed when she passed by. The way the other young women moved together like a school of fish, seamlessly closing ranks whenever she drew near. If not physically, verbally, as if they raised a conversational wall as she approached.

She preferred to stay home to worship, but her pa had long since dismissed that notion.

"We need fellowship with other believers, Catherine. God didn't mean for us to be alone. That's when the devil has an advantage, because there's strength in numbers, you know. If he can isolate us, he can infiltrate our thoughts, whispering his lies unchecked, until our doubts and despair take root. Besides, are you sure it's not your imagination? Perhaps these girls might be too shy to talk to you, have you thought of that?"

She had. But she knew better.

Her pa didn't understand. This wasn't a thing she imagined—it was something she felt. She had always had the ability to read beneath the surface, to catch what lay just beyond the pleasantries. The slight hesitation in a voice. The weight of an unspoken judgment in the flicker of an eye. The forced quality of a smile that did not reach the eyes.

They did not like her. Even if they never said so. Even if they never would. She could address it, confronting them with the question, but she knew they'd answer with a response that shifted the responsibility to her.

She exhaled and stepped inside, her footsteps muted against the worn wooden planks of the floor. The air inside the sanctuary was thick, heavy with heat and the lingering scent of candle wax and aged wood. The walls, once whitewashed, had dulled with time, the edges darkened by the smoke of lanterns and the press of passing years. The pews stretched in rigid rows, polished by the shifting weight of countless sermons, of restless bodies enduring long hours of preaching. The air hummed with the mingling voices of the congregation, laughter and conversation rising in bursts between the walls. Catherine wanted to laugh with them, but her tears sat just at the surface, willing her to let them fall.

She swallowed hard, then followed her pa to their usual wooden pew, settling onto the hard, unforgiving surface. The ache that would settle in her bones before the service's end was a familiar one.

She felt eyes on her.

It wasn't the first time.

She turned her gaze toward the front, resisting the urge to glance at the ones who watched her with the eyes that didn't smile back.

Zeke sat in the pew ahead of her, his posture relaxed, his arm draped over the back of the bench. When he turned and caught her eye, he grinned, his dimples flashing in that easy way of his. The dim morning light softened his face, casting shadows along the sharp line of his jaw, highlighting the green of his eyes. She knew the look well—the kind that made the other girls preen and whisper, their admiration shining in their eyes. Eyes that smiled back at him.

He had been in the area for only a short while, and already the young women had taken notice. Handsome, new, unattached. That was all it took.

Her pa liked him, and she knew he thought he might make a fine match for his daughter.

Catherine was not convinced.

Zeke flirted with everyone. He liked attention. And he assumed, like so many others did, that she would simply accept his interest, as if she had no choice in the matter, as if he was doing her a favor. Why did his confidence bother her so much?

She wondered if Matt attended church, too. If so, perhaps he attended the larger Baptist congregation on the other side of town. He showed confidence, too, but he also exuded a quieter confidence, while Zeke shouted his from the rooftops.

The sanctuary filled, the aisles growing crowded, while the pews creaked beneath the weight of more bodies pressing in. The sounds of laughter and chatter swelled, then hushed as the first strains of a hymn stirred the air.

Catherine pressed her hands against the leather cover of her Bible, grounding herself.

A holy place.

A house of worship.

She had learned long ago that church was not always a refuge for everyone. Yet, she still loved the little sanctuary, despite the scornful looks around the room. Bro. Amos Whitmore, the interim pastor, strode up to the pulpit, his heavy boots echoing in the hush that settled over the congregation. The sun filtered through the church's high, arched windows, dust motes drifting in the golden shafts of light like restless spirits caught between this world and the next. The scent of wax-polished pews and aged hymnals mixed with the lingering warmth of summer air that refused to leave, making the room feel almost stifling.

His voice, rich with fire-and-brimstone authority, rolled over the wooden beams like a storm cloud preparing to burst. "Welcome, welcome. Before we lift our voices in song, I'd like to extend a warm greeting to our visitors today. We hope you find your home and family here among us."

Funny. He'd said the same thing when she and her father first arrived.

Catherine kept her face smooth, hiding the pull of discontent that twisted inside her. A family. A home. How easily people spoke such words, not realizing how often they rang hollow. Or how little they meant what they said. Their welcomes were reserved, not open.

Her father, sitting beside her, gave a hearty "Amen," his deep voice sure and unwavering. She held back a sigh. Across the aisle, Rosalind Greer's gaze locked onto her, and Catherine turned away from the ice-thin glare that cut sharper than any blade. The weight of being an outsider pressed down on her shoulders, familiar but never welcome.

If only she could slip away. Back to the river, where the bridge stood in quiet witness to the passage of time, where the water hummed beneath its timbers, a lullaby she understood better than the clipped niceties exchanged in church pews.

She had tried. Oh, how she had tried to fit in, to forge friendships where none had been freely offered. She had smiled. She had helped. She had served in ways that should have softened their hearts toward her. But their cordial words never stretched into anything deeper.

Perhaps she'd rather be alone in the woods than alone in a crowded sanctuary.

When the service ended, the air outside carried the scent of damp earth, the promise of coming rain woven into the breeze. The congregation spilled out of the church in clusters—laughter, chatter, the rustling of skirts and the scuffing of boots against the dry earth.

As expected, Zeke had drawn a gathering of admirers, the young women fluttering around him like a cloud of honeybees eager for their share of sweetness. He, of course, welcomed their attention, flashing that easy grin, all dimples and mischief.

Catherine turned to follow her father, but something made her glance back.

Zeke's gaze met hers.

He tipped his hat, the smile that curved his lips edged with amusement, as if he caught her staring. She scowled and quickened her pace, feeling the warmth of her own irritation prickle her skin.

Her father had already made his way into conversation with Mr. White, the shopkeeper, whose wide, toothy grin contrasted with the sharp shrewdness in his eyes.

"Have you had any flooding along the bank since you settled there?" Mr. White asked, his hands clasped loosely behind his back, giving the impression of a man at ease—though Catherine suspected few things escaped his notice.

"I haven't seen it yet, but I know it's happened in the past," her father replied. "Depends on how much rain we get. Is your land flat or on an incline?"

"It's on a slope, like most. Close enough to the river for convenience, but far enough back to keep dry."

"I guess we all run a risk, depending on how high the water crests." Her father nodded toward the road. "Most newcomers with businesses stick to town, though. You must like a little quiet if you settled out there."

Mr. White shrugged, his smile never faltering. "The country suits me fine. But I do keep a room above the store. It's useful on late nights when I don't feel like making the ride back."

"Must be nice," her father mused. "Gives you the best of both worlds, I suppose."

Catherine barely heard them.

Something—or rather, someone—unsettled her.

Mr. Blythe, the blacksmith, leaned against the side of the church, talking in low tones with Bro. Whitmore. He wasn't even looking at the preacher. His gaze was locked on her.

Not just watching—studying.

A shiver crept along her spine, her instincts prickling with unease.

She shifted closer to her father, linking her arm through his, grounding herself in his steady presence. Mr. White excused himself to speak to another man, and her father turned to her with a questioning look.

"Lovely service, don't you think? Strong preaching and good fellowship," he said, his tone warm, but his eyes keen.

Catherine hesitated. "It was fine."

"You don't seem convinced."

"I suppose I'm just tired." She avoided mentioning the women who still huddled together, whispering, their glances darting toward her like arrows tipped with something sharp.

"I didn't know Mr. White lived near the river," she said instead, hoping to divert his attention.

"Neither did I. But a lot of folks do." Her father nodded toward the crowd. "Zeke does, remember?"

Catherine barely stifled a groan. "Oh, Pa. Not this again."

He grinned, undeterred. "I didn't see your Mr. Sanderson today. Think he's a churchgoer?"

She folded her arms. "Since he's not my anything, I wouldn't know."

"Well, he certainly intends to court you."

Zeke, of course, chose that moment to appear, his dark locks tousled by the wind, his hat tipped just enough to shadow one eye. The black of his coat contrasted with the sun-warmed bronze of his skin, and when he smiled, he looked every bit the rogue he was.

"Who wants to court you?" he asked, his eyes flicking toward her pa before settling back on her, unreadable.

Catherine gave her pa a withering glare, but he chuckled.

"There's a newcomer showing interest in Catherine, Zeke."

Zeke's smile faded. His gaze sharpened, while his voice tightened. "Oh? I'll have to meet him."

"It's none of your business," Catherine muttered.

Zeke arched a brow. "Isn't it?"

Before she could respond, her father lifted a hand in farewell, signaling that it was time to leave. As she climbed into the wagon, she spotted movement in the distance—Matt Sanderson, dressed in a dark coat and vest, his pocket watch glinting in the sunlight. He was breathless, his face glowing with perspiration.

"Mr. Sanderson, you're out of breath," her father said as the young man approached. "Is something wrong?"

"I overslept." Matt exhaled heavily. "My horse is missing. Had to walk."

"You didn't report it to the sheriff?"

"I wanted to make it to service."

"Well, the sheriff's right there." Her father nodded toward the man in question. "Once you're done talking with him, you're welcome to ride with us. Where do you live?"

"Along the river, across the bridge." Matt glanced at Catherine. "How are you?"

She tilted her head, taking in the dampness of his collar, the slight strain around his eyes. "Better than you, I think."

He chuckled. "I must look a sight."

"You do."

A small smile ghosted across his lips before he turned to find the sheriff. Zeke had joined another group who welcomed his conversation.

Catherine expected to feel relief that his attention left her. Instead, unease crept in—subtle but undeniable.

She glanced back toward the church.

Mr. Blythe was still staring.

And now, so was Zeke.

Their gazes flicked toward Matt, then back to each other. Tension coiled between them, unreadable but unmistakable.

Rosalind Greer saw it, too.

Catherine could see the wheels turning in the girl's mind before she turned to whisper to the others.

The wagon jolted forward, pulling them away from the church. Catherine exhaled, rubbing her arms as the weight of unseen things pressed down.

Sundays should have been a day of peace. A day of rest.

Instead, she always left feeling more exhausted than when she arrived.

Catherine clung to the hope that she had a place in God's house.

———

She looked perfect in yellow. The color softened her, made her glow. It caught the light as she moved, as if the sun had chosen her, draping her in something pure, something untouchable.

Others noticed. He saw it in the way they watched her—the admiration, the curiosity, the quiet longing in their glances. They didn't even try to hide it.

His fingers flexed against the worn leather of his Bible.

He hated it. Hated them.

It wasn't jealousy, not in the way a man might covet a woman for himself. It wasn't about possession. If anything, the thought of claiming her made his skin crawl. She was an obstacle, a distraction, a flickering light that refused to be snuffed out. If he couldn't kill, all other desires fell short.

And yet, something about her held him in place.

A fascination, perhaps. An irritation, definitely.

The urge clawed at him, that sharp, familiar itch rising in his chest. He had thought it might ease in time, that his restraint would strengthen, that he could be a new man. But the sound of laughter grated in his ears, their voices rising and falling in a symphony of carefree existence.

He could end that laughter.

He knew how.

But he shouldn't risk it. Not yet.

His grip on the Bible tightened, the edges biting into his palms. No, not her.

She had ties here. People would ask questions. She was not some nameless drifter or some fool who wandered too close to the river alone. Or a horse assumed stolen for practical purposes. He smiled. If they only knew—it was practical. To him.

He exhaled slowly, forcing the tension from his shoulders.

Patience. There were ways he could settle his cravings without exposing what they couldn't imagine.

He needed to build something here—a name, a role. He had to play it well, and he had to keep playing it. A church-going man. A good man. The kind of man who knew the scriptures and nodded at the right moments. The kind who smiled, who blended in, who shook hands without squeezing too tight.

So he'd sit through the sermons. He'd murmur his "Amens," and he'd play the part they expected him to play.

Even if it meant smiling at those he longed to kill.

But as Catherine smiled again, as the sunlight caught the golden strands of her hair, something in him coiled tighter.

One day, she wouldn't smile.

One day, that light would fade, swallowed by something darker, something final.

And maybe, just maybe, he'd be the one to snuff it out.

Echoes of Stuckey

Reese

Reese watched as James checked every corner of the house. Addie stood by, gripping Cash's leash, but this time the dog wasn't trying to yank away. He stood rigid, his ears back, letting out a low whine every few minutes.

"Nothing. Looks like you're all clear," James finally said.

The lights had flickered back on since their arrival, but that didn't shake the unease settling in Reese's chest. The storm outside had passed, yet she still felt like something pressed against the walls of the house, unseen but present.

"Of course, it's all clear," Addie muttered, shaking her head.

James sighed. "Gram, not now."

"It's him," she said, voice low. "He always shows up."

Reese swallowed hard. "Him? You mean Stuckey?"

James waved a dismissive hand. "Ignore her. Are you sure you saw someone standing on the deck? Maybe there are footprints leading away from it." He pulled the hood over his head before heading toward the back door.

"You're wasting your time! Stuckey never leaves tangible evidence behind!" Addie called after him. Cash barked, straining at the leash.

Reese turned to the older woman. "Are you going to tell me what's going on? Or at least what you think is going on?"

Addie exhaled, rubbing Cash's head. "Guess since you've seen him more than once now, it's about time I do." She settled onto a box marked "Books" and patted the empty space beside her, but Reese shook her head and remained standing.

"Stuckey lived here in the late 1800s. Folks later found out he probably had ties to the Dalton gang—those bank robbers that got themselves caught. But Stuckey escaped and ended up here along the Chunky River."

Reese folded her arms, waiting.

"He didn't go by Stuckey in Meridian, but when they searched his house, they found old papers with that name. He had official papers for his river property with another name he used as a disguise, but most folks thought he killed someone for the property and the identity. Who knows what his real name was? Either way, he lived in a house on the river, lured travelers to trust him for different reasons—then killed them. Some say he killed for money. Others say he killed because he liked it."

Reese shivered.

"Finally caught up to him, though," Addie continued. "They hung him on that bridge out there. But they didn't cut him down right away. Sheriff wanted him to be an example, so they let him rot in the sun for three days before cutting the rope. Dropped him straight into the river."

"That's awful," Reese whispered.

"Awful?" Addie raised a brow. "He butchered people like livestock. They found bodies all along the riverbank. He didn't deserve a grave. Besides, you know how legends go—there's so many versions of the story, you don't know fact from fiction. But one thing's for sure, most agree he's still hunting this river, searching for his next victim. And he hasn't forgiven those who stopped him the first time."

Reese ran a hand down her arm, smoothing the goosebumps. She thought of the rope she'd seen swaying beneath the bridge, the shadowed figure outside her deck.

"I know what you're thinking, but don't worry," Addie said, misreading her silence. "The worst he can do is scare you. He's been dead a long time."

Reese didn't tell her she saw two men. James already thought she'd imagined one. Cash whined, and a floorboard creaked somewhere in the house. She swallowed hard. Was one of them a ghost? She didn't believe in ghosts. Did she? Demons, maybe, but not ghosts. She wanted to believe Addie, but she didn't know what she believed anymore.

"Maybe it's just kids messing with me," she muttered.

Addie scoffed. "In the middle of a thunderstorm? I doubt it."

Something creaked down the hall.

Reese stiffened, her mind racing through rational explanations, but nothing stuck. The house had settled plenty since she moved in, but this sounded deliberate.

Addie sniffed. "You don't have to believe it. Doesn't mean it ain't real."

The back door swung open, and James stepped inside, his soaked pants clinging to his ankles. Reese grabbed a thick beach towel from an open box and held it out to him.

Their eyes met as he took it from her.

"Thanks."

She nodded, watching as he wiped the rain from his face and hair.

"She hasn't been feeding you stories about Stuckey's ghost, has she?" James muttered, throwing the towel over his shoulder.

"James Wendell McCoy, you know good and well it's not just a story," Addie shot back. "You've got your own tales to tell, too."

James' jaw tightened. "We've all got stories, but none that prove anything. Most of it is from years of hearing that legend. Imagination has a way of manifesting itself."

Reese looked between them. "So you have seen something?"

"Who? Stuckey?" James forced a short laugh. "Of course not. And neither did you. Probably just some vagrant looking for food."

"With a rope around his neck? In a storm?" Reese asked. She almost told him about the other man, but stopped herself.

James crossed his arms." Are you sure it was a rope? Couldn't it have been your imagination playing tricks on you?"

"She didn't even know the story yet," Addie cut in. "I only told her a few minutes ago."

Reese frowned. She didn't like being talked down to like a scared child. She had seen something. Someone. Or two someones.

James sighed and raked a hand through his damp hair. "Look, are you afraid to stay here alone?"

"No," Reese said immediately. But even she could hear the hesitation in her own voice.

James smirked. "You're as bad as that dog—brave on the outside, whimpering on the inside."

Reese opened her mouth to snap back, but he turned toward his grandmother.

"Come on, Gram. It's late."

"I suppose it's time to get Cash to bed." Addie rolled the leash around her hand and leaned toward Reese, lowering her voice. "Don't let Jamie fool you. He's scared of Stuckey, too."

Then she was gone, leaving Reese alone with James.

"What'd she say?" he asked.

Reese tilted her head. "She said you're afraid of the ghost, too."

He rolled his eyes. "I guess we're all afraid of something, but ghosts? I doubt that's what you saw."

"Maybe not," Reese admitted. "But until tonight, I thought ghost stories were just for campouts and slumber parties."

James grinned, shocking Reese. "You want to have a slumber party? I can camp out here if you need protection."

Was the man flirting with her now?

Her face reddened. "I'll be fine, thanks."

James chuckled and strode to the door. "Good night, then."

The screen door slammed behind him.

Reese locked the deadbolt and leaned against the frame, exhaling, and wondering why she thought a deadbolt could make her feel safe after what she saw. If she really saw it.

The wind had died down, but she still felt unsettled. She shut off the last lamp, telling herself she wouldn't glance at the deck. The clocks along the hall ticked wildly before chiming all at once—deep, hollow, unnatural.

Reese squeezed her eyes shut.

She wouldn't look at the deck.

She wouldn't.

But as soon as she left the living room to head toward her new bedroom, she felt tempted to call James back and take him up on his offer. But as much as she loathed the idea of staying alone in the house, letting him in felt riskier than whatever waited outside on the deck.

The Watchers and the Wicked

The Unseen, 1878

Belias bared his teeth in a grin, his forked tongue flicking between them as he watched the smaller demon, Sleim, rub his hands together, eager to stir the man's mind into deeper depravities. His amusement at Sleim's enthusiasm was short-lived, though. The weak-minded fool thought this was as simple as whispering into the ear of a killer, but Belias knew better. This was delicate work. The urges had to fester, had to rot him from the inside out, seeping into his bones until he was beyond saving.

It wouldn't take much longer. The man was already unraveling, piece by piece. The bloodlust grew stronger each day, creeping back into his waking thoughts, writhing through his nightly dreams. Even his twisted fascination with the woman couldn't drown out the deeper hunger clawing at his gut. Lust came in many forms. Theirs was not to lead him to mere physical desires—but to stoke the fire of something far greater, far darker.

"Remember not to get eager, Sleim," Belias said, his voice curling through the air like smoke. "He must be protected from them." He flicked his claw toward the trees, where Raphael and his warriors lingered, silent sentinels of the light. "If they intervene too soon, they will ruin everything. And we can't have that. Not yet."

Sleim's eyes darted to the angels, his shoulders hitching as he shrank into himself. "They're just watching."

"For now." Belias tilted his head, his black eyes gleaming. "They always watch before they strike."

Sleim twitched. "Maybe we should work faster—before they have a chance."

"Fool." Belias snarled and shoved Sleim back a step. "We don't rush. We let the cracks spread, let them think they have time. And while they hesitate—" he grinned, slow and malevolent, "—we devour."

Sleim bobbed his head in agreement, though his hands trembled at his sides.

Belias rolled his shoulders, stretching his talons wide. "Keep the church distracted in their own worlds. Keep them murmuring, divided. Let their envy fester. Let them sit in their pews, blind to what happens beneath their very noses. If they're too busy gnashing their teeth at each other, they won't remember the power that prayer and that book gives them."

Sleim shifted, uneasy. "I thought their greatest weapon was—" He swallowed hard, his voice barely above a whisper. "His name."

At the mention, the trees around them seemed to shudder, the air growing heavier. The light warriors didn't move, but Belias felt their focus sharpen.

His nostrils flared. He reached out and wrenched Sleim forward, his grip like iron. "And what do you think happens when they pray, you pathetic wretch?" He hissed, pressing his talons into Sleim's flesh until the smaller demon whimpered. "That is their weapon. That is what burns us. And that is what you will keep them from doing."

Sleim yelped as Belias shoved him toward the girls who had begun their walk home, their heads bent close, whispering in haughty tones. They didn't need much interference—humans never did. Their jealousy and pride had already done most of the work. All Sleim had to do was stir the embers.

"Go," Belias ordered. "Keep her isolated. Keep them sneering at her, doubting her. If she has no refuge, if she has no allies, she will be ripe for our master's plans." He grinned, slow and venomous. "Her isolation feeds his darkness."

Sleim hesitated for half a second too long, his gaze flickering back to the light warriors.

They hadn't moved.

They simply watched.

It was worse than an attack, and they knew it.

With a growl, Belias raked his talons down Sleim's back, forcing him forward. "Move, coward." He hissed a laugh. "If they meant to strike, you wouldn't have time to tremble."

Sleim scurried away, disappearing into the shadows after the women.

Belias turned, his gaze settling on the angels once more. The golden glow of their weapons gleamed in the dimming light, their unreadable faces carved from stone. He did not fear them. He feared their master. But their master only intervened when men's willing hearts surrendered. And he'd make sure that didn't happen.

Smirking, he raised a single talon in a mock salute.

They couldn't stop what was coming.

Not even Raphael could halt the sickness blooming in the man's soul, because the most delicious truth of all wasn't that monsters were made.It was that they were awakened.

And Belias was more than happy to be the one to do it.

The night air pulsed with unseen movement. Shadows stretched longer than they should, twisting and curling where they had no reason to be.

Above the town, Raphael stood with his centennial comrades, unseen, unshaken. Below them, the streets buzzed with chatter, Sunday afternoon fading like a dying ember. Churchgoers exchanged pleasantries, their minds already shifting to business, to gossip, to everything except what had just been preached. The weight of it settled over the town—a slow decay, not seen with human eyes, but felt in the spirit realm.

"Do we know the mission here, Raphael?" Uriel asked, his arms folded across his broad chest.

"Only to watch for now but also protect the girl." Raphael spoke quietly, but his voice held its usual strength.

"Why not the others?"

"We have our orders to protect the girl and the one she'll marry."

"Do we know why?"

"We only know what's ordered, and we cannot ask more; you know that."

Uriel exhaled hard, eyes scanning the spiritual landscape. The demons were already working—twisting, whispering, feeding small offenses and enflaming old resentments. It was so easy. Too easy.

"We need more prayer, Raphael. Like so many other times, we lack the prayer cover, and we lack earnest devotion from these believers. They're too busy looking at each other and not Him. They're too caught up in their own feelings."

"And so it has always been, and so it will always be. But there are still those who are faithful, even if they're not so obvious. Sometimes the most faithful are overlooked." Raphael's gaze flickered toward a few scattered individuals who left the church in silence, heads bowed, prayers still lingering on their lips. They weren't the loudest voices in the congregation, but their prayers carried further than any sermon spoken today. "I'll follow the girl and her father home, while you stay and watch. Don't engage, just watch."

Uriel's expression darkened. "That's what Belias told that nasty little demon just now."

"Make no mistake. He's not little. Nasty, yes, but not little."

"Noted." Uriel nodded, his eyes assessing the spirit realm around the storefronts. He frowned as he felt the Sunday reverence already dissolving, as if it had only been a thin veil that quickly faded once the pews emptied. A shopkeeper who had just come from the service muttered under his breath about a new competitor stealing his customers. A woman who had sung a hymn of grace minutes ago now whispered harshly about a neighbor she despised.

They had already forgotten.

Raphael left him to mind his post as he flew up and over the small southern town who had no idea what went on right under their noses. Uriel was right. They were too busy fretting over their own interests, trying to best each other, or snubbing those they didn't value—whether through jealousy or ignorance.

Below, the demons stirred, slithering between the people, inflaming bitterness, feeding resentments. It was so subtle, so insidious.

Why couldn't these Christians love each other as Christ loved them?

Didn't they know that unbelief only surged when outsiders looked in and found strife, judgment, and hypocrisy among those who claimed to follow the light?

Uriel was right about something else, too. Without praying believers, this town risked losing its light to a great darkness that grew stronger with every sick thought that ran through the spaces in Stuckey's mind.

———

Catherine and her pa invited Matt for Sunday dinner, and he provided delightful company and conversation. She found herself drawn to his calm charm, but her mind also drifted to another man's charm, though not quite so calm. Matt didn't kiss her hand again when saying goodbye, but he did grasp it gently, his touch lingering, making his attraction for her known.

Her pa drove Matt home to his place that afternoon, promising to help him repair his pump at the well. Catherine busied herself at home, baking bread and putting up vegetables. She didn't like to work on Sundays, but winter waited in the distance, creeping closer each day. The garden would soon wilt under frost's icy fingers, and she'd learned well in their first winter here how quickly the river's beauty could turn harsh.

She finished her work, wiped her hands on her apron, and glanced at the clock. Still enough daylight left. She threw on her bonnet to protect her hair from the wind and stepped outside, exhaling as she took in the sight of the sun lowering against the tree line. A hush had settled over the river, the kind that came before nightfall, where the world felt suspended between light and dark.

She needed space. Air. Somewhere the walls didn't press so tightly around her. She needed to enjoy the outdoors before winter shut her inside for months.

Clutching her copy of *Pride and Prejudice*, she started toward the bridge.

The wooden planks groaned beneath her step, a familiar, almost reassuring sound. This place had become her refuge, the only place she could breathe without the weight of unspoken judgments pressing against her chest. The river whispered below, slow and steady, its surface catching the final threads of golden light. Shadows stretched long over the water, curling at the edges like fingers reaching for something unseen.

The wind stirred, carrying with it the scent of damp earth and decaying leaves, and she pulled her shawl tighter. A crow cawed in the distance—a sharp, jarring sound that made the hairs on her arms rise.

She wasn't alone on the bridge.

A figure sat near the railing, legs dangling over the edge, staring into the slow-moving current. A girl—slight in frame, but unafraid. The soft sway of her feet told Catherine she wasn't waiting for anyone. She was simply there.

Catherine's fingers slipped, and her book nearly tumbled from her hands. She caught it just before it could fall into the murky water.

The girl jumped, startled.

"I'm so sorry," Catherine said. "I never meant to frighten you."

The girl turned, and Catherine met a pair of hazel eyes—open, searching, with something unreadable behind them. She was younger than Catherine had expected. Fourteen, maybe? There was a quiet, timid beauty about her, but something else, too. Something familiar.

Something Catherine couldn't quite place.

"Don't apologize," the girl said, steadying her breath. "You only startled me. I often get lost when I'm daydreaming."

Catherine studied her. Why did she seem so familiar?

"I don't think I've met you around before. Are you new here?"

The girl hesitated, then gave a small smile. "I saw you at church. I'm Ellen."

Catherine blinked. She saw *her*?

She tried to remember. She always noticed the way people looked at her—the polite distance, the stiff smiles. But she hadn't seen this girl at all. Not in the pews. Not in the crowd. Not in places she expected to feel unwelcome.

How could she miss her?

"You go to my church?"

"Yes, but we've only been twice," Ellen continued, pointing down the river. "My grandfather and I are camping on the riverbank until he finishes his business in town. Then we head to Jackson. He's opening a shoe repair store there, and we're going to live above it. He's been working and saving a long time for this, so he's excited."

Catherine's chest tightened at the warmth in Ellen's voice—a girl with no permanent home, yet so full of hope.

"Where are your parents?" The question slipped out before she could stop it.

Grief flickered across Ellen's face, quick but unmistakable.

"My pa and ma got Typhoid fever," she said softly. "They couldn't recover. I'm blessed to have my grandpa with me."

Catherine swallowed, guilt settling in. "I'm sorry. I lost my ma as a baby, so I'm thankful for my pa. He's taken care of me alone for years. Now I take care of him, too. And I'm guessing you help your grandpa?"

Ellen's smile returned, softer this time. "I do. He's ornery and doesn't always listen, but he loves me and wants what's best."

Catherine smiled too, because she understood that kind of love. She realized she never gave her new friend her name.

"I'm Catherine," she said, reaching out a hand. Ellen grasped it without hesitation, and Catherine's fingers brushed against the calluses on her palm.

A girl who had endured a hard life but still carried a soft smile.

A girl she hadn't noticed until now. Because she'd been too busy noticing those who didn't want to notice her.

A Bridge to Question

Reese

The bridge looked like many early twentieth-century bridges, with an overhead truss structure, other than the blockades on either end that prevented vehicles from passing over its fragile platform. Reese didn't know why her footsteps that afternoon led her to explore the legendary spot in Lauderdale County that brought outsiders to take photos and videos of their visit, exploiting the local legend of a murderer's story for their followers on social media. The stories of hauntings would have amused her any other time, but now that she'd been experiencing some strange sightings and phenomena herself, she didn't know how she felt about what she'd read on the internet. At least now she had internet service, even if it failed at a consistent connection.

Stepping past the overgrown vegetation to walk onto the bridge, she observed the faded graffiti paint that looked more like sidewalk chalk on the old wooden planks, while the gaps in between them allowed her to peer below to the murky water flowing underneath the creaky structure. If it wasn't for the graffiti on the blockades and the bridge, the site might be like any other country bridge you'd encounter. Different birds chirped, and water trickled in a rhythm, creating a serene setting for an afternoon walk. She liked it, but only in the daytime. It didn't seem so scary, as she listened to the peaceful sounds surrounding her and watched a fish surface as it jumped, before heading back into the depths where the muddy waters hid its descent.

A dog barked, so she looked up to find Addie and Cash approaching from the other side of the bank, on the opposite side of their houses.

"So you decided to brave a walk on the creepy bridge, eh?" Addie asked, her spiked hair glistening with hair spray or gel, which held it in place. Her makeup line ran along her jawline, and Reese resisted the urge to smooth it out and blend it with her sleeve.

"It's a nice walk. What's over there?" She looked past Addie at the path that led behind some trees.

"It's a nice walk, too, and if you go right, you'll run into the little beach area down there. See?" She pointed to a sandy area where a boat launch held a couple of kayaks and a small fishing boat.

"People kayak in that?" She scrunched her nose at the brown water, thinking about what might lurk underneath. She doubted the fish she'd seen earlier swam alone in the river. Though beautiful, the river's mystery was best observed, not experienced.

"They sure do, and they love it. It's quite the popular activity every season. You should try it sometime. Jamie can show you some tricks since he kayaked often during his summers here."

"I think this is as close to that water as I'd like to be."

Addie laughed, petting the top of her dog's head. "Hear that, Cash? We finally found someone more afraid of the river than you."

"Cash doesn't like the river?"

"Cash doesn't like water at all. You'd think he'd been born a cat, and this is his last life, but he came back as a dog."

Reese laughed with Addie at Cash's expression, like he knew they talked about him and his fear of the river. He whined and pulled at his leash, ready to go down the road to his house.

Addie looked toward Reese's house and squinted. "Are you expecting company?"

Reese turned in the direction of Addie's gaze, and there right outside her house stood a woman, looking down at them.

"No, I'm not. What do you suppose she's doing?"

"Well, I don't know, but you might want to go see. Probably one of those multi-level marketing people. I've lived through a few generations, and they seem to pop up anew every decade. They might have different products, label them differently, or modernize them, but it's all the same. Good luck!"

She left Reese, struggling to keep up with Cash as he raced toward home. Reese sighed, wishing she could follow them. She wasn't in the mood to deal with a salesperson, but even if this woman wanted to sell her something, why was she at the back of the house,

staring at the river? Something about it didn't sit right. Southern hospitality was one thing, but strangers lurking uninvited on her property wasn't part of the deal.

After exiting the bridge, she walked down the road toward the driveway, bracing herself to reject whatever the woman was selling—makeup, essential oils, miracle vitamins. She loved essential oils, and some supplements were worth their salt, but that didn't mean she wanted a stranger pitching them in her backyard.

She could use a real money-making opportunity, though. A real one. Something sustainable. Not another side hustle with empty promises.

Her bank account wouldn't be kind to her if she couldn't replenish it soon with a consistent flow of income.

As she rounded the house to the back, her steps slowed.

The woman stood motionless, her back to Reese, staring at the riverbank below. A light breeze ruffled the hem of her floral-print skirt, but she didn't move, didn't acknowledge Reese's approach.

Reese swallowed. Something about the way she stood—rigid, arms wrapped tightly around herself, shoulders trembling ever so slightly—made Reese pause.

Not a salesperson. She stepped closer.

"Can I help you?"

The woman jumped as if Reese had blasted an air horn next to her ear.

Reese raised her hand in apology. "I'm sorry. I didn't mean to startle you. I live here."

The woman turned, her tear-streaked face catching the late-afternoon light. Her shoulder-length blonde hair needed a root touch-up, but the soft, sweeping style framed her features beautifully. She looked about forty-something, her striking features shadowed by the unmistakable weight of recent trauma.

Reese didn't know how she knew that—not exactly—but ever since her failed marriage, she'd developed a keen sense for recognizing pain in others.

"Did you say you live here?" The woman's voice wavered, and she dropped her arms, grasping the fabric of her skirt as if she needed something to hold onto.

Reese hesitated. "I just moved in. My uncle left it to me when he passed."

The woman's face went bone white. She swallowed hard.

"You okay? Did you know my uncle?"

The woman's breath hitched. "Not exactly. My mother did."

She bit her lip and turned back to the river, blinking rapidly as fresh tears slipped down her cheeks.

Reese stepped forward, an unease curling in her stomach. "Did you—did you not know he passed?"

The woman's voice dropped to a quiet, brittle whisper, so faint Reese had to lean in to hear.

"I know. I'm the one who found him."

Reese stiffened.

"What? What do you mean, you found him? They said a neighbor discovered him."

The woman finally met Reese's gaze, her expression unreadable. "I live about ten miles from here, so no, I'm not exactly a neighbor. But my mother lived down the road aways. Maybe that's why they got it confused. Besides, everyone's considered a neighbor here."

Something about this conversation pressed against Reese's nerves in all the wrong ways. It wasn't just the words—it was the way the woman spoke them. She wasn't just mourning.

She was hiding something.

Reese's initial wariness softened into something else—concern? Pity? An odd pull toward her? She had to be at least ten years older than Reese, yet something in her demeanor made Reese feel like she needed to protect her.

"Would you like to come inside?" Reese offered. "I'm still unpacking, but I finally set up my coffee pot. I can make you a cup of coffee or tea if you'd rather. I have one of those off-brand machines with the pods, though, so if you prefer a good old-fashioned drip, you might be disappointed."

The woman shook her head sharply, like she had just remembered she wasn't supposed to be here. "No, thank you. I've taken up enough of your time. I need to go before it gets dark."

She turned to leave.

"Wait," Reese called. "I don't even know who you are. How did your mom know my uncle?"

The woman's back stiffened. Every muscle in her body seemed to coil.

"Like I said," she murmured, "I have to go."

Then she moved. Fast.

She darted to her car, her long skirt swaying with each hurried step.

Reese's pulse spiked. "Wait! How did you know my uncle? At least tell me that!"

The woman skidded to a stop at the edge of the road, hesitating just long enough to turn back.

For a moment, she only stared.

Then, in a voice low and final, she said, "I shouldn't have come here. It's best you don't know. You don't want to know."

She spun and rushed toward a silver Toyota parked just beyond the trees.

Reese didn't hesitate. She yanked out her phone, aimed the camera, and snapped a picture, her heart pounding as the car roared to life and sped away.

The taillights vanished around the curve of the road.

Reese stared at her screen, flipping through the photos.

A clear shot of the license plate.

Her hands trembled slightly as she lowered the phone.

So odd.

She had never experienced a conversation so laden with mystery, so thick with unspoken meaning.

And she knew exactly who to ask about it.

She turned back toward the house, scanning the yard as if the shadows might reveal more than she wanted to see.

When she opened the front door, the clocks chimed again.

The sound crawled over her skin, thick and heavy, as if time itself was trying to tell her something.

She crossed her arms over her chest, gripping them tightly.

A whisper of a thought pressed against the back of her mind.

Uncle Art... what did you get me into?

The Gathering Darkness

Stuckey

The night pressed in close, thick with the damp scent of earth and pine, the musk of decay rising from the underbrush. The woods listened. Not empty but waiting. Their silence was the kind that swallowed men whole.

Moonlight slashed through the canopy, carving the forest floor into jagged shadows that stretched and writhed as the wind stirred the trees. Something scurried through the brush—quick, nervous. Insects droned, their ceaseless dirge weaving through the trees. An owl's cry split the night, high and mournful, before the hush devoured it again.

He moved through the undergrowth, his boots grinding against the brittle remains of last season's leaves. The knife rested easy in his grip, its handle warm against his palm, fitting there as if it had always belonged.

Ahead, the coyote lay still. The trap had done its work.

Moonlight glinted off the steel jaws clamped around her hind leg, blood pooling into the dirt in dark rivulets. She should have been thrashing. Howling. Fighting with everything left in her. Instead, she only panted, chest rising in uneven bursts, her yellow eyes locked onto his.

She saw him.

A flicker of unease coiled in his gut.

She should be afraid. They all were. He'd seen it in their eyes before—wild, desperate terror, the last pathetic struggle before the inevitable. But this...

This was something else.

The wind stirred the branches overhead, sending shifting shadows flickering over the ground like restless specters. Beyond the ridge, the river gurgled as it passed, its sound distant now, muffled—as though he stood just outside the reach of the world.

He crouched beside the coyote, pressing his knee against her ribs. A tremor ran through her body, but she didn't fight. Didn't flinch. Didn't beg.

She was waiting. Not out of resignation—but determination. There was something behind those yellow eyes. Not terror but resolve. She wasn't just staring at him. She was holding his attention.

The hunger gnawed at him, curling sharp and deep in his gut. He had done this before, again and again. The release should come now. It always had before.

His fingers tightened around the knife.

The first strike. The first howl of terror as the pain ripped through her.

Another strike. Then another.

Warm muscle surrendered to steel, but the rush never came.

The coyote's breath left her body with barely a sigh, the woods swallowing the sound before it could settle. No struggle. No fight.

No satisfaction.

His pulse pounded slow and heavy in his ears.

He wiped the blade clean, pressing it into the damp earth. Blood stained the dirt beneath him, already darkening, sinking into the hungry ground. He pried open the trap, plucked a tuft of fur from the bloodied metal teeth, and tucked it inside his coat.. But the trophy felt as empty as the eyes that stared back at him.

Without another glance, he turned toward the tree line. His shadow stretched long before him, bent and twisted in the moonlight.

The exhilaration faded before he reached the edge of the woods.

It hadn't been enough.

It never would be.

Not until he fed it properly.

Not until he felt the heat of human blood and he had a trophy worth keeping.

Catherine settled onto the worn wooden planks, shifting to find a comfortable position. She tucked her skirts beneath her, careful to keep them from dragging against the dirt, and leaned back on her hands. The bridge became hers at this hour—her refuge, her quiet place away from crowded places and awkward stares.

The evening air cooled her skin, a welcome relief after the lingering warmth of the afternoon sun. The river moved below, slow and lazy, rippling with the occasional fish darting beneath its surface. She flipped open the book in her lap, brushing her fingers over the familiar pages.

Her lips moved silently as she read, but the words didn't sink in. Something felt... different.

She glanced up, frowning toward the trees on the far side of the river. The woods had always felt wild to her, tangled and unbroken by the hands of men. But today, the trees seemed taller, their shadows longer. A weight pressed against the air, thickening it. The usual chatter of birds and insects had softened, a hush spreading through the branches.

Catherine swallowed, shaking her head. She was being ridiculous, like a child scared of silly ghost stories.

Still, she let her gaze drift over the tree line one more time before forcing her attention back to her book.

A sudden creak beneath her sent a jolt through her spine.

Her heart leapt. She whipped her head around.

It seemed as if something breathed deep, heavy breaths nearby. Scanning the river's edge, then behind her once again, she saw nothing. Heard nothing.

The wind moved through the bridge's beams, stirring the loose boards beneath her. She let out a small, breathless laugh, placing a hand over her chest to still her racing pulse. Her imagination painted shadows where there were none.

The bridge had always creaked—it was old, worn by years of wind, rain, and footsteps. She had no reason to feel watched. No reason to feel the weight of something unseen, hovering just beyond the edge of her vision.

And yet...

She rubbed her arms against the sudden chill.

A rustling, a shift in the underbrush.

Her breath caught, fingers clenching the spine of her book. Something was there.

Catherine turned her head sharply, once again scanning the woods where the sound had come from.

The trees swayed, while the wind stirred the dying leaves, sending a soft whisper skimming across the bridge. A trick of the wind. That's all.

Still, her pulse refused to slow.

"Catherine?"

She gasped, her book slipping from her lap onto the planks. She turned to see Ellen standing a few feet away, her hazel eyes wide.

Catherine let out an unsteady breath, shaking her head. "You startled me."

"It seems we easily startle on this bridge." Ellen glanced toward the woods, as if she, too, sensed something lingering there. "Are you all right?"

Catherine hesitated. She didn't want to sound foolish. If she said she felt as though something unseen had been watching, Ellen might laugh—or worse, believe her.

"I'm fine," she said, bending to retrieve her book. "Just... lost in thought."

Ellen didn't look convinced, but she didn't press. She studied her a moment longer before plopping down beside her friend on the bridge, her thin legs stretched out, swinging gently.

Catherine smiled, grateful for her friend's presence, and refusing to give in to the feeling that something—or someone—remained behind, watching.

Shadows and Faces

Reese

Reese leaned against the bridge's railing, watching the murky water churn beneath them. The river always moved, always shifted, yet somehow, it felt as though it hid something beneath its restless surface—like a secret waiting to be discovered.

"So, you think that could have been Patricia's daughter?" She and Addie had been talking more and more, but Reese wasn't sure how she felt about it. She spilled her guts about her divorce and how Dylan and her friends had betrayed her, and now she figured Addie probably told her grandson, too, since James now looked at her with sympathetic eyes. She should have told Addie to keep it to herself. Despite her spunky, nosy personality, Reese somehow knew that the older woman wouldn't gossip if she'd asked her not to say anything. For Reese, that would be an unspoken agreement, but for some, it didn't work that way.

Addie sighed, rolling Cash's leash around her wrist as they strolled along the old bridge. "Maybe, but I don't know her name. Fact is, I barely remember Patricia at all. I'm surprised I even remembered that much."

"Who was she?"

"She dated Art for a while." Addie squinted, as if searching through years of forgotten memories. "Didn't last long, maybe a few months, but I don't remember when exactly. Just before he passed, I reckon."

Reese frowned. "What happened to her?"

"That's the thing—I don't know. I mean, I do know she went missing a little while before Art died, but nobody could figure out what happened to her." Addie's voice darkened slightly. "One of those cases where people had their suspicions but no real answers."

Reese's stomach twisted. "So she disappeared, and then Uncle Art died soon after."

Addie nodded. "That's right."

Reese hesitated. "She suspects he had something to do with her mother's disappearance."

Addie shrugged. "People wondered, but there wasn't anything solid to go on. Art wasn't exactly a popular man around here, but no one disliked him. They just didn't really know him. And no one pegged him for a killer. And with no body, no evidence, what could they do, anyway?"

Reese wanted to dismiss it—the very idea of her uncle being involved in something like that made her skin crawl.

But the truth was, she hadn't known him well, either.

She only knew what her mother had told her about him.

He had always been that distant relative, the one who sent the occasional Christmas card but never really inserted himself into her life. She had assumed he was just a loner, someone who preferred his own company.

But what if there had been another reason he kept his distance?

She exhaled, rubbing her arms. "This just keeps getting stranger."

Addie tilted her head, studying her. "Did the girl say why she came to Art's house?"

"No, and that's what bothers me. And how did you not know she was the one who found him when he died?"

Addie's expression turned slightly sheepish. "Oh, right. I forgot—you don't know about my accident."

Reese straightened. "Accident?"

"Got hit by a semi on the highway, right before your uncle died. I ended up in the hospital for weeks. Lacerated spleen, cracked ribs, fractured pelvis—the works." She scratched Cash behind his ears, and he leaned into her touch, panting in appreciation. "By the time I found out about Art, he was already in the ground. I had some family visit me in the hospital, but their minds weren't on the happenings on this road. Jamie wanted to tell me, but he said later he didn't want to upset me." She chuckled dryly. "Imagine not wanting to upset a woman with a fractured pelvis."

Reese winced. "That's awful, Addie. I'd have never known." The older woman walked with a determined gait, as if she dared her own body to slow her down.

"Well, we keep going till we can't." Addie gave a knowing nod. "No use in stopping 'til we have to."

Reese offered a half-smile but sighed, looking up at the empty spot where the woman had stood yesterday in her backyard. The memory sat uneasily in her mind. "None of this makes sense."

Addie smirked. "Things around here rarely do, girl."

"Then why stay?"

"Because home is home. Quirks and all."

"I don't call mysterious women and murdering ghosts quirks."

"What do you call 'em?"

"Freaky. And certainly not welcome in my home."

Addie threw her head back and laughed, the sound rolling across the water and echoing through the trees. Cash's ears perked up, clearly unimpressed that her amusement had interrupted his attention.

"Have you had any more Stuckey appearances?"

"No," Reese admitted, glancing back toward the house. "Not since that night. But other strange things have been happening. I guess the wiring's bad in the house."

"The wiring?"

"The lights flicker all the time. And the clocks... they chime when they shouldn't. Not just one—all six of them."

Addie whistled. "That is strange. You want Jamie to check it out for you?"

Reese caught the sly look in the older woman's eyes and shook her head. "No, thank you. I'm more concerned with my real surprise guest yesterday." She hesitated, then added, "I got her license plate number in a photo."

Addie's eyebrows lifted. "Smart thinking."

"You got whose license plate number?"

Reese turned at the sound of James' voice. He strode onto the bridge, hands in his pockets, his face unreadable.

Addie smiled. "How lucky it is that you show up now."

"Why lucky?"

"Because Reese needs your help. I think it's time you tell her what you do for a living." She winked at James before tugging Cash's leash. "Come on, boy, let's get home before the rain comes."

Reese watched the dog follow eagerly, his tail wagging, but his pace quickened as they left the bridge behind. Maybe Cash had the right idea.

James turned back to her. "What did you mean when you said you got someone's license plate number?"

Reese folded her arms. "What did she mean about you needing to tell me what you do?"

James smirked. "Oh no. You first."

She sighed, rolling her eyes. "Fine. But I just felt a raindrop, so let's go to the house."

A loud splash from the river cut through the air. Reese stiffened, spinning toward the railing, peering down at the water below. Bubbles and ripples spread across the surface.

"Did you hear that?"

"Hear what?"

Reese squinted. The muddy river stretched below them, its surface thick and swirling—but something about it felt wrong. For a second, she swore she saw something just beneath the water. A shape. A figure floating just below the surface.

A body.

She blinked hard, then the vision was gone. Only the dark, restless water remained.

James exhaled. "It's a river. Water splashes."

Reese forced herself to nod, before turning and following him up the road as more raindrops hit her nose.

Inside the house, Reese flipped on the lights, half-expecting them to flicker again. They didn't. The clocks stayed silent. The air, thick with humidity, carried the faint scent of rain drifting through the open window. For once, the house felt still, as if mocking her.

James shrugged off his rain-spattered jacket and draped it over a chair. The distant roll of thunder vibrated through the walls, a low hum beneath the silence.

"Do you drink tea or coffee?" Reese asked, filling the vintage kettle with water.

"Coffee, mostly. But I don't mind tea." He leaned against the counter, watching her. "Do you have local honey?"

"I do. I stopped at a roadside market outside of Meridian. I also picked up some peaches."

"Ah, the last of the season." He smirked. "Not that Gram would admit it. She says fall forgets Mississippi most years."

Reese chuckled. "She's got a point. It's different from what I'm used to, although I can still feel the change."

"You miss Missouri?"

She hesitated, pouring the steaming water into their mugs. "Some."

James took his tea and stirred in a spoonful of honey, watching the golden liquid dissolve into the dark swirl. "I live in Biloxi, near the coast. But I'm thinking of moving back here."

Reese arched a brow. "Oh, why?"

"Gram only has me now. My dad was her only child, and I'm her only grandson. She has nieces and nephews from siblings who've passed, but as for immediate family, I'm it. With both my parents gone, She's it for me, too. And it's nice that she can fill me in on the parts of Dad I never knew."

Reese nodded, a quiet understanding passing between them. She knew all about being an only child, and she knew what it was like to lose someone—to be left sorting through their life like a puzzle, trying to understand the pieces they never shared. If only she knew more about her own father, about her uncle, too. Why hadn't she pressed her mother to share more?

Outside, the rain picked up, pattering against the porch steps.

James took a slow sip of tea before setting his mug down. "So," he said, "why were you getting someone's license plate number?"

Reese set her own mug aside and told him about the woman from the day before—her sudden appearance, the cryptic remarks, the way she had fled. James listened without interrupting, fingers drumming lightly on the countertop, his expression unreadable.

"I remember speaking to the detective on your uncle's case," he said finally. "He told me they had no evidence or reason to suspect foul play. They questioned the woman who found your uncle deceased, but had no reason to suspect her, either. She didn't even go in the house, but called them right away. The coroner said he fell and hit his head."

"That's what I was told when they contacted me."

Did you get a good look at this woman?"

Reese nodded. "Blonde, tall, mid-forties. Pretty. Dressed boho-style."

James smirked. "Boho?"

"Flowy skirt, baggy blouse. Cute—on the right people."

He nodded, but seemed bemused. "You still have the license plate number?"

Reese pulled out her phone and swiped the photos, then turned it so he could see.

James leaned in, studying the screen. "Mind if I send these to my phone?"

She hesitated. "Why?"

His gaze flicked to her. "Because Gram was right. I should probably tell you what I do for a living." A slow smile tugged at his lips, but his eyes were serious. "I'm a detective with the Biloxi Police Department."

Reese blinked. That explained a lot. His natural suspicion when they met. His attention to detail. It all made sense.

James tapped his phone against his palm, then turned his attention back to the screen. He started to send the photos to himself—then stilled. His brow furrowed.

"What is it?" Reese asked.

"When did you take these photos of the bridge?"

"Same day I took the ones of her license plate."

Without a word, he turned the phone toward her.

"Do you know this man?"

Reese's heart flipped. The screen showed the bridge, its wooden planks stretching over the dark river, mist curling along the edges. The trees loomed in the distance; skeletal branches blurred in the background. She had posed her selfie just right, to catch the river in the background, and in the afternoon light of the golden hour.

But she wasn't alone in the picture.

A figure stood in the background, half-hidden in the deepening shade of the late afternoon. Tall. Dressed in vintage clothing, with a long coat with tails, a vest, and a top hat.

His face was sharp, his features stretched into something unnatural—not quite a smile, not quite a sneer. It was the expression of someone who had already won a game she didn't even know she was playing.

Her fingers turned numb, the air around her suddenly colder.

"He looks like he knows you," James said.

Reese's throat tightened. Her stomach curled in on itself, twisting into something sharp and unfamiliar.

"I know him, too."

The words came out hollow, barely above a whisper. She barely got them out before the weight of recognition crashed down on her.

That face. That smile. She had seen him before.

Outside. On her deck.

With a noose around his neck.

———

Sleim snarled, his clawed fingers twitching as he loomed in the darkness, his molten gaze fixed on the two humans at the table. He watched their faces—watched the fear creep into the girl's eyes as she stared at the photo, the troubled hesitation in the man beside her.

"She sees too much," Sleim spat, his voice a guttural growl. "I say we finish her now."

Belias didn't even glance at him. He stepped forward, his own gaze never leaving Reese and James.

"No. We wait."

Sleim bristled. "Wait? Wait for what?"

Belias moved in a blur. One moment he was still, the next his boot slammed between Sleim's shoulder blades, driving him to the ground with enough force to rattle the very air.

"I said wait." His voice was a whisper of venom, but the weight of it sent tremors through the room.

Sleim writhed beneath his grip but didn't fight back. Not against Belias. Not yet.

Then, a slow, rhythmic clap echoed behind them.

The temperature in the room spiked in an instant, suffocating, thick with sulfur. Heat rippled across the air like waves rolling from an open furnace.

Belias went still.

Sleim whimpered.

Sonnellion had arrived.

The greater demon stepped forward, his black wings brushing the ceiling, their edges charred as if the fires of Hell had never stopped licking at them. His grin was carved like a blade, his eyes burning coals beneath a heavy brow.

"You disappoint me, Sleim." His voice slithered through the air, an oily mixture of mockery and malice. "I expected more."

Sleim straightened, masking his tension beneath a cool expression.

Sonnellion strolled past, exhaling heat with every breath, the walls themselves seeming to shudder. He glanced toward the two humans, tilting his head as he studied them like insects under glass.

"Look at them," he mused. "So engrossed. So oblivious to what lurks just beyond their sight." He smirked, his lip curling with amusement. "And yet... they feel us, don't they? They sense the shift in the air. The shadows creeping closer. Even if they don't admit it."

Sleim, still pressed into the ground, growled through his fangs. "She is ripe for an attack. Just like him."

Sonnellion's grin widened, then vanished in an instant.

The room darkened.

In a movement faster than a human eye could track, he crouched, seizing Sleim by the jaw, his claws sinking into flesh and bone. Sleim's body convulsed, his eyes bulging in agony as black veins spidered out beneath his skin.

"You don't understand, do you?" Sonnellion's voice was velvet-wrapped steel, a whisper laced with impending doom.

He squeezed.

Sleim choked on a strangled cry.

"He did not need much prodding," Sonnellion continued, his voice calm, almost pitying. "The filth of his own soul was already an open door. He welcomed us. He reveled in what we gave him." His grip tightened, claws burrowing deeper, filling Sleim's throat with fire. "She is different. If you act too soon, you will ruin everything. It's a slow burn with some of them, and it takes patience to feed that fire."

Belias smirked. "That's what I tried to tell him."

Sonnellion shoved Sleim back with a flick of his wrist, sending him sprawling. The lesser demon scrambled to his knees, eyes burning with resentment but wisely holding his tongue.

Sonnellion straightened again, his attention flicking toward James now, his smile stretching into something dark and satisfying.

"We must remind her of how they betrayed her," he murmured. "Isolate her. Make her doubt. Make her weak."

He took a slow step forward, shadows clinging to his form like mist.

"And what better place to start..."

Another step.

The light in the room flickered.

"...than with him?"

Belias chuckled, low and knowing.

"Yes," he agreed. "That part has already begun."

Sleim's lip curled, though he remained kneeling. "And what of her church invitation?"

Belias' smirk faded.

Sonnellion's expression twisted into something unreadable, something... dangerous.

"Ah," he muttered, his wings shifting. "That."

They turned their attention back toward James, watching the flicker of hesitation in his expression. Watching as Reese's words still lingered in the air between them. She was considering it.

Sonnellion sneered. "That seed must not take root. Work on him, too. Remind him why he shouldn't trust another."

Belias nodded, his voice cold. "We'll make her too familiar. Too easy to believe in. Then remind him how that ended last time."

Sonnellion exhaled another blast of scorching air, his satisfaction palpable.

"Do whatever you must," he said, his voice like a death sentence. "But if she steps foot inside that church... if she begins to pray..."

His wings unfurled, blocking out the dim light as his voice reverberated through the space, ancient and full of fury.

"...it will be your head on the floor beneath me."

Belias stiffened. Sleim let out a strangled whimper.

Then—the light returned.

Sonnellion was gone, but the air still simmered with the memory of his presence, the shadows still darker than they should have been.

Sleim remained crouched, seething. He lifted his head slowly, fury burning behind his ember-like eyes.

"A day will come," he hissed, barely audible.

Belias turned to him, the ghost of a smirk still on his lips.

"You'd be wise not to dwell on that," he murmured. "Focus on what needs to be done here."

Sleim flexed his claws. "And what is that?"

Belias gestured toward the humans, still oblivious to the darkness lurking around them.

"Keep watch. Alert me if you see any light warriors. But do not engage."

Sleim's jaw tensed. "And where are you going?"

Belias' gaze flickered with something colder than before.

"We'll need reinforcements."

He glanced toward Reese again, the locket at her throat catching the dim light, and his smirk returned.

"His plans for her cannot unfold."

With that, he vanished into the shadows.

Sleim remained, his claws flexing against the floor, his eyes smoldering.

A moment later, the lights in the house flickered.

And the clocks chimed.

Blood and Innocence

Catherine

The bridge had become their meeting place—a sanctuary between two lives that neither fully belonged to. The sun, pale and hazy, barely broke through the thick clouds above, casting the world in a strange, silver gloom. Below, the river flowed sluggish and dark, like ink pooling in the earth.

Catherine had hoped Ellen would come today. They had met twice before, each time discovering more similarities, more unspoken understanding. Catherine had never met another girl who truly loved books—who could talk about characters in stories like they were as real as the people around them. She had never met someone so unassuming, who wanted to know Catherine as much as Catherine wanted to know her.

"I wish I could stay and talk," Ellen said, shifting the small sack slung over her shoulder. "But my grandpa wants to move camp. He says the fish are better downriver, so we're packing up. I need to grab some things from town before nightfall."

Catherine tucked a loose strand of hair behind her ear. "Then let me walk with you. There's a shortcut I can show you, and then I can ride home with my pa after he finishes work."

Ellen's face lit up. "That'd be great! It's so nice to talk about something other than politics for once."

Catherine chuckled. "Sounds like my pa. Though sometimes he tells me to stop talking about politics. We women aren't supposed to worry over such things, you know."

Ellen smirked, lifting an eyebrow. "Sounds like you do worry over such things."

"For someone so young, you're quite perceptive."

Ellen shrugged. "Maybe. Do you care about politics?"

"Sometimes. But mostly, I don't like people telling me what I should care about," Catherine said.

A sharp, shrieking cry ripped through the woods.

Both girls stopped mid-step.

Ellen swallowed. "Catherine... is this the shortcut? Aren't we headed away from town?"

Catherine blinked, realizing she had veered off the main path. The underbrush here was thick, twisting, more overgrown than she remembered. "Oh—sorry. This way."

Ellen didn't move. She turned her head slightly, listening. The wind had died completely, the branches overhead still and watchful.

"What is it?" Catherine asked.

Ellen hesitated. "Didn't you hear that? It sounds like—Never mind. Maybe I imagined it."

Another cry—this one high, agonized. A mixture of desperation and fear.

"That wasn't your imagination," Catherine said, already stepping forward.

"Catherine, wait!"

She didn't.

The woods seemed to breathe around them, swallowing the sound of their footsteps as they wove deeper into the trees. Every branch they passed felt like it held a presence, like the forest braced itself for something.

Then Catherine saw it.

The coyote's body lay twisted and brutalized, its fur slashed apart and hacked in pieces, but with frenzied precision. Dark stains soaked the dirt around it, like a crude altar made of blood and soil. No, not an altar. An evil and barbaric sacrifice.

Four pups cried near the corpse of their mutilated mother. Tiny, shivering, pressed against the cold and stiff body that could no longer warm them.

Catherine fell to her knees, barely breathing, as she scooped up the nearest one. It fit inside her palm, trembling.

"Oh—" Ellen gasped, stepping back so quickly she almost tripped. "Oh, no—what—what could have done this to her?"

"Not what. *Who*. It was a man," Catherine said, her voice hollow. "A man did this."

Ellen clutched at her shawl, her eyes darting wildly across the clearing. "But why? If someone wanted its fur, they would've skinned it. If they were hunting—"

Catherine swallowed, staring at the deep, jagged wounds carved into the coyote's side. No clean cuts. No mercy.

"He did it for sport," she murmured.

Ellen's breath hitched. "That's—" She turned, her hands shaking as she wiped at her eyes. "Last night... My grandpa and I heard something."

Catherine looked up sharply.

Ellen's voice dropped to a whisper. "Howling. And then... something else. Squealing. Crying." She sucked in a breath. "We heard it happening."

A weight settled deep in Catherine's stomach, and she felt sick.

Ellen picked up a pup and hugged it close to her chest, her face pale, lips pressed tight as if holding in something she wasn't ready to say.

Catherine felt the same. The kind of fear that clung to your ribs and made you doubt your own reality.

She looked down at the tiny, helpless pup in her hands.

Just like them, it had lost its mother to cruelty. Someone out there had taken pleasure in this barbaric act.

And somewhere in the woods, maybe something-or some-one-really was watching.

———

Stuckey watched the girls from the shadows of the trees, their arms wrapped around the pups, their faces pale with the fresh taste of fear.

Their fear pleased him.

The coyote had been a paltry distraction, something to hold him over, to keep the hunger from consuming him whole, but it didn't work for long.

And now...

He needed to kill again.

Perhaps if he had smashed the skulls of those pups, it would have lasted longer. But he hadn't known about them. That coyote had diverted his attention for a cause. Her silence hadn't been resignation. It had been a bargain.

Even so, coyote pups wouldn't feed him. Not for long.

No—he needed human cries.

Her cries.

Some men longed for a woman's companionship. A wife. A house. A family.

But he longed for the smell of fear and death.

For the moment the soul broke free of its body.

The Dalton boys killed for gain, for greed, for practical necessity. He killed because it he needed the act itself. He sought it like a drunk pursued his bottle.

He inhaled deeply, savoring the last remnants of their horror-stricken expressions.

Then he turned and walked away from the instincts that pumped the blood in his veins.

And every step grew heavier, like wading through the sinking, relentless riverbed of mud.

———

Raphael stood at the edge of the bridge, watching the shadows coil at the edge of the trees, shifting with the restless wind. The river beneath whispered, a sluggish murmur, as if unwilling to bear witness to the darkness gathering in the woods beyond.

Tyrius stepped beside him, his expression grim. "He's escalating." Though he towered over Raphael, he inclined his head slightly—a silent deference to the leader he followed.

Raphael, pensive, nodded. "Yes."

Uriel said nothing, but his pinched expression and the set of his shoulders said enough.

"We need more protection," Lior added. Though shorter than the others, his lean, sinewy frame carried an unyielding strength. All four of them had sent demons shrieking into the abyss, but the darkness here festered, thick and stubborn, emboldened by the complacency among believers.

"We are all that's sent for now," Raphael said. "It's up to us."

Tyrius's gaze drifted toward the forest. The canopy shuddered, restless, though no wind stirred. "There are many of them. These evil minions twist his thoughts, whisper to him, fuel his desires."

"We need revival in God's people," Raphael said quietly. "Evil thrives when the righteous do nothing."

Uriel exhaled, his breath misting in the cool air. "His army here is weak. Distracted. Selfish."

"Then we strengthen the ones who aren't."

A snarl tore through the air.

The ugly little demon appeared in front of them, hissing, and baring jagged teeth before shielding itself against His light, then slinking back into the trees, its presence retreating like a stain bleeding into the night.

Lior smirked, but Raphael's expression remained unchanged, his gaze dark and knowing. "It wouldn't be so bold unless their forces were growing."

Beyond the bridge, the town stirred beneath a sky heavy with clouds, its people oblivious to the battle waging in the unseen. The angels turned toward the heart of it—toward the man who burned with holy fire.

But Raphael lingered. His eyes fell on the two girls below, their figures small beneath the sprawling reach of the bridge's shadow. A whisper of grief stirred in his chest—faint, but insistent. He wished he couldn't see what the Almighty allowed, especially when his duty extended to only a chosen few. It wasn't his place to question, to understand. A single tear traced his cheek, the light catching in the darkness of the moment. For some, it was already too late.

The Ghosts of Betrayal

Reese

The little church's steeple rose into the sky, its sharp peak piercing the soft, rolling clouds above. The cross atop it glinted in the late afternoon sun, a beacon against the endless blue.

Reese stood at the bottom of the steps, her stomach tightening. The building itself wasn't intimidating—grayish brick, white double doors, nothing grand or ornate. But small churches always felt suffocating.

In a crowd, she could disappear. Here, she'd stand out like a stain on a starched white shirt.

She adjusted the strap on her purse, stalling. She still wasn't sure why she had agreed to this.

Well, she was.

James had asked. Addie had insisted. And something in her—something she wanted to ignore—whispered that she needed to be here.

Not that she expected much.

Her last church had crushed her in ways she hadn't realized were possible. The very people who had prayed with her, shared meals with her, and studied scripture alongside her had turned their backs on her and followed her Judas.

She had expected grief over her husband's infidelity. She hadn't expected exile.

But exile came quickly when Dylan introduced them to his mistress.

When her supposed friends had fawned over the new woman, gushed over her engagement ring, and—worst of all—celebrated the baby Reese could never have given him.

That had been the worst. She should have known Dylan's popularity played a bigger role in those friendships than she did. They had all but patted Reese on the head and told her to move on, as if a broken heart and ten years of marriage was something to dust off like crumbs on a table. As if she had been the problem all along.

So, Reese had moved on. Right out of church and away from their rejection and betrayal.

She still loved Jesus. Still believed in Him with every fiber of her soul.

But she wasn't sure how to love His people anymore.

A quiet voice stirred in her mind, steady and familiar.

I have commanded you to love one another.

Reese's breath caught. It wasn't a thought she had summoned. It was just there, absolute and unmoving.

Her pulse quickened.

She knew the voice.

She just didn't know how to obey it.

The wooden steps creaked as a shadow moved beside her.

"Are you going in, or did you change your mind?"

Reese turned. Addie watched her, arms crossed, head tilted.

Despite her spiky hair and over-applied eyeliner, Addie saw too much. Her sharp gaze cut through Reese's defenses like a scalpel, and Reese had the distinct feeling she wasn't fooled by any excuses.

"I was just... enjoying the weather."

Addie squinted at the sky. "Enjoy it while you can. Droughts in Mississippi often hit like a curse."

"Gram, let her enjoy the sunshine without a guilt trip."

James' voice was easygoing, his smile a little too knowing. He had a presence that Reese found both frustrating and steady.

Then they stepped through the double doors at the top of the church steps.

Warm air met them, thick with the scent of old wood and faded hymnals. The soft murmur of conversation hummed through the sanctuary, people greeting one another, the occasional laugh breaking the low chatter. It wasn't a large congregation, but the energy of a hundred people could feel just as heavy as a thousand.

And then came the first roadblock.

A woman with caramel hair and French-manicured nails glided toward them, her smile sweet but sharp.

"Well, James, you brought a visitor."

The words were polite, but Reese wasn't stupid. Women like this had mastered the art of a slight wrapped in sugar. Take a bite, crack a tooth.

"Cassie, this is Reese Hayden. Reese, Cassie Milton."

Cassie's lips curled ever so slightly as she took in Reese, as if inspecting damaged goods. Then, as if Reese had ceased to exist, she turned her attention back to James.

"We went to school together, didn't we, James?" Cassie's hand rested on his arm. "Though it was a bit more than that, wasn't it?"

Well, that was subtle. Reese stiffened. She knew this game. Cassie wasn't just here to smile sweetly at James—she was marking her territory.

James only offered a sheepish smile, expertly steering the conversation elsewhere. "Where's Gage?"

Cassie's posture softened. "Running around with his little crew out back. He'll come in when the music starts."

James glanced at Reese. "Cassie has a son."

Addie chimed in. "How's his dad doing, Cass?"

"Oh, we're getting along better. He sees Gage on weekends now, and the strife has settled, so I can't complain." Her gaze slid back to James, her expression coy. "I guess it's lucky for you that you and Lynette never got married, huh?"

James flinched, and his jaw tightened. Barely noticeable, but Reese caught it. So did Addie, who shot Cassie a pointed look.

The woman immediately turned and drifted back to a cluster of other women, their gazes darting toward Reese with barely veiled interest.

Then the whispering began.

Reese tried not to grit her teeth and tighten her jaw. She didn't need another headache.

"Ignore that," Addie muttered. "Hens don't like a new hen prancing around their rooster."

Reese's head snapped toward her, scandalized. "Hens don't like who doing what?"

Addie smirked. "You heard me."

Flustered, Reese plopped into a seat beside her, putting distance between herself and James. This is why she had hesitated to attend church again. All she needed was a bunch of church women circling her like vultures.

Addie leaned in again, voice low. "You and Jamie—you're the same, you know. Running from hurt. But hiding won't keep it from finding you."

Reese glanced at James, who was speaking to an older man, his expression unreadable.

"Keep what from finding us?"

Addie patted her hand—a solid smack, not the gentle, grandmotherly kind. "Never mind."

Reese hesitated, then whispered, "What happened to him?"

Addie sighed, eyes flicking toward James. "He used to have a partner on the force-a woman. They were close; in fact, they dated, even though it was frowned upon in the department. We thought they'd marry, though. I liked her myself. Jamie brought her here a few times; they even sat together right here on this pew, which is how Cassie knows about her. Anyway, she betrayed him, and not only him, but the code they lived by as police officers. She took bribes and sold out people she was supposed to protect. And when James threatened to turn her in, she made sure the fallout landed on him instead."

Reese's stomach tightened. James had been betrayed, too. By someone he loved and trusted.

Addie paused, making sure Jamie was out of earshot. "But he never wavered. Even when they put him through rigorous interrogations, even when other friends on the force doubted him. He stood tall and answered their questions with the truth, and God took care of my boy. A witness came forward with evidence that Lynette had been the one involved, not Jamie. She's in jail today, and I'm afraid his trust is locked up with her," Addie murmured. Then she glanced at Reese, her lips twitching. "Though I have a feeling some folks might surprise him."

Reese blushed at what she implied, then cut her eyes to James again, this time with a different view of him. He caught her staring but said nothing as he sat down beside her.

Then the service started, and the first notes of the piano filled the sanctuary, followed by the familiar rise of voices singing an old hymn. Reese recognized it instantly.

Great is Thy Faithfulness

O God my Father

Something inside her cracked.

The last time she had heard this song, she had been sitting in a pew with Dylan, right after she found out about the affair, and she hadn't even told him she knew yet. Nor had she told their friends she knew they helped him cover it up. The irony of singing that song had hit her back then, and she had left church that day with the intention of never going back.

No one had missed her.

Her own church had left her to hurt alone, not even calling her husband out on what he had done but embracing him and his new wife.

The words of the hymn blurred as her memories sharpened.

Morning by morning, new mercies I see...

She couldn't do this.

She stood, headed for the back of the church, desperate for an escape. She barely heard James calling after her, barely saw Addie's confused frown.

All she saw were a hundred judgmental eyes watching her go.

Sleim laughed as Reese strode out of the church, her retreating figure stiff with tension. He could still taste the sting of rejection rolling off her like smoke curling from a dying fire.

Wounded believers were the easiest prey. One nudge, one whisper of isolation, and they pulled themselves out of the fold willingly. And the best part? Their own kind made it so easy. The righteous weren't just quick to cast stones—they tore each other apart, feeding on the wounded like vultures over a carcass, never realizing they were doing the enemy's work for him.

They hadn't been able to use her uncle the way they had wanted, but Reese? There were other ways to twist a wounded soul. He relished the thought of dismantling what remained of her fragile faith. To keep her blind to what had been set in motion long before she was born.

She didn't realize how close she had come to something bigger today.

Too close.

He and the others had seen to it that her husband never stood by her, never valued her. That her friends had abandoned her. That her sorrow had driven her here—to the very place where his plans had once been unraveled.

A shadow shifted beside him, the air thickening with heat.

"Are you ready?"

Belias.

Sleim hated the way the higher demons could slip in and out of the void at will. He still lacked that skill, forced to slink through shadows like a second-rate servant.

He straightened, brushing off his irritation. "Like I said, she's ripe. They make it too easy for us, don't they?"

Belias didn't answer at first, his yellowed eyes scanning the storm clouds gathering over the trees. When he finally spoke, his voice was a slow coil of contempt.

"They are notorious for eating their own." He let the words settle. "The ones who claim to serve Him do our work for us, tearing each other apart under the guise of righteousness."

Sleim smirked. "Then we should win this battle easily."

Belias turned, sharp and sudden, flicking a talon in the air. A ripple of energy pulsed between them, and an image materialized.

A woman praying.

Sleim recoiled. "Her? She's not the type."

Belias slammed him into the wall before he could react, claws twisting into his shoulder. "They're all the type, you worm."

Sleim choked on sulfur as Belias' breath scorched his face.

"When are you going to learn?" Belias hissed. "You don't need brute force to be truly evil. Their own evils will destroy them—a single unchecked grudge, a selfish ambition, a bitter wound left to fester." His sneer darkened, but his grip did not loosen. "That is where our strength lies."

He leaned in closer, his voice a growl. "But one praying believer—one who surrenders completely—can ruin it all." His claws dug deeper into Sleim's shoulder. "We had an entire stronghold once, back when we could have destroyed the fabric of faith in the early days of this country, but a single woman praying in her kitchen shattered it. A village bowed in darkness, and one intercessor brought it to its knees. You think flesh is weak, but you should remember when they cry out to Him, when they wield the power of His name, we are the ones who flee. Have you forgotten again, Sleim?"

Belias shoved him away with a final snarl. "Your arrogance already cost us before, right here, with Stuckey. One praying man stalled his evil then. Don't let it cost us now."

Sleim gasped for air. Then, despite the pain, a smirk curled on his lips.

"Speaking from experience, Belias?"

The larger demon went still.

Sleim pressed on, the words like poison-tipped daggers. "I know the stories. You failed once, didn't you? The village woman you speak of—Rebecca. Her prayers destroyed your plans in Salem, and you lost your chance at a promotion."

Belias' face darkened, his eyes like flames. "What do you know? We changed the court systems. They were never the same again after that. What's that saying? They threw out the baby with the bath water."

"Hmmm...maybe. But you cost us the chance at changing this nation for good."

Belias' claws tightened, puncturing Sleim's skin, but the jab was worth it.

Sleim wasn't finished.

"And Sonnellion—he lost, too, didn't he? All because of a single woman and her pitiful prayers." He coughed, tasting blood and sulfur. "Pathetic."

Belias' grip tightened for a heartbeat. Then, he shoved Sleim back, disgust curling his lips.

"You don't know what you're playing with."

Sleim spat, grinning despite the searing pain in his ribs. "I know enough."

Belias ran a talon down Sleim's cheek, slow and deliberate. Fire burned where he touched, and Sleim barely held back a cry of pain. When Belias pulled his hand away, a seared brand remained—marking him like Sonnellion had marked Belias back then.

"There's only one difference between me then and you now, Sleim," Belias muttered, voice dark as a dying star.

Sleim clenched his teeth. "What's that?"

"I had the wits to fear my superiors." He stepped back, eyes gleaming. "Good luck."

Then, in a rush of searing air, Belias vanished.

Sleim had barely caught his breath before a sharp stab sliced into his back, twisting him around with brutal force.

A wall of heat engulfed him. The ground beneath him burned as though he had been cast into the deepest pits of their domain.

He didn't have to turn to know who had arrived.

Sonnellion.

As his superior's claws dug into his throat, lifting him off his feet, Sleim no longer found much satisfaction in provoking Belias.

Not when his own torment had only just begun.

———

The knock at the door came just as Reese was about to turn off the porch light.

She sighed. She hadn't been expecting company. And she wasn't in the mood for it, either.

Opening the door, she found Addie standing on the other side, a Tupperware dish in her hands and a look that said she wasn't leaving anytime soon.

"Thought you might be hungry," Addie said, pushing past Reese like she owned the place. "Made gumbo. And before you say you ain't hungry, I don't believe you."

Reese exhaled, rubbing a hand over her face. "Addie, I appreciate it, but—"

"Don't start," Addie interrupted, setting the dish down on the counter. She turned, hand on her hip. "You ran outta church like a sinner caught stealin' the offering plate. And I'm just supposed to let that be?"

Reese stiffened. "I'm fine."

Addie narrowed her eyes. "Mmm. And I'm the Queen of England."

Reese let out a dry laugh. "Look, I just don't think church is for me anymore." She moved toward the counter, pulling open a drawer just for something to do. "It's too much. The whispers. The way people stare." She swallowed, gripping the edge of the counter. "I've been through enough, Addie. I don't need the judgment on top of it."

Addie leaned against the table, arms crossed. "Ain't nobody perfect, girl. Not me, not them, not you. But I'll tell you somethin'—the enemy loves when we think we're better off alone."

Reese clenched her jaw. "I never said I was better off. Just that I'm done."

"You done with God, too?"

Reese turned sharply. "Of course not."

"Could've fooled me," Addie said, not unkindly. "Faith isn't just you worshipping Jesus, Reese. The enemy loves when folks think that way."

Reese huffed. "So now I need people to be saved?"

"No," Addie said simply. "But you sure do need 'em to stand."

The words cut through Reese's carefully built walls.

Addie sighed and stepped closer. "You think I don't know? That I haven't been there? Sometimes church folks hurt worse than the world ever could. But you know what's worse than dealin' with 'em?" She nodded at Reese. "Doin' this. Lockin' yourself up. Pullin' away from the people who'd fight for you—*with* you." Reese's chest tightened.

Addie shook her head. "This fight you're in? It ain't just physical, and you know it. The worst thing you can do in spiritual warfare is isolate yourself." She crossed her arms. "I've lived here for years, seen things, experienced things—but for whatever reason, Stuckey, or whatever evil's at work, chose you. And you know why?"

Reese stayed silent.

"Because you're isolating yourself, and that weakens your resolve," Addie said firmly. "You think Jesus meant for us to fight battles alone?"

Reese swallowed hard, looking away.

Addie stepped closer, her voice gentler but no less certain. "Remember, Jesus loves His church—flaws and all. You can't love Him and hate what He died for."

Reese tensed, longing to tell the other woman to leave, so she could breathe in some space from the truth that threatened to suffocate her.

Addie continued. "You may not think you need the church, but you do. And what if the church needs you, too?"

Reese nearly scoffed at that. No one had ever needed her before. No one had ever sought her out.

And then she heard His voice, as clear as if He spoke as Addie just did.

I sought you out. Isn't that enough? How many have you sought to love? How many suffer alone as you do?

The room fell silent except for the faint ticking of the clock.

Addie gave her a knowing look. "I'll leave you be now." She tapped the container of gumbo. "Eat that. There's rice in a separate compartment—real rice, not that instant stuff." Her face softened. "God brought you here for a reason, Reese. He brought you to me, so don't go thinkin' I won't be back."

She walked to the door, pausing before stepping out.

"You weren't made to fight alone, Reese. None of us were."

Then she was gone.

Reese, for all her frustration, felt something shift inside her.

Swallowing back the tears, she had to admit—Addie's words of truth didn't suffocate, but cracked a window in a room she thought was sealed shut. She still wasn't ready to go back, though. Wasn't ready to step into that place where she had only known rejection.

But maybe... just maybe...she wasn't ready to be alone, either.

A Town's Secrets

Catherine

Catherine pulled on the heavy wooden doors of the livery stable, but they didn't budge. The latch held firm.

"It's closed. Now what?"

Ellen shifted the coyote pup in her arms, its small body warm against her chest. "Maybe he had to leave early. Is there another livery?"

"No. Blythe's is the only one in town." Catherine frowned at the empty hitching post and the dark interior of the stable. "That's odd. He's usually here until my pa leaves. They ride home the same way until the road splits before the bridge."

The earlier unease from the woods tightened in her stomach again. Something about this didn't feel right.

Across the street, Mr. White stood on the steps of his store, fitting a key into the lock.

"There's Mr. White," she said. "Maybe he'll know what to do with these pups."

They crossed the dusty road as the sky deepened into dusk, the scent of chimney smoke curling through the crisp autumn air.

"Hello, Mr. White."

He turned, a warm smile spreading beneath his neatly trimmed shadow of a mustache. "Catherine! Whatcha got there? Puppies?"

Catherine shifted the bundle in her arms so he could see. "Not exactly. They're coyote pups. Their mama is... gone. We couldn't leave them out there alone."

He frowned, glancing toward the livery stable. "Did you ask Mr. Blythe to take them? He's always had a soft spot for strays."

"We tried. But he's gone."

"Gone?" Mr. White's brows lifted. He turned his gaze to the livery again, his expression unreadable. "Strange. I've never seen him leave this early."

Catherine exchanged a glance with Ellen, the feeling of unease growing heavier. But why? Mr. Blythe leaving his business early shouldn't alarm her. She needed to calm her paranoia.

Pushing open the heavy oak door to his store, Mr. White stepped inside, the bell overhead jingling. The familiar scent of kerosene, fresh tobacco, and dry goods wrapped around them as they followed him in.

"Well, hello, young lady," Mr. White said, turning to Ellen. "Are you a newcomer?"

"Yes, sir. But only for a few days."

Catherine listened as Ellen repeated her story, but her thoughts drifted, her gaze sweeping over the busy street outside.

The town had changed since she and her father arrived a year ago. It was fuller now, buzzing with strangers—railroad men, travelers, merchants looking to take advantage of the town's growth. She barely knew half the people who passed by anymore.

And somewhere among them was someone cruel enough to kill for sport. No, not just kill. Brutalize. Torture.

"Catherine?"

She turned back to find both Ellen and Mr. White watching her.

"Sorry, Ellen. I got distracted."

Mr. White grabbed a crate and a burlap sack, then placed it on the floor in front of them.

Catherine cleared her throat, looking down at the pups she held, then up at the storekeeper. "Mr. White, would you—"

He was already shaking his head. "Sorry, dear, but no. I've been staying above the store lately, and I doubt the hotel guests next door would appreciate the yapping at night."

Catherine sighed. "What about your place on the river?"

"I have free range chickens, you know," he said, rubbing his chin. "They wouldn't get along too well, I'm afraid."

He looked down at the pups, then back at the girls. With a sigh, he gave a small, defeated smile. "Oh, alright. My hens can stay in the run for a while. Hard enough to reject a group of pups, but to reject two pretty ladies, too? I didn't have a chance, did I?"

Catherine smiled, relieved. But as she stepped forward to place the pups in a crate, something in her hesitated.

The pups whimpered, pressing against each other, their tiny bodies trembling. They pawed at the wooden slats of the crate, tongues out and panting.

Her hands stretched out as Mr. White reached down to lift the crate.

"Wait, Mr. White."

He paused, glancing at her in mild surprise. "What is it, Catherine?"

"It's just—"

"It's just that we should take them to my grandpa," Ellen cut in.

Catherine blinked at her. "Your grandpa is okay with that? I thought you needed to leave soon."

"Oh, we do, but... but..."

Before Ellen could scramble for an excuse, a voice interrupted from behind.

"What do we have here?"

Catherine turned to find Zeke striding into the store, his boots scraping across the wooden floorboards. He crouched beside the crate, studying the pups with lazy interest.

One pup yipped at his appearance. He reached in, grasped it by the loose scruff of its neck, then lifted it to eye level.

"Zeke! That's mean!" Catherine almost slapped his arm, but stopped herself.

"No, it's not mean. That's how their mama carries them." He smirked and lowered the pup. "Where'd you find these little fellas? There's probably an angry coyote mama out there, ready to tear into whoever took her babies."

Catherine swallowed. "We found them. Their mother is... gone."

Zeke's smirk faded. "Gone?"

"Someone killed her."

His jaw tightened. "Killed her?"

She nodded, her fingers tightening around her sleeves as she cradled her own chest.

"Stripped of its fur?"

"That's just it. It seems they killed it for sport. Not just killed it, but tortured it."

"Tortured?" His voice had lost all its usual teasing edge. He said nothing, but reached out to pet a pup, before it snapped at his fingers.

He pulled back, chuckling. "Hey now. Be nice."

Catherine smirked. "Maybe she just doesn't care for you."

Zeke shot her a sidelong glance. "What, you training them already?"

"Perhaps."

Ellen shifted, nervously twisting the chain of a locket Catherine hadn't noticed before.

"Ellen, what a beautiful locket."

Ellen glanced down, running her fingers over the delicate etching. "Thank you. It belonged to my ma."

She flipped it open, revealing a faded portrait of a woman with Ellen's eyes and cheeks.

Catherine smiled softly. "You look like her."

Ellen returned the smile, but it didn't quite reach her eyes. She shifted her eyes to Zeke, questioning.

"Oh, right. Zeke, this is Ellen. Ellen, Zeke."

Zeke nodded and tipped his hat. "I've seen you at church, haven't I? You're with a man, usually. Older gentleman. He your grandpa?"

Ellen nodded, smiling sheepishly, but Catherine felt shame. Even Zeke had noticed a young girl at church, and Catherine hadn't noticed her at all. If it wasn't for their affinity for the bridge, they might not have even met.

Zeke leaned against the counter. "So, you two decided to play mother to wild animals, huh?"

"Wild orphans. We couldn't just leave them," Ellen said.

Zeke tilted his head. "Well, if you need a place for them, my barn's open."

Catherine gawked at him. "Are you sure?"

"They'll be safe there. Besides, you can visit them anytime," he added with a wink.

Her face warmed, but she ignored him, focusing on the pup nestled against her chest.

"Alright," she said finally.

Zeke grinned. "Good. You're riding home with your pa, I assume?"

"Yes."

He tipped his hat. "Then I'll see you later, Cat."

Catherine narrowed her eyes at his use of her pa's nickname, but she didn't argue. She and Ellen said goodbye to the pups while Zeke spoke to Mr. White about an order.

As she, her pa, and Ellen drove out of town, Catherine looked at Blythe's Livery. Mr. Blythe stood in the doorway, watching White's General Store across the street.

His face was blank, and his stare, unblinking. Something powerful coursed through her veins when his eyes met hers.

A cold shiver ran through her.

After she and her pa dropped Ellen off at the bridge, Catherine leaned against the worn seat of the wagon, the steady clop of hooves stirring up the dusty earth beneath them. Twilight had begun its slow descent, casting long shadows over the road. A cool breeze carried the scent of pine and distant smoke, curling from the chimneys of homes nestled beyond the river. She tried to focus on the beauty of her surroundings, but all she could think about was two sets of eyes. One held mischief, another held mystery.

"Pa, have you noticed Mr. Blythe acting strangely lately?" she asked, keeping her voice casual.

Her pa didn't look over, his focus on the winding road ahead. "No, but I haven't been looking for anything, either. Why do you ask?"

Catherine hesitated, her fingers tracing the ridges of the wooden seat. "I don't know. He was just... different today, that's all. I'm sure it's nothing."

She didn't mention how his eyes had lingered on her Sunday after church, how the weight of his stare had made her feel like a butterfly pinned beneath glass.

Her pa let out a thoughtful hum. "He's probably just juggling too much at once. All these railroaders and their families coming into town call for a lot of business, and he works alone. Probably needs some help to manage his customers."

"But isn't that a good thing?"

"For business, sure. Not always for a man's sanity." He gave the reins a light flick, guiding the horse around a bend. "I'm swamped at the post office, too, but sometimes Zeke helps when the trains are slow. I'm grateful for that."

She glanced over. "Do you need me to help, Pa? I don't mind."

"That's no place for a lady, Cat. Best you steer clear."

Her brow furrowed. "The post office?"

"No, the train depot. And it's near the post office, so I'd thank you to mind me and stay away from there, too. The language those men speak ain't fit for a young lady."

She crossed her arms. "It's not like I haven't—"

The horses slowed as her pa tugged gently on the reins. He turned to her, his expression expectant. "Haven't what, Catherine Grace?"

She pursed her lips. "Oh, Pa. Men talk that way everywhere, if you have ears to listen."

He frowned. "Then stop listening."

With a click of his tongue, he urged the horses forward again. Catherine exhaled, staring at the trees as they passed in a blur of green, brown, and color shades hinting at autumn's arrival.

"This Ellen," her pa said, shifting the conversation. "You know much about her or her grandpa?"

"Not really. She only said they'd be here a couple of days, then they're heading to Jackson. Her grandpa's starting a shoe repair business."

"Well, that's nice. I wonder why he's here now?" He shrugged. "Anyway, I wish we had someplace for them to sleep, but I suppose her grandpa knows how to set up a camp properly."

She laughed, nudging his arm. "I'm sure he does, Pa. But no one sets up camp like you, do they?"

He chuckled, giving her an affectionate shove in return. "You'll never let me live that down, will you? It was one camping trip. I didn't know the tent would rip a hole through the canvas, and I sure didn't expect it to rain that night, either."

Catherine grinned at the memory. That miserable night, curled up beneath a leaking tarp, with the sound of rain drumming like a war march against the ground—it had been awful, but she wouldn't trade the memory for anything. She giggled and her pa joined her.

Her pa's voice quieted. "Why don't you invite your friend Ellen and her grandpa to supper tomorrow evening? Don't let them take no for an answer."

"Okay, Pa. I won't."

"You like her, don't you? She's quite young for a friend of yours."

"I guess she might be, but she's kind, and we have a lot in common. I'd take a younger, kind friend over an older, unkind acquaintance any day. A friend is a friend, right?"

Her pa nodded. "Right." He paused, then continued. "Cat, are you still not making friends here? I mean, there's your Mr. Sanderson and Zeke, but what about the other girls at church?"

She rolled her eyes. "Pa, Matt and Zeke are not my anything, and no, no girls. I just don't seem to get on with people the way others do. I don't know what's wrong with me, but even when I'm kind to others, they don't seem to receive me well."

He was quiet for a moment, then said, "Cat, I'm going to tell you what I told your mother, when she had the same problem. Sometimes, people just don't know what to do with a pure heart."

She scoffed. "Pa, I'm not so pure. I have mean thoughts, too, you know."

"Oh, I know you're not perfect. I don't mean perfect. I mean a pure heart with pure intentions and an honest view of them-selves. It's rare to find someone who truly sees themselves as they are. Most folks walk around with blinders on, only seeing where their comfort zone leads them. That comfort zone often leads to others with the same blinders on. If someone comes along and lifts those blinders, it disturbs their comfort, and well... they get jittery-like. Then those nerves turn to resentment."

"You're saying they don't care for me because I'm honest with myself?"

"There's a little more to it than that, but yep. That about sums it up."

Catherine frowned. "I'm not sure I understand that at all."

"I don't think you're meant to, Cat." He patted her hand. "Just keep being you. Folks like Ellen and your old pa appreciate who you are, and don't you forget it. The Good Lord, too."

She sighed, turning her gaze to their little cabin in the clearing. As much as she loved and appreciated her pa and Ellen, she wished others could appreciate her, too.

A familiar smile flashed through her thoughts, and she exhaled sharply, frustrated by it. Zeke. Always so confident, always so sure of himself. He seemed to appreciate her, but Zeke smiled at all the girls—she wasn't about to mistake his charm for anything more than what it was. She didn't want to be like the other girls. She wanted to be *the* girl. That realization hit her like a hammer strikes a nail. No, he couldn't be someone she needed.

Matt Sanderson, though...

Her fingers traced the edge of her sleeve as she thought of the other man, of the way he had only looked at her. He had a quiet sort of charm, a steadiness that made her feel seen in a way she hadn't been seen before.

Maybe she'd sit with him at church on Sunday. Let the other girls see.

That would ruffle a few feathers. They hadn't seen him yet, but they would. Zeke would face competition.

She smirked at the thought, watching as the sun dipped lower behind the trees, painting the sky in streaks of gold and violet.

She wouldn't need to compete for Matt's attention, but she hated that she wanted to compete for Zeke's.

Even worse, she hated that those girls at church knew it, especially Rosalind. Somehow, she knew how Catherine felt about Zeke, even though she tried her best to hide it.

And if Rosalind saw it, who else knew?

———

Darkness curled thick and hungry around them, coiling like smoke from a dying fire. The air pulsed with an unnatural weight, charged with the anticipation of something unholy.

A voice, smooth as silk but sharp as a dagger, slithered through the black void.

"We must continue to isolate her, Sleim."

A shadow shifted—crouched, waiting. Its breath rasped through yellow teeth, eager, restless.

"The deed must take place soon," the voice continued, resonant with authority. "He must burn with the need to complete his destiny here. Get going. He resists, but that resistance is fragile. Make sure it shatters."

Sleim's misshapen body tensed, his sinewy fingers twitching with the thrill of the command. His yellow and red eyes widened.

"You're letting me fuel that fire?" His voice was guttural, thick with glee.

A pause. Then the voice, cold as winter's breath.

"I am. But you'd better not do anything to dismantle the plan, or you'll face the pit."

Sleim recoiled at the mention of it—the searing torment, the endless void, the eternal gnashing of teeth.

"I'm not going to that hole," he hissed, his voice trembling with loathing.

"Then don't disappoint me, Sleim." A whisper, yet somehow deafening. "Make sure he thirsts for blood. Make sure he cannot escape it. Do not let him rest until he feeds his hunger."

A low growl rumbled from deep within Sleim's twisted frame, and then he moved—crawling fast, his bent legs skittering like an insect over the darkened earth. His elongated fingers scraped against rock and root as he surged forward, his back arching with each lurching step.

His eagerness to walk upright spurred him on. One day, he would stand tall. One day, he would shed this cursed, slinking form.

But first, he had work to do.

The pawn lay in his bed, dreaming dark and twisted things. Sleim wound himself through his mind like a maze, slipping into the cracks of his thoughts like ink seeping into paper. He would stoke the fire of bloodlust until it burned so hot, so insatiable, that resistance would turn to recklessness.

A smile—thin and malevolent—curved Sleim's cracked lips.

He could almost hear the screams already.

Whispers of the Dead

Reese

Stepping out of the car, Reese inhaled deeply, the scent of damp earth and sunbaked grass filling her lungs. The little yellow house with its white trim sat at the end of a winding dirt drive, nestled among pastures that stretched wide and golden under the setting sun. Behind it, a dense tree line loomed, dark and secretive, as if it swallowed the world beyond. Though modest, the house had charm—a quiet defiance against the wilderness pressing in on all sides.

A wind stirred, carrying the faint, acrid scent of something burning in the distance. Reese glanced toward the trees. A smattering of crows gathered on the fence line, their beady eyes fixed on the house, their presence unsettling in a way she couldn't explain.

James watched her as they approached the porch. "You ready?"

She adjusted the strap on her purse. "I guess so." She appreciated James' offer to go with her once they found out where her unexpected visitor lived. She figured James could get in trouble for using his connections to get the address, but she needed to find out what this woman had to do with her uncle.

Before her knuckles met the door, it swung open.

A girl—twelve, maybe thirteen—stood in the threshold, an apple in her hand, green and tart-looking, jagged bite marks along its surface. She didn't greet them. Instead, her gaze swept over them, detached and unimpressed, as she slowly, deliberately chewed.

"Mom! Some people are at the door!" she called, voice flat.

James smirked, clearly amused, but Reese felt the awkward weight of being an outsider.

A moment later, Sharon Langton appeared, wiping her hands on a dish towel. The second she saw Reese, the light in her face dimmed, her body tensing like a startled animal.

"Tiffany, go unload the dishwasher," she said.

The girl sighed. "I already did."

"Then load it."

Another exaggerated sigh. "Fine. But tomorrow it's your turn."

The girl stomped off, leaving behind a wave of adolescent attitude, but Sharon didn't watch her go. Her focus remained locked on Reese and James, her grip tightening on the doorframe.

"Why are you here?" she asked sharply. "I don't want my daughter involved in any of this."

James's voice was cool, measured. "And what exactly is 'this,' Mrs. Langton?"

Her eyes darkened. "Oh, don't act like you don't know. You're an attorney, aren't you?" A humorless laugh left her lips. "That's rich. Bringing your lawyer to scare me off. You didn't need to do that. I already left, didn't I?"

James raised a brow, but Reese spoke first. "He's not an attorney, Sharon. Can I call you Sharon?"

Sharon didn't answer, but she didn't correct her, so Reese pressed on.

"He lives down the road from me. I asked him to come with me because I wanted to talk."

Sharon exhaled sharply through her nose. "You're wasting your time. There's nothing to talk about."

"I don't think that's true." Reese held her ground. "You came to the house for a reason, didn't you? Please, I just want to talk for a few minutes."

Sharon hesitated, glancing back into the house. Dishes clattered in the kitchen. For a brief moment, something in her face softened. Then, as if catching herself, she squared her shoulders.

"Fine. Let's go to the patio."

She led them around the house, past an overgrown hydrangea bush drooping with the weight of late summer blooms. Reese noticed how the leaves curled inward, dry despite the humid air, as if the plant itself recoiled from the lingering summer heat.

The small patio huddled beneath a gnarled pecan tree. A wrought iron table and chairs sat in the shade, their once-white paint now chipped and rusted. Rain had pooled in the seat divots, and Sharon wiped them down with a towel before gesturing for them to sit.

"I only have a few minutes," she said. "Tiffany has a band concert tonight."

"What does she play?" James asked, leaning back, casual but attentive.

"Clarinet."

He nodded. "Band kids are good kids. I played saxophone."

A flicker of something crossed Sharon's face—not quite a smile, but something close. James had a way of disarming people, Reese noted. Maybe that was part of his job, or maybe it was just him.

"We won't keep you long," Reese said, steering the conversation back. "But can you tell me why you came to my house? And why you left so abruptly?"

Sharon's fingers knotted together in her lap. Her eyes drifted toward the tree line, beyond the fields, beyond the present moment.

"I was hoping for answers," she admitted, then looked at James. "If you're living on that road, then you know about Art. And if you know about Art, you know about my mother."

Reese exchanged a glance with James. He cleared his throat. "Well, I don't live there. I'm visiting my grandmother, but I did grow up here. I do know about your mom, though. I'm sorry."

"She's been missing for over two years," Sharon continued, her voice tightening. "She just disappeared. No car, no note. Nothing."

Reese's stomach sank. "I'm sorry, too. I can't imagine how hard that must be."

Sharon's jaw clenched. "You're right. You can't imagine. It's a nightmare I don't wake up from." Her fingers curled against the table. "I know she's gone. But I want to know how. I want to know where."

A chill settled over Reese's skin.

"What does this have to do with my uncle Art?"

Sharon hesitated, her expression unreadable. "They were together for a while. And then my mother started acting... different."

"Different how?"

"She was nervous all the time. Jumping at shadows. Acting like something was after her." Sharon shook her head. "I asked her about it, but she brushed me off."

"What makes you think Uncle Art had anything to do with it?"

Sharon's expression hardened. "Because the last time I saw her, she was heading to see him. At that house on the river."

Reese's grip tightened on the chair.

"She never came home," Sharon continued. "And when I went to Art's house the next day to ask about her, he swore he hadn't seen her. But something was off. He looked scared."

Chill bumps surfaced on Reese's arms.

"What have the police told you?" James asked.

Sharon scoffed. "The same thing they always say. That they're still working the case."

James leaned forward. "Tell me about the day you found Art."

Color drained from Sharon's face. Her shoulders locked, stiffening.

"I went over there again that day," she admitted. "I guess I was harassing him, but I didn't care. I just wanted the truth."

She swallowed hard.

"He wouldn't answer the door. So I went around back." Her voice turned hoarse. "I saw him through the glass. Facedown on the floor. I knew—" Her voice faltered. "I knew he was gone."

The silence that followed was thick, suffocating.

"Is there anything else you remember?" Reese asked, softening her tone.

Sharon's hands balled into fists. "Why does it matter? Are you asking for my mother's sake? Or for him?"

"Both," Reese admitted. "Something isn't right, and we need to figure out what happened."

Sharon scoffed. "The police haven't found anything. What makes you think you can?"

James met her gaze, steady and unshaken. "Because I am the police."

Sharon's head snapped up. "What?"

"I'm a detective. Biloxi PD."

Her face darkened. "And you didn't think to mention that before?"

"We didn't want to spook you," Reese said. "We just need the truth."

Sharon sat motionless for a long moment. Then, at last, she sighed, the fight bleeding out of her.

"My mom's things are still in her room," she said. "Just as she left them."

James nodded. "Can we take a look?"

She hesitated, then finally gave a slow nod. "Come back tomorrow. Like I said, we have a band concert."

Reese saw something shift in her eyes—a crack in the wall she had built around herself. And for the first time, she knew Sharon wasn't just looking for answers.

She was looking for hope.

A Table in the Dark

Catherine

Ellen's grandfather, Thatcher Hollis, had an easy charm about him, the kind that filled a room with warmth. His jokes carried a teasing lilt, his eyes sparkled with mischief, and when he spoke of his new adventure, his voice crackled with energy, drawing everyone into his excitement. Catherine liked him immediately, though she secretly marveled at the sheer amount of food he could put away. Every time her pa passed him the plate of biscuits, Thatcher took another without hesitation, splitting it open and slathering it with butter—Catherine's butter, churned after hours of arm-numbing labor. She whispered a silent prayer that he wouldn't clean them out.

"When do you leave for Jackson?" her pa asked, offering Thatcher the plate yet again.

The older man took another biscuit without a shred of guilt, nodding before answering. "Thank you, Eli. We'll be leavin' come morning, I reckon. Now that I've collected on a loan, it's time to mosey on, ain't that right, Ellen?"

Ellen's face fell as she glanced at Catherine, a quiet plea flickering in her eyes, the kind only those who had known loneliness could recognize.

"Oh, Grandpa, do we have to leave Meridian so soon?"

"I'm afraid so, Cricket. We'll be leavin' at first light."

Catherine's pa leaned back in his chair, tapping a thoughtful finger against his chin. "Where you headed first?"

"We'll take the river down a ways, then find a place to dock before headin' to Jackson on foot. I expect we'll come across a horse we can bargain for along the way. Maybe trade the fishing boat."

Catherine sat up. "The river's a good way to travel if you want to avoid the roads, but you'll need to watch out. There's more than fish and driftwood in those waters."

Thatcher chuckled, his weathered face splitting into a grin. "Ain't my first time takin' the river, little lady. Ain't nothin' like it in the world, is there, Cricket?" He nudged his granddaughter, who nodded, though her smile was a touch too thin.

"Grandpa, maybe we could stay a little longer? Just until the pups grow a bit more?"

Thatcher sighed, reaching for his tin cup and taking a long drink. "Ellie, I told ya. It's gonna get cold soon, and we can't be campin' on that riverbank much longer."

Catherine's pa cleared his throat. "There's room and board to be found in town. Might not be a bad idea to settle in for a bit before moving on. Give you a chance to get your business started in a place that's already growing."

"Naw. Can't afford it if I'm a mind to setting up shop when we get to Jackson."

Her pa slid his gaze at Catherine, who dropped her lids in disappointment.

"Well, it won't get cold for another couple of weeks, and if you need more blankets, we have plenty. You can camp on our place if you need to."

Thatcher rubbed his beard, his sharp eyes flicking to Ellen, who held her breath like a girl clinging to hope. His gaze softened. "I guess that's an idea, but we'll stay on the river. I like fresh fish. Alright, Ellie. A few more days. But just a few, you hear?"

Ellen exhaled, breaking into a wide smile. "Thanks, Grandpa."

Thatcher shook his head, chuckling. "Coyote pups. Whoever heard. That girl would bring along every livin' thing she found, if she could." He scooped up the last of his tomato gravy with his biscuit, chewing with the same enthusiasm as his first bite. "Sometimes I wonder if she'll prefer critters to a husband and children." He reached over and patted Ellen's hand, winking as she flushed pink.

Catherine laughed. "Animals are easier to understand than people."

"Ain't that the truth," Thatcher agreed.

As the meal and the chatter wound down, Catherine stood and began gathering the dishes, moving toward the wash basin with Ellen beside her. Across the room, the men continued their talk, their voices dipping into the deep rhythms and gruff tones as they discussed the political climate.

Ellen let out a sigh, scrubbing a plate. "I just don't want to leave yet. I like it here. Grandpa thinks Jackson will be good for his shoe shop, but I don't see why we couldn't stay here instead."

Catherine handed her a towel. "He'd have plenty of business here. We have new families arriving all the time. Just last week, six moved into the county, and that's not counting the bachelors."

Ellen perked up. "Speaking of bachelors... what do you think of Zeke?"

Catherine nearly dropped the tin cup in her hand. "Zeke? Why do you ask?"

Ellen shrugged, feigning innocence. "I saw the way he looked at you. He's handsome."

Catherine smirked. "He knows it, too."

"Confidence is attractive," Ellen teased.

"It is. But sometimes I wonder if his confidence is so great that he forgets to make me confident in him."

"I see." Ellen eyed her curiously. "So you and Zeke aren't..."

"No." Catherine narrowed her eyes. "Why? Are you sweet on him?"

Ellen's cheeks flamed. "No! He's much too old for me. But I like him for you, I think."

Catherine scoffed. "For me? No, I don't think so. Besides, I'm courting Mr. Sanderson. At least, I think I am."

Ellen tilted her head. "The new man I saw talking to you at church?"

"That's the one."

"Hmmm. He is handsome. What's it like, Catherine?"

"What's what like?"

Ellen lowered her voice, as if asking for some great secret. "Being so beautiful that men flock to you all the time?"

Catherine blinked. Then laughed outright. "Ellen, I don't have men flocking to me."

Ellen rolled her eyes. "I've only been here a few days, and I've already seen it."

Catherine nudged her with an elbow. "Well, it's going to happen to you soon enough. You're beautiful, too."

Ellen snorted. "I don't think so. My ma was beautiful. Graceful. I don't think I take after her at all."

Catherine frowned. "Why do you say that?"

Ellen sighed, glancing down at herself. "My legs are too skinny, my chest is too small, and my hair just falls in strings, no matter how I twist it up. It's not thick like yours, and it's not a pretty color, either. My ma had pretty hair, too."

Catherine turned fully to her, setting the dish aside. "You have lovely hair, Ellen. And the rest will take care of itself soon enough. Besides, there's more to life than looks."

Ellen gave a weak smile. "The only people who believe that are the ones who don't have to worry about it."

Catherine sighed, wrapping an arm around her friend's shoulder. "Then you should believe it, too."

Ellen leaned into her slightly, and Catherine felt something stir inside her. She had always wanted a sister. Maybe if Ellen stayed, she could have that—someone to talk to, to laugh with, to share secrets over warm biscuits and candlelight. A sister, a friend. Catherine had always wanted both. Right now, she'd take at least one.

"I don't want to leave here, Catherine. I think we could be best friends."

"I know we could."

Ellen fingered her locket. "My ma's best friend gave this locket to her, you know. When my ma died, her friend had her picture put inside so I could wear it. She said Ma shouldn't ever be forgotten."

She hesitated, turning the locket over in her fingers. "My ma was like that with people. Always loved. Always treasured."

She looked up, her voice softer now. "I think it would be nice to be remembered like that. Like someone treasured me for all the right reasons, skinny legs and all."

Catherine's smile faltered.

The words settled deep in her chest, pressing against something she couldn't name.

"Well, you can be sure I'll never forget you, Ellen," she said, trying to keep her voice light. "And I don't need a locket to keep your smile right here with me." She tapped her chest.

Ellen smiled at that, but Catherine saw something behind it. A flicker of doubt.

"Let's just hope we can change your grandpa's mind about staying here."

"Ellen," Thatcher called from the table, stretching with a groan. "We best be getting on."

Catherine's pa followed him out the door, but she held Ellen back for a moment.

"Listen. Maybe we can convince your grandpa to stay. If he sees how much demand there is for a shoemaker here, he might change his mind. I know there's business waiting for him."

Ellen's eyes flickered with hope, but then she bit her lip. "He's made up his mind, though. Once he does that..."

Catherine grinned. "I'll have my pa talk to him again. He can be convincing. After that, I guess that's all we can do."

Ellen tilted her head. "Well, we can pray, too. Right?"

Catherine nodded. "Of course. If God brought us together, He can keep us together, too. And in that case, your grandpa doesn't have a choice."

Ellen chuckled, fiddling with her locket. When she looked up, her eyes shined—not with tears, but with something lighter. Hope, maybe.

Catherine didn't know how such a pretty girl could ever doubt her own worth, but she suspected someone had once made her feel that way. Because that's how most people came to believe such things about themselves.

And Catherine had never been more determined to make sure Ellen knew just how much she mattered.

Catherine vowed she'd never let Ellen be overlooked again.

———

He shouldn't be here.

The darkness inside him pulsed, coiling tighter with each passing day. The urges gnawed at the edges of his mind, whispering, clawing, demanding.

The pups whined. Small, pathetic things, their cries sharp in the stillness of the barn. He scowled down at them, their tiny bodies huddled together in the crate. Weak. Helpless. Just like everything else.

His fingers curled around the scruff of one, lifting it. The pup yipped, squirming in his grip, its dark eyes round with confusion, then fear.

That was better.

He squeezed, just enough to feel its little pulse hammering against his fingers, just enough to savor the way its body tensed. But it wasn't enough. Not nearly enough.

He needed something more.

Something human.

A noise outside jolted him. Footsteps approached the barn.

He dropped the pup. It hit the floor of the crate with a soft thud, its tiny limbs scrambling to right itself, whimpering. But he wasn't listening to the pup anymore.

He turned toward the slats in the barn wall, breath steadying, pulse slowing. Watching. Waiting.

Someone was there.

He didn't expect her.

Her silhouette shifted in the late afternoon light, casting long shadows across the packed dirt. Unaware. Alone.

He stilled.

She was close. Too close. If she came inside...

His fingers twitched.

The thought took root before he could stop it. How easy it would be. One swift movement, a hand over her mouth, the sharp, startled intake of breath before the struggle began.

A thrill crawled up his spine.

Another sound.

More footsteps. Another voice, low, indistinct.

His jaw clenched.

Too risky. Not here. Not now.

He backed away, forcing himself to move in slow, measured steps. The urge burned in his gut, hot and hungry, but he couldn't be reckless.

Not yet.

He slipped out the back, his body tense, his breath controlled. Whatever life he had planned here, whatever mask he needed to wear—he couldn't afford to lose it. Because it was no longer about fitting in, and it was no longer about hiding out. No, his place in this little town meant much more. But he needed to satisfy his cravings or he'd make mistakes.

He'd finally feed the impulses that starved inside since he'd arrived. Now that he'd made the decision, he had to plan how to do it without getting caught.

Because his hunger had only just begun.

———

Sleim bared his jagged teeth, nostrils flaring as he crouched in the shadows, his elongated fingers curling into the dirt beneath him. The accursed warrior of light stood near the barn's entrance, his presence a blinding disruption in the carefully woven strands of corruption Sleim and his minions had worked so tirelessly to cultivate. The man—their pawn—had been on the brink, teetering at the precipice of his own depravity, only to be pulled away.

But not by chance.

No, this was an interference, an unwanted interruption summoned by a voice lifted in prayer. Someone had spoken against the darkness, called for help, petitioned the heavens—and their plea had been answered.

Sleim curled his talons against the earth, rage simmering in his gut.

He despised the warriors, but he hated prayers even more.

Prayers were weapons. Prayers were shields. Prayers called the warriors down from the heavens and disrupted the carefully sown seeds of blood and sin. Prayers invited His intervention, and Sleim had no way to fight Him.

The celestial loomed in the barn's entrance, golden light bleeding from the edges of his armor, his massive wings arched like a shield around the girl. She had no idea what had nearly befallen her. How close she had come to death. How close he had come to finally surrendering to the gnawing hunger inside him.

But it wasn't over.

This was only a delay.

The warrior may have intervened, but the seed had already taken root. The man's urges were festering, multiplying, rotting inside him. Soon, the itch would be unbearable, the craving too strong to resist. His master had ensured it.

Some darkness could not be penetrated by light.

The humans had left their town defenseless. Their shepherd was distracted, his prayers weak, his sermons routine—nothing more than an echo of dead faith. He did not see. Did not feel the decay spreading beneath his very feet. He spoke of righteousness but did not wield it.

They had no leader to lead them, protect them as a shepherd should. No shield.

And yet...

Sleim's lips curled in irritation. Someone had interfered. Someone had prayed.

And that meant they had a problem.

It didn't matter.

A single prayer warrior would not be enough. Not against the hunger rising, not against the storm Sleim's master was preparing to unleash.

Yes.

Sleim's tongue flicked out, tasting the decay already spreading.

The man would fall.

The town, the church, would fall.

And when it did, the light warriors would watch as their feeble, flickering flames were smothered into the abyss.

Of Men and Devils

Reese

The door creaked on its hinges as James and Reese stepped into Patricia Langton's bedroom—a space long abandoned to dust and memories. The scent of lavender hung faintly in the air, the kind that lingers in forgotten sachets tucked away in drawers, now stale and faded with time. It mingled with the deeper scent of old wood, dust, and something else—something harder to name. A weight in the air. A sorrow that had seeped into the walls.

Tiffany stood in the doorway, arms crossed over her chest, her expression unreadable.

"So," she asked, her voice flat. "You think you can find my nana?"

James thumbed through a dog-eared notebook, the pages whispering as they turned. "I don't know, but we'll try."

"She wouldn't have left me like this."

Reese heard the quiet grief beneath the words, the gravity of loss carried for too long. Tiffany was young, but her voice had the brittle edge of someone who had stopped expecting answers. Reese offered a steady smile.

"Of course not. Do you remember anything from back then?"

Tiffany leaned against the wall, chewing the inside of her cheek. "Some. I remember she told me not to let anyone in the house. And that I shouldn't answer the phone."

Reese frowned. It wasn't unusual advice for a grandmother to give a child, but something about the way Tiffany said it—how her voice dipped into something close to fear—sent a chill up Reese's spine.

"Do you remember anything else?" she pressed, careful not to spook her.

The girl hesitated. "I did tell the police something, but they ignored it. Said it didn't matter."

James set down the notebook. "Everything matters."

Tiffany gnawed on her lip before speaking. "One day, Nana said she needed to go to the library. She came home with a bunch of books on demon possessions. Crazy stuff. I told the cops, but they just kinda nodded and moved on."

Reese exchanged a glance with James. "Did she say why she needed them?"

"Only that I shouldn't look at them because they might scare me." Tiffany shrugged, but the flicker of unease in her eyes betrayed her. "I asked her why she had them, but she just said she needed to learn about something. That's all she ever said."

She crossed her arms, looking away. "Nana prayed a lot. She used to say that faith was the only thing keeping the bad stuff away. But she still went missing. So what good did all that praying do?"

Reese hesitated. "I don't think faith works like that." But Reese wasn't so sure herself, anymore. Tiffany had a point. Good didn't show up just because you prayed for it. Evil didn't always lose because you're on the winning side, either. Sometimes the demons weren't just in the stories or haunted places. Sometimes they wore human faces, and sometimes, worst of all, they kissed you goodnight.

Tiffany gave a half-hearted laugh. "That's what my nana would have said, too."

A tightness curled in Reese's stomach. Something about all of this was wrong, as if some force worked behind the scenes. She sensed it in the air around them.

Shivering, she turned to the vanity dresser, where a cluster of photos sat yellowing in their frames. She picked one up. Patricia stared back at her—blonde hair, green eyes, high cheekbones. A beautiful lady. Could her uncle have hurt this woman? Maybe in the house she now slept in? Or maybe Addie had been right and it *was* Stuckey. Maybe he still hunted for new victims after all.

Reese tilted the frame, frowning. Something in the reflection caught her eye. A shape? A shadow? For a heartbeat, she wasn't sure. As she leaned closer, the faint outline sharpened. A man. A man's face, twisted into a grin—not friendly, but dark, sinister. Her chest tightened, a chill sliding down her spine. She blinked, heart hammering. When she looked again, only Patricia stared back, smiling softly from the frame. She set the picture down quickly, pulse thrumming in her ears.

"Something wrong?" James asked.

"No." She forced a laugh, but even to her own ears, it sounded brittle. "Nothing."

Her fingers hovered over the next frame, a different photo of Patricia—one where she stood near the river, her hands clasped in front of her. Something about the image felt off, like Patricia had been uncomfortable when it was taken. Her eyes caught on the delicate glint of a necklace resting at Patricia's throat.

A locket.

Reese leaned in, narrowing her eyes. "That locket... it's beautiful." She couldn't explain it, but it seemed familiar in some way, as if it held memories meant for her.

James peered over her shoulder. "Looks antique."

"It is," Tiffany said from behind them, her voice quieter than before. "It was passed down in our family. My great-great-great-grandmother had it first, and every woman in the family since then has worn it."

Reese's fingers brushed the edge of the frame. "And now it's missing?"

Tiffany nodded. "Nana always wore it. But when she disappeared, so did the locket."

Reese exchanged a glance with James. "Did she ever tell you where it came from?"

Tiffany hesitated, then shrugged. "Not really. Just that it had been in the family for generations. There's a letter that was supposed to go with it, explaining its history, but I've never read it."

James exhaled, rubbing a hand along his jaw. "Maybe that letter is still somewhere in the house."

Tiffany frowned but didn't argue. Instead, she shrugged. "Maybe. Mom probably knows where it is." She turned toward the door, pausing just before stepping out. "Did you wanna see her storage room? The cops barely looked in there, but she kept a lot of stuff. Maybe you'll even find the letter." She dropped her gaze for a moment, before looking back up at them.

Reese and James followed her outside. The barn loomed ahead, its weathered boards gray with time, the roof sagging as if the weight of the years had pressed it into submission. The stench of mildew and old hay clung to the humid air.

Tiffany led them past a German Shepherd chained near the entrance. The dog rumbled deep in his throat, watching them with suspicion—until Tiffany patted his head, and he melted into a puddle of wagging affection.

"He acts tough, but he's a pushover," she muttered.

Inside, the barn was dim. Dust motes danced in the slanted light from the loft above, shifting like restless spirits in the gloom.

"She kept everything organized." Tiffany gestured toward the metal shelves lined with plastic bins. "Nana was big on categories."

Reese let out a small laugh. "She and I would've gotten along. I love my label maker."

Tiffany rolled her eyes. "How exciting."

James ignored them, stepping toward the shelves. "Are you sure your mom won't mind us looking through this?"

"She won't care. She's been meaning to throw most of it out anyway."

Tiffany hesitated at the door, fidgeting with the edge of her sleeve. "I'll leave you to it. Mom wants me to help with dinner, and I don't really like being in here anyway." She turned, pausing at the threshold. "If you find something... something weird... let me know, okay?"

James nodded. "We will."

With a small, tight-lipped nod, Tiffany disappeared into the humid afternoon, her retreating footsteps crunching against the gravel path.

A long silence stretched between Reese and James once she was gone.

Reese exhaled, glancing back at the shelves. "So, where do we start?"

James pulled down a dusty photo album from the shelf, flipping it open. A few loose pictures fluttered to the ground like dead leaves.

He and Reese reached for them at the same time, their hands brushing. Reese yanked hers back. James arched a brow at her but said nothing.

He studied the images, frowning. "Looks like family pictures. Nothing unusual."

Tossing it aside, he reached for another bin, pulling out a stack of books, fanning through them. His frown deepened.

"Didn't Tiffany say Patricia got books from the library?"

Reese nodded. "Something about demons and possession."

James turned one of the books open and pointed at the inside cover.

A name scrawled in ink.

Reese's breath caught. Her uncle's name.

She swallowed hard. "But... these books belonged to Uncle Art, not the library. Why would he have books about the occult? Have you seen his house? It's not exactly *The Addams Family* mansion."

James exhaled. "Yeah. We came looking for answers, and all we got were more questions."

The storm had settled in by the time they pulled into Reese's driveway. The sky bruised deep purple, thunder rolling in low, muttering threats in the distance.

James killed the engine.

Then he froze.

His arm shot out in front of Reese just as she reached for the door handle, barring her like an old Southern mother slamming an arm across the passenger seat when hitting the brakes.

"What on earth?"

"Stay here." His voice was sharp, eyes locked on something inside the house.

Reese followed his gaze—and her blood ran cold.

A shadow moved inside.

"I locked that door," she whispered.

James slid out of the car, hand resting on his holstered gun, his body tense. Reese, ignoring his order, followed on his heels.

James glared at her and gritted his teeth but said nothing.

He reached for the doorknob. Twisted it.

It swung open.

Her ex-husband, Dylan, stood in her living room, grinning, a bottle of her water in one hand, a peach in the other.

"Reese, babe. Where've you been?" He took a slow, deliberate bite of the peach, juice running down his chin. He wiped it with the back of his hand and smirked at James.

"I see you've moved on. Got this one fooled, eh?"

Reese steeled herself and inhaled. "Dylan, what are you doing here?"

"What, no warm welcome?"

Exasperated, but not surprised, Reese turned to stare out the sliding glass doors and take another deep breath but found herself staring into Dylan's reflection instead. Would she ever rid herself of his imprint on her life?

The clocks chimed all at once, their discordant echoes filling the house.

And in the window—his reflection changed.

It wasn't him staring back.

It was another figure.

Full-bodied. Staring. Waiting.

The glass fogged for a brief second, as if breath had passed over it.

Her pulse spiked. She sucked in a sharp breath, whirling around.

Dylan stood where the reflection had been.

He laughed. "What's the matter? You look like you've seen a ghost."

Reese didn't answer. She studied him, her pulse still uneven. How could he be so unaware? Dylan just stood there, casual, unaffected. As if nothing had happened at all.

But he had no idea how right he was.

She looked back at the glass, but Stuckey's face had vanished. Reese knew his presence lingered. It remained in the air. The room still felt wrong, thick with something she couldn't name.

Or maybe she could name it. She swallowed hard.

Stuckey.

———

"You break in?" James asked, voice calm but edged in steel. He pulled back his blazer, revealing his badge at his waist.

"Whoa, officer. Relax." Dylan held up his hands for effect. Then he laughed, unfazed. "You call it breaking in, I call it checking in."

He took another slow bite of the peach, chewing leisurely. "Door was unlocked."

Reese knew that was a lie.

James didn't blink. "That so? It's still not your house, so not your door to open, locked or unlocked."

Dylan's smirk widened. "Just thought I'd stop by, see how my ex-wife was settling in. Thought we could... catch up." His gaze flickered to Reese, lingering in a way that made her skin crawl. She found it hard to imagine how just months ago, she mourned their relationship. Now, she just wanted the space to be free of him, once and for all.

James didn't move. "You done eating your snack?" Brilliant, how he spoke to Dylan like you'd speak to a child. Reese almost smiled.

Her ex raised a brow, amused. "Why? You want some?" He held up the peach. "Plenty in the fridge. I figured since I used to live with this woman, that makes me a guest in this house."

Reese felt her stomach turn. He was enjoying this—taunting her. Reminding her that he used to have power over her.

Used to.

James' jaw ticked, but his expression didn't change. "Nah. I figure now you're done, you'll have no reason to stay." The double entendre wasn't lost on Dyaln, and he chuckled, shaking his head.

"Man, you play the tough guy really well. I bet that works on most people."

James didn't speak, but just stared back. Smooth, calm, steady.

But Reese saw the slight narrowing of his eyes. The shift in his stance—just enough to make Dylan aware that this wasn't a game he wanted to play.

Dylan licked peach juice from his fingers. "You always gotta have someone watching out for you, huh, Reese?" His voice dipped lower, mockingly sweet. "First your mama. Then me. Then Art." He gestured to the house, looking around. "And now you found your own personal guard dog." His eyes flicked back to James. "How long do you think she'll keep you around?"

James didn't hesitate. "Much longer than you."

The words landed like a hammer, and not just with Dylan. Reese's heart pounded. *What did he just say?*

Dylan's smirk faltered. Just for a second.

"I think I'm the one that got rid of her. Didn't she tell you?"

James took a single step forward. "You're done here."

Something dark flashed in Dylan's expression, but he didn't argue. He glanced back at Reese. "Like I said, you always did need someone to fight your battles, huh?"

Reese's fists clenched. "Get out, Dylan."

Dylan lingered a second longer, like he wanted to say something else, but then he just smiled. Slow. Calculated.

He set the half-eaten peach on the counter. "Always a pleasure, Babe." He turned to leave, then stopped. "Well, not always. Enjoy your new home in the sticks."

Was that why he came? An interest in the house?

James didn't move until Dylan was out the door, down the steps, and into his car. Only then did he glance at Reese. "You okay?"

Reese exhaled, her pulse still pounding. "Yeah." She wasn't, and from the way he studied her, he knew it. He looked at the door where Dylan retreated only seconds ago, as if he expected the man to return.

"What a piece of work. If he comes back, you tell me."

Reese nodded, then hesitated. "Thanks, but despite what he said, I don't need anyone fighting my battles." She crossed her arms over her chest, waiting for him to argue.

James studied her for a moment longer, then picked up Dylan's half-eaten peach from the counter. He turned it over in his hand once before tossing it—hard—into the trash.

Shadows and Suspicions

Catherine

T he store buzzed with townspeople bustling between the crowded aisles, voices rising in chatter about winter stores, the latest shipments, and town gossip. The scent of kerosene, tobacco, and burlap mingled in the warm, slightly dusty air. Shelves overflowed with goods lined up in a row—sacks of flour, jars of molasses, bolts of fabric stacked unevenly near the counter. Not only was it the tidiest shop in town, but Mr. White's fair prices kept it busier than its competitors. People often speculated about how he kept prices so low, but they were too grateful to question it too much.

Catherine navigated the narrow space, tugging her shawl tighter around her shoulders as she searched for the last of her provisions. A sharp shift in the air warned her she was being watched. She turned just as Matt Sanderson stepped into view, a crate of goods balanced under his arm, a roll of material slung over his shoulder.

"Hello, Catherine." His voice was smooth, steady. "Finding what you need?"

She glanced at his load. "Looks like you found more than enough of what you need, Matt. What on earth are you going to do with all that material?"

He smirked. "Taking it to Mrs. Foley at the dressmaker's shop."

Catherine lifted an eyebrow. "Oh? A frock for yourself? I'm not sure that'll be too flattering on you."

The words were light, but she didn't miss the heat creeping up her neck. He could wear rags and still look striking.

"She's not the one making my clothes, if you must know," he replied easily. "There's a new tailor setting up in her shop. He'll handle the men's garments while she keeps to the ladies'."

"I didn't know Mrs. Foley had that much room in her shop."

"She doesn't, but they're making it work until they can rent a larger space."

Catherine nodded, glancing toward the shelves, but Matt's gaze stayed on her. There was something about his expression—interested, yet unreadable.

"What about Mr. Spinks?" she asked. "He already tailors at the other end of the street."

"He's got more orders than he can keep up with. The new tailor will give him some competition."

"Seems like the town's expanding in ways I never imagined when we first arrived." She hesitated before adding, "Speaking of businesses, do you know if there's a shop space available? I have a friend who's considering settling here—a shoemaker."

Matt frowned slightly. "There's that space on Second Street, but it's rough. Needs tar paper for the winter, but it could work."

"I thought my pa said a man was selling farm equipment from there?"

"He was, but he decided he needed a bigger place. The space is empty now."

"That might be perfect for my friend. Thank you."

Matt adjusted the crate under his arm, studying her. "This friend of yours... what kind of friend is he?"

There was more than jealousy in his voice, something obscure—curiosity? Concern?

A mischievous thought flitted through her mind. Letting him believe Mr. Hollis might be a gentleman caller was almost too amusing to resist. Her lips curled as she fought back a giggle.

"What's so amusing?"

"Oh, nothing," she said, brushing a stray curl from her face. "Mr. Thatcher Hollis is the grandfather of a new friend I met. They're considering settling here."

His shoulders eased. "Ah. Will they live in town?"

"I'm not sure yet. They like the river—been camping out there the past couple of weeks."

He nodded but didn't reply. His gaze flicked around the store as if suddenly restless.

"Don't let me keep you from your duties, Mr. Sanderson," she said. "If you need to go—"

"I told you, call me Matt. And no, I'm not in a hurry." His tone turned quiet. "Actually, I wanted to speak with you about something." He motioned toward the quieter corner of the store.

Catherine hesitated. "What is it? Why so secretive?"

"Not secretive," he murmured. "Just... better to keep it between us."

Something in his voice sent a shiver down her spine. Still, she followed him to the corner by the window.

"I found something," he said, voice lowered. "And I just want to warn you to be careful."

Her breath caught. "What did you find?"

Matt leaned in, his voice barely above a whisper. "A bloody knife. Near my property."

Her fingers slipped on the sack of flour in her hands, nearly sending it tumbling to the floor. She caught it just in time, pulse hammering.

The image of the coyote mother flashed in her mind.

"I don't mean to frighten you," Matt continued. "But after what I heard about that coyote and the pups you found, I thought you should know."

"Did you give it to the sheriff?"

He hesitated. A flicker of something—guilt?—crossed his face. "I didn't," he admitted. "I should've, but... I found it near my fence, right where someone would put it if they were trying to spook me. I figured it was a warning."

"A warning?"

He exhaled through his nose, shifting the crate. "I've got competition. Some men don't like me selling game—they want the business for themselves. I've done well here in a short amount of time, and not everyone's happy about it."

Her stomach twisted. "You think they're the ones who hurt the coyote?"

"I don't know. But after my horse was stolen, and I found my place ransacked a while back, I assumed it was them. I told the sheriff, but he didn't have much to go on, so I let it be. Then

I found the knife." His jaw tensed. "I reacted. I threw it in the river."

"The river?"

"Either it's sunk in the mud, or it's floating downstream by now."

Catherine's heart pounded. "But what if it wasn't them? What if it was the same person who—" She stopped, pressing her lips together.

Matt's expression darkened. "I don't know. But I figure you and your pa should be careful. Your new friends, too."

A chill swept down her spine. "Thank you for telling me."

She should've felt gratitude. Instead, she felt trapped. He had only spoken out of concern, but now, the thought of walking home alone made her throat tighten.

Matt must have noticed her unease, because his brow creased. "Will you be alright? Should I walk you home?"

"I'll be fine, Matt, really. Pa's driving me home in the wagon. I'll wait for him."

He nodded, watching her for a moment before exhaling. "Alright." A beat of silence passed. "Would you and your pa be free for a picnic on Saturday? The weather's cooling, and I'd like to enjoy a day on the river before winter locks us indoors."

Catherine hesitated. "That sounds lovely. Do you mind if I invite Ellen and her grandpa?"

"Certainly. I'd like to meet your friends." A small grin played at his lips. "Maybe we'll play some horseshoes. I'll bring the stakes and hammer—see if Blythe's got any bent shoes we can use."

She smiled. "Ellen would love that. I'll get her to help me with the food."

Matt shifted the weight of his crate again. "I'll see you then."

He turned, sauntering away with his easy, confident gait.

Catherine watched him go, unease curling around her ribs. She should feel reassured by his kindness, yet something lingered at the edge of her thoughts—something uncomfortable.

She wasn't sure if she felt relief or regret.

"Miss Catherine, do you need something today?"

She turned and smiled at Mr. White, but his eyes weren't on her. They lingered out the window, watching Matt Sanderson cross the street. His expression was blank, but something about the prolonged stare made Catherine shift her weight.

"Oh, no, I'm fine. I think I'm ready to pay for these things now."

"I'll tally them at the counter, then." He sighed as he moved behind the register. "We're finally at a lull after several hours of constant shoppers coming in and out of here. I'm glad for the business, but I'm also glad for this break."

Catherine glanced around. She hadn't even noticed that, at some point during her conversation with Matt, most of the store patrons had cleared out. The once-cluttered space now felt strangely hollow, as if she stood in a different shop altogether. Had she really been that lost in her discussion with Matt?

As Mr. White counted out her goods, the front door creaked open again.

"Did you hear, Mr. White?" a breathless voice called.

Catherine turned to see Mrs. Laney, one of the town's busiest gossips, bustling into the store, her cheeks flushed from the autumn wind. She carried a basket of bread in one hand and waved the other excitedly. Her gaze slid to Catherine, and she nodded politely, before turning her attention back to her latest gem of gossip.

Mr. White straightened. "Hear what?"

"The travelers—Henry and Louise Harrington. They never arrived at the boarding house last night."

Catherine's hands tightened on her crate of goods.

"What do you mean?" Mr. White asked, his face drawn with concern.

Mrs. Laney lowered her voice, glancing around. "Mrs. Webb, the woman who runs the boarding house just past the river bend, sent word this morning. She had a room waiting, said they sent a telegram from Jackson saying they'd be there by nightfall. But they never showed."

Catherine frowned. "Maybe they had a delay?"

Mrs. Laney shook her head, her expression dark. "No, Zeke said he saw them step off the train. They even asked him which road to take. But somewhere between the station and the boarding house, they vanished."

A hush settled over the store, thick and uneasy.

Mr. White rubbed his jaw. "That's a quiet stretch of road at night. Lots can happen on a road like that."

"A horrid thought," Mrs. Laney said, her voice dropping lower. "Mrs. Webb sent her son to look for them first thing this morning. He found nothing—no footprints, no wagon tracks, nothing."

Catherine's stomach twisted.

The missing travelers. The coyote mother's brutalized body. The bloody knife Matt found. The rumors circling town like vultures over carrion.

Something dark was stirring in Meridian. Maybe it wasn't her imagination at the bridge that day.

Mrs. Laney glanced at Catherine, then back at Mr. White. "I don't want to spread fear, but—"

"Then don't," Mr. White interrupted sharply. "You don't know what really happened to them, do you?"

She pursed her lips. "No. But the sheriff has already sent out men to search. Besides, Reginald Buxton found his cow mutilated, just like that coyote mama in the woods, only his cow was right in his barn. Somebody slaughtered that animal, and not for the meat, either. He said he'd never seen anything like it. And what of all these missing animals? Horses, chickens, and the like. It's getting so a person can't feel safe around here anymore."

"Mrs. Laney, you're saying Mr. Buxton's cow was mutilated?"

The older woman patted her hand. "I know, it's a terrible business, and right here in our own community. This is what happens when you let all these people in-that railroad might be good for progress, but murder ain't no progress."

"We don't know anyone was murdered yet," Catherine said, but her words sounded hollow, even to her own ears.

"I guess the sheriff and the others will let us know if they find anything."

"I doubt they find much," Mr. White murmured, his fingers drumming against the counter. "If anything happened, whatever-whoever-did it likely already covered any traces of a crime."

Catherine shivered at the certainty in his tone.

Mrs. Laney huffed. "Well, we can at least pray they show up safe." With that, she adjusted her basket and bustled back out into the street, calling a greeting to someone passing by.

Catherine turned back to Mr. White, who was watching her too closely.

"Before you go," he said, lowering his voice, "there's something else I need to tell you, I'm afraid."

She exhaled sharply. "Oh?" Wasn't that what Matt had said only moments ago?

A flicker of something crossed Mr. White's features, but it passed too quickly for her to be sure.

"I'm sorry to deliver this tidbit of information, but I'm too fond of you and your pa to let it go."

Catherine tilted her head. She noticed him glance past her, toward the door. The store felt even quieter than before. Even the old wood beams, which always creaked with the wind, had gone still. A hush, as if the building itself listened.

She frowned but waited.

"That Mr. Sanderson of yours said something odd to me today, and I figured you might want to know."

"Mr. White, he's not 'my Mr. Sanderson.' Matt is a friend, and for now, let's stick to that reference."

He held up his hands. "I understand. It's just—everyone's noticed the way you two carry on these days. People naturally assume."

"Well, let's not assume."

A small chuckle left his lips, but his eyes remained sharp.

"Fair enough. Back to my story, then—I waited on him earlier, just before he spoke with you over in the corner."

"We weren't in the corner, Mr. White," she corrected. "He needed to discuss a concerning matter, and my pa will know all about it. There was nothing clandestine about our conversation."

He waved off her irritation. "I didn't mean anything of the sort, Miss Catherine, but I feel it's my duty to warn you about my concerns with this young man."

She folded her arms. "And what exactly is your concern?"

He hesitated, as if choosing his words carefully. "We spoke about his property, and he started complaining about the coyotes hanging around his livestock. He said, and I quote, 'As far as I'm concerned, those coyotes are the enemy to our small farms around here.'"

Catherine stiffened. The words alone didn't unsettle her, but in light of the mutilated coyote mother she'd found...they took on a different weight.

Still, she shrugged. "A lot of folks feel that way, Mr. White. Even my father has had to shoot one or two. Why is this a cause for concern?"

"Well." Mr. White scratched the back of his neck, his gaze drifting slightly past her before snapping back. "It's just—after the state you found that animal in, and now hearing Matt speak like that... it made me wonder."

Something in his tone irritated her, but she supposed he did mean well.

She softened, unwilling to insult the man's concern. "I appreciate that, Mr. White, truly. But Matt's not the type."

An emotion flashed in his eyes, just for a second. Then he smiled, warm as ever.

"Just remember, Miss Catherine," he said, voice lower now, "you never really know what type men are. Just when you think you do, they go and surprise you with another version of themselves."

Her brow furrowed. "What an odd thing to say, Mr. White." Did he have experience with men who are posers?

He didn't respond. Instead, he simply smiled again—too polite, too practiced. Mr. White had always been kind, but like most, tried to tell her how to behave, to think.

She turned to go, but he stopped her.

"I didn't tell you all of it, Miss Catherine," he murmured, voice almost conspiratorial. "But I think your pa should hear it, too."

"My goodness. Is it really that serious?"

"I'm not sure," Mr. White admitted, rubbing his jaw. "At the time, I didn't think much of it. But now, with everything happening, I wonder." He leaned in slightly, lowering his voice to a hushed whisper, causing goosebumps to grow along her arms. "He came into the store one day with blood stains on his pants and his right shirt sleeve. When I asked him about it, he claimed he'd been cleaning a deer."

Catherine straightened, resisting the urge to roll her eyes. "Matt's been hunting and fishing for trade, Mr. White. That explanation makes perfect sense."

"The blood patterns didn't." His words came slowly, deliberately. "It didn't look like the kind of mess you get from dressing a kill. It looked... like something attacked him. Or rather, like he attacked something."

She shifted her crate of goods on the counter. "That's quite an assumption. Or accusation." Her eyes narrowed but he didn't flinch.

"I just thought you and your pa should know, that's all," Mr. White said, watching her closely. "A lady such as yourself shouldn't have to worry over the ugliness in the world."

Catherine bristled. "And what should we worry about then? Hair ribbons and baking socials?"

His brows lifted at her sharp tone, but then he reached across the counter, patting her hand lightly. "I'm sorry, Miss Catherine. I really didn't mean to stir up a hornet's nest—just to warn you about one. The coyote incident, Matt's remarks, the blood-stained clothes…" He sighed. "A man can't help but wonder about such coincidences."

A voice cut through the air, startling Catherine.

"I highly doubt Matt Sanderson is bold enough to stroll into town with bloodstains on his clothes after what happened to that coyote."

Catherine turned to see Zeke standing in the doorway, his hat in his hands, gaze locked on Mr. White.

The storekeeper's face shifted from smug to sour in an instant. "Hello, Zeke," he said, voice tight. "I didn't hear you enter."

"I guess not." Zeke stepped further inside, his broad shoulders casting a shadow over the counter. He took his time adjusting his hat, leveling Mr. White with an even stare. "You've been too busy stirring the hornet's nest."

Catherine fought the urge to smile as Mr. White's face darkened, either from embarrassment or irritation—or both.

Zeke tilted his head slightly. "Maybe we should all be careful about throwing around accusations. Especially with missing and brutalized animals, and now two missing travelers with no clear answers."

The tension in the store thickened like August heat before a storm.

Mr. White pursed his lips but said nothing.

After paying for his own items, Zeke helped Catherine carry her goods to her pa's wagon outside the post office, balancing the weight with one arm as if it were nothing. Before she could thank him, he caught her hand lightly.

"I need to talk to you a minute."

She sighed dramatically, resting her free hand on her hip. "Not you too, Zeke. What is it with everyone today? Everyone's talking about suspicious happenings and suspicious people."

Zeke chuckled. "Fair enough. I won't tell you if you don't want me to."

She sighed again, exasperated. "Fine. What is it?"

Instead of answering, he watched her, his gaze shifting from the way she rubbed at the nape of her neck to the subtle tension in her shoulders. He leaned back against the wagon, crossing his arms, his blue eyes sharp against the late afternoon light.

"Catherine, do you remember when Mr. Blythe closed early the day you found the coyote pups?"

She hesitated. "Yes. What about it?"

"He's been closing early every day since."

That gave her pause after hearing about Mr. Buxton's cow and the missing couple.

"No one knows where he's been going," Zeke added.

Catherine frowned. "That is odd, but—"

"The day you found the pups was the first day he started closing early, right?"

"Yes, I suppose so."

"Well, on that day, a friend of mine swore he saw Blythe rushing back to the livery. Said he had blood on his hands and clothes."

She froze for a fraction of a second before shaking her head, laughing dryly. "This is the strangest day of my life."

"Why?"

"First, Matt tells me he found a bloody knife on his property. Then Mr. White tells me Matt had blood on his clothes and a vendetta against coyotes. Now you're telling me Mr. Blythe is sneaking off early, and he had blood on him the same day we found the dead coyote?" She huffed. "What next? Mr. Blythe accuses you? Should I start looking at my own pa sideways?"

Zeke let out a low whistle. "That's a lot of coincidences to untangle."

She smirked. "You're telling me."

Zeke turned his gaze toward the livery across the street. "You know, typically, a dead coyote wouldn't garner this much attention. But the way that animal was killed...and I'm sure you heard about Buxton's cow. Both mutilated in the same way."

"How do you know?"

"I went by Buxton's when I heard. I wanted to investigate to see if whoever did it left us some clues."

"What did you find?"

"Nothing. Other than the sheer brutality of the kill."

Catherine shivered. "I know. I can't stop seeing the way that mama coyote looked, the way she must have suffered."

"Have you ever heard of such a kill by a man before?"

She shook her head. "No."

"I have."

She looked at him sharply.

"I was just a small boy," Zeke said, his voice quieter now. "but I know men did terrible things during the war. Things no one wants to talk about. I think...I think violence—true, deep violence—stains a place forever."

A chill crawled over Catherine's skin. "You mean... like a curse?"

Zeke nodded, staring past her. "Maybe. Or maybe places don't forget the things done on their soil. And maybe people don't forget it, either. Maybe a man gets stained, too." He hesitated, blinking as if shaking himself loose from memory. "Forget it. I get lost in my thoughts sometimes, you know."

Mr. White called from his store. "Don't forget your shovel, Zeke!"

Later, as she rode home, her pa broke the silence.

"I noticed you talking to Zeke outside in what seemed like a serious conversation. Anything I should know?"

Catherine hesitated, then told him everything.

Her pa whistled low. "Sounds like we have a Bona Fide mystery on our hands."

"Pa, do you think Mr. Blythe could torture an animal like that?"

Her father's expression grew grim. "A week ago? I'd have said no. But now... I'm not so sure. I guess you never really know a man until he shows you the most recent version of himself."

"That's odd. Mr. White said almost the same thing."

Her father frowned. "Did he?"

"Almost." Catherine thought back on her talk with Zeke. "Pa, Zeke said some strange things today about death, or about death's memory."

Her father's hands tightened on the reins. "Oh?"

"He said death can leave a mark, like a curse. Why would he say such a thing?"

"Cat, do you not know what happened to his mother?"

Catherine blinked. "I—I know she died, but—"

"She was attacked during the Sherman raids. Two Union soldiers." His voice was quiet, heavy. "A slave heard her screams. Caught them in the act, then grabbed a gun from the wall and shot them both. They hung him for it."

Catherine stared.

"She survived long enough to give birth to Zeke's baby sister, his half-sister."

She didn't miss the implication. "What happened to her? Did she die in childbirth?"

Her pa didn't speak for a moment, then he spoke so softly, she had to lean in to hear over the sound of the wagon wheels grinding against the dry, hard earth.

"No. She hung herself two days later."

Her throat tightened. "Zeke found her, didn't he?" She didn't know how she knew things sometimes. She just did.

Her father nodded confirmation. "He did. I wouldn't know about it, if not for Jenkins telling me. He and Zeke moved here at the same time, remember? He knew Zeke's family for years."

"What happened to his pa? And his sister?"

"His pa remarried, but Zeke didn't get along with his stepmother, so he left Atlanta when he was old enough to come here with Jenkins, hiring on with the railroad. Jenkins helped him get his job and brought him along.

"But what happened to his baby sister?"

"That's the worst part, I think. His pa took her to an orphanage and dropped her off on the steps. Jenkins said Zeke was never the same after that."

Silence stretched between them as the wagon rocked along the road.

Finally, her father sighed. "There's something else I can't figure."

Catherine looked at him, waiting.

He tapped the reins lightly. "Why does Zeke need a new shovel... when he bought a brand-new one just two weeks ago?"

———

He needed to keep her close. Not for love—he had no use for such nonsense—but for control. She asked too many questions, saw too much. If he didn't find a way to tether her, she might stumble onto something she shouldn't.

Marriage had its uses. A wife could serve as a distraction, a shield. A woman like Catherine, with her good name and respectable father, would make him appear like any other man. Settled. Safe. Unremarkable. If people saw him as a devoted husband, they wouldn't suspect the hunger lurking beneath his skin, the need that gnawed at his insides like a starved animal.

But things were growing...complicated.

People were asking too many questions. Whispers about the missing travelers already spread through town like wildfire, tongues wagging with speculation. The couple was missed. He should have chosen better, those with no ties or connections, where they wouldn't be missed for a while, if ever. He'd know better next time.

Next time.

The thought of the next time simmered in his blood, a fever rising like the fog on the river—hovering, waiting. Yet, with the talk of the mutilated coyote, of bloodstains and knives, the town grew restless. Curious. Anxious. Some, like Catherine, weren't content to let mysteries lie.

He had to find a way to stop the questions. And her. He had to find a way to make her trust him.

The others hovered around her like flies, but she was already his. Even if she didn't know it yet. He saw the flicker of something in her eyes whenever they spoke—hesitation, curiosity. She was wary, but that didn't matter. He was patient. He needed to charm her, play the role she expected, not the one that came naturally to him. And once she belonged to him, once she was tucked away in his home, raising children and tending to her duties, she wouldn't have time to dig where she shouldn't.

That was the key. Keep her busy. Keep her distracted. Keep her blind.

And in the meantime, he'd have to be more careful. The last one had been a mistake. A thrill, but a mistake. He'd have to make sure no one would miss them. Make sure no one would ever find them. And he needed to make sure no one had a reason to suspect him. Ever.

Most of all, he had to make sure they never caught him.

Because they'd never take him to the rope. Not alive.

The Man in the Middle

Reese

James and Reese managed to rid themselves of Dylan's toxic presence once he left, exchanging a few sarcastic remarks about his audacity. But even as they laughed, a strange, unsettled quiet remained in the house, settling like dust in the corners. Reese realized just how much lighter the space felt without him. For so long, she had carried the burden of his absence like a wound, jagged and raw. But now, standing here in this house, her house, she saw the truth.

It wasn't an absence at all.

Dylan had never truly belonged to her, had never even belonged in her life, really. The gaping hole she had imagined him leaving behind had never been his space to fill. It had been something else all along. Something waiting. *Someone* waiting. She felt him tugging at her heart, whispering into the broken corners, but she just wasn't prepared to trust that he wanted the best for her. Not after all she'd lost. Not when it was in the sanctuary of His people where she had felt the most broken.

They spread the boxes from Sharon's barn onto Reese's carpeted floor, the dim glow of a single lamp casting long, creeping shadows along the walls. The scent of dust and aged paper thickened the air, blending with the lingering traces of Dylan's cologne that still clung to the furniture. James stretched his legs, flipping open a photo album, while Reese sifted through a box of newspaper clippings, old bills, and receipts. The mundane nature of the items didn't fool her. Somewhere in all of this was a truth waiting to be discovered. She'd been surprised when Sharon offered them the boxes to take home and sift through. Maybe she just couldn't do it herself because the grief sat too heavy, weighing against her need to know more. Grief had a way of exhausting—not just the body, but the hope that anything would ever feel normal again.

The quiet between them wasn't uncomfortable, but it carried a weight, an expectancy, as if both sensed that something was about to be uncovered, along with what transpired only moments before. James flipped another page, his fingers trailing over the yellowed edges of a photograph. He stilled.

"This is odd."

Reese looked up. "What?"

He held up a photo, studying it before handing it to her. "Looks like it was taken with an old Polaroid camera."

Reese took it, tilting it toward the light. "There's a Polaroid in the back room. My uncle didn't throw much away." The faded and blurred image was grainy, capturing Patricia and Art mid-laughter. But another figure stood just out of frame. The man's face wasn't visible—only his torso, clad in a faded t-shirt with a logo across the chest. The logo blurred with the image, but the words were sharp enough to read them.

"George's Gas 'n' Goods," James said.

A flicker of recognition sent a shiver up Reese's spine. "That's the gas station off the highway." Why did that unsettle her?

James nodded. "Do you recognize him?"

"No," she admitted, studying the picture closer. "It's just a man's torso, after all, but maybe Sharon will know who he is."

"Judging by his build and hands, he looks around their age," James noted.

Reese frowned. Something about the photo pricked her emotions in a way she couldn't name. Like something else lingered just outside the frame, something unseen but present.

"The expressions on Art and Patricia's faces—they're too forced, too deliberate. As if whatever they had been laughing at hadn't been funny at all," she said.

James shifted closer, his shoulder brushing hers as he took the picture back. The warmth of his nearness didn't escape her notice, but she forced herself to focus.

"Good job, detective." He smirked. "Maybe you should help us on the force."

Reese snorted. "Except I have no desire to move to Biloxi."

"The coast has it great points, but it's nice here, too. How's the job hunt going, anyway?"

"It's not," she admitted. "Honestly, I think all this sleuthing is killing my chances of finding something. But I also feel like I've exhausted every position available in the area."

James leaned back against the couch, his eyes narrowing thoughtfully. "What did you do before?"

She hesitated. "Not much. Just college jobs. Dylan wanted me to support his dreams, so I never built a career for myself. And then... I thought we'd have kids, so I didn't mind at first."

The words sat between them like a weight.

She didn't look at him, didn't want to see the reaction on his face when she admitted what had been left unsaid—that children never came. Somewhere deep down, she wondered if that was why the silence around her felt so loud now.

After a beat, he asked, "What did you study in college?"

She forced a small laugh. "Believe it or not, journalism."

James lifted an eyebrow. "Why wouldn't I believe it?"

"I don't know. People have always seemed surprised when I told them."

He tilted his head, studying her in that quiet, unnerving way of his. "Really? I would have thought it suited you well."

She scoffed. "Why?"

"For starters, you're observant. Inquisitive. Persistent." He grinned. "Aren't those traits every reporter should have?"

"That's a nice way of saying I'm a nosy pest, but I'll take it." She hesitated, then added, "Truth is, I've always wanted to write."

"I can see that about you."

"Really? Thanks." She didn't know why that touched her so much, but she swallowed a lump and smiled.

James smiled back, before turning the photo over in his hands again, his smirk fading.

"Who do you suppose this guy is?"

Reese shrugged. "There's only one way to find out." She reached for the photo, but when their hands brushed, something in her flinched, unexpected and sharp. And James reacted, too. He stiffened and pulled back, his usual stoic mask slipping for just a second, betraying a flash of the same unease that rippled through her.

Before either of them could speak, a door slammed somewhere down the hallway. They both jumped.

Reese's eyes met James' widened stare, before he smiled. "It's just a draft," he said. "Addie's stories are getting to you. All is well." But his voice faltered on the last word, like he wasn't sure if he believed it — or if he just *needed* to.

Reese wasn't sure which startled her more — the door slamming or the warmth that lingered where their hands had touched. Maybe it was nothing. Maybe it was something. But she didn't know if she wanted to discover the truth either way.

———

George's gas station sat just off the highway, wedged between an auto shop and a field of kudzu that had swallowed an abandoned house long ago. The lot wasn't built for more than a few cars at a time, but it didn't stop the steady flow of customers stopping in for cold Cokes, cigarettes, or a quick bite from the grill inside.

Reese wasn't much for fried food, but the moment she stepped through the door, the scent of seasoned batter, hot grease, and something sweet curling through the air made her pause.

James leaned in, his breath warm against her ear. "Might smell good, but if you saw the kitchen, you'd never eat here again."

A shiver ran down her spine—though she wasn't sure if it was from his proximity or the mental image. She smirked. "Thanks for ruining my appetite."

He smirked back. "Just looking out for you."

They approached the counter.

"Hey, Julie," James greeted the redhead behind the register.

Julie glanced up, her lashes thick with mascara. She smiled at James—until her gaze flickered to Reese. A sideways glance of disdain. Reese knew that look well.

"James," she said, smoothing her top, "I didn't know you were in town again."

He gave a polite nod. "Is George around?"

Julie's lips pursed, but she turned and called out, "Hey, George! You got visitors!"

George emerged from the back, wiping his hands on a grease-stained rag. His thick glasses magnified his eyes so much that Reese had to avoid looking directly at them, afraid she might laugh.

"James! Well, I'll be. What brings you to our neck of the woods? Thought those gulf waters would have swallowed you up by now."

"I come to shore every now and then." He gripped the other man's hand in a solid shake. "How've you been, George? Looks like business is still good."

"Can't complain. If I did, it'd be to Uncle Sam, but he ain't listening, so what's the point?"

James chuckled, then slid the photo across the counter. "George, you remember Patricia Langton?"

George's smile faded. "Yeah. Shame about what happened."

James held up the picture. "Recognize this guy?"

George squinted. "Hard to say without a face. I do remember Patricia and Art coming in with another fella a few times. Strange man. I remember when he bought that t-shirt he's wearing there, just after he spilled chili on his over there in the diner."

"What was strange about him?" Reese asked.

"Can't say I know to be exact. Just something...off...about him. Art and Patricia seemed real tense-like, too. Why you asking about him? He got something to do with Patricia? You on this case, now, James? Is that why you're back?"

"Not exactly. Just helping Reese in her uncle's house, and we came across this picture. It made us curious."

George sized her up, a knowing glint in his eye. "Ah. I see."

Reese shifted uncomfortably, moving slightly away from James. He peered at her, but George spoke, diverting his attention back to the reason they came.

"That's all I know, I'm afraid. Julie you got anything to add?"

"I'd appreciate any help," Reese said, hoping to soften the other woman's attitude.Julie didn't even glance at her."I don't know much, other than what George already told you. I know that he never came in here again once Patricia disappeared, but I didn't think anything about it. Art came in a couple of times before he—well, that's all I know. Sorry."She shifted her focus to James, flashing him a quick, familiar smile, then turned away to ring up another customer.

They left with more questions than answers.

Back in the car, James turned to her, suddenly too close. The space between them charged with something unspoken.

His gaze flickered to her lips for a second—barely noticeable, but enough.

James exhaled, low and quiet. "You have nothing to worry about there, you know."

She swallowed. "About what?"

James turned to her, his gaze heavy, searching. "What George implied in there. I don't—" He stopped, rubbing a hand over his face before exhaling sharply. "I'm not looking for anything here, Reese. I don't let people in easily, not anymore."

She swallowed, forcing herself to hold his gaze. "Neither do I."

The honesty sat between them, vulnerable, raw.

James let out a slow breath. "I think I'm starting to trust you, though, and that scares me."

Her heart clenched. He was giving her something real, something she hadn't expected.

"I think I might trust you too," she whispered, then laughed bitterly. "And that scares me."

James shifted closer, his voice quieter now. "I'm not him, Reese, any more than you're her." When she gave him a surprised look, he smirked. "I know Gram told you about Lynette." At her acknowledgment he continued. "Again, we're not them."

"I know," she murmured. "But neither of us know how to do this anymore, do we?"

James smirked, but it was tired, worn. "Nope."

A pause. Then, softer, he said, "But maybe-when we're ready-we can figure it out together."

Reese felt something shift inside her. It wasn't just about the ghosts of the past anymore. It was about what came next.

She nodded. "Yeah. Maybe. But right now, I need to focus on my uncle and all these secrets. We can worry about anything else later."

The admission settled between them, heavier than it should have been, yet somehow freeing. And for a fleeting second, Reese thought she felt the weight of something else watching, but then it was gone.

And she realized there was no taking it back.

And she didn't know if she wanted to.

WHISPERS IN THE WIND

Catherine

The town buzzed with its usual late-afternoon activity, but a weight lingered in the air—thick, unshakable. The missing travelers dominated the day's conversations, spoken in hushed tones and marked by uneasy glances. Even the wind carried the unease, rustling through the streets in chilled gusts, stirring fallen leaves along the wooden sidewalks like restless spirits.

Catherine and Ellen walked side by side along the main road, Ellen pulling her scarf tighter around her neck, bracing against the autumn air.

"I know we need to head back to the post office, but do you mind if we stop at the church first?" Ellen asked. "Brother Whitmore mentioned holding a prayer vigil for the missing couple, and I'd like to see if there's a time set."

Catherine hesitated but nodded. "Alright. Pa probably doesn't expect us back yet, anyway."

As they neared the church, a familiar sight made Catherine's stomach tighten. A small group of girls stood near the steps, their skirts fluttering in the cold wind. Rosalind Greer stood at the center, as always, her posture poised, her chin slightly lifted—a queen among her court. Mary Beth Turner leaned in close, speaking in a hushed whisper, the others nodding, their expressions tense.

Ellen's pace quickened. "Oh, look! The girls from church. Let's say hello."

Catherine forced a half-smile to hide the churn in her stomach. Say hello? As if that was all it took.

Rosalind was the first to notice them. Her sharp blue gaze flicked toward Catherine before settling on Ellen with polite curiosity.

"Oh." Rosalind's voice was smooth, unbothered. "Hello, Catherine."

Catherine forced herself to return the greeting, smiling a thin smile. "Hi, Rosalind."

Mary Beth's gaze shifted toward Ellen. "I don't think we've met."

"I'm Ellen Hollis," Ellen said warmly. "My grandpa and I are new to Meridian."

Rosalind inclined her head slightly. "Welcome. That's a pretty wildflower in your hair."

Ellen beamed. "Thank you. Catherine helped me weave it into my hair. Wildflowers are my favorite."

Rosalind arched a brow, assessing. Judging. "How nice of her."

Ellen frowned, while Catherine said nothing. It was always like this—every interaction laced with subtle exclusion, an unspoken understanding that they tolerated her, but never truly welcomed her.

Hannah Simms folded her arms and cleared her throat. "I still can't believe those travelers are really gone. How does someone just vanish without a trace?"

Mary Beth shivered. "It's awful. Ma says we need to be more careful, and she insists I stay here at the church until she and Pa are ready to go home. I mean, we live right here in town, but she doesn't want me home alone."

Rosalind pressed at the pins in her hair behind her ear. "I've heard my father and some of the others talking. People are wondering if... well, if someone in town had a hand in it." She lowered her voice. "Just think. It could be anyone we know. Even someone in the church."

Ellen's eyes widened. "You really think someone here at the church could do something like that?" Her gaze flickered toward the heavy wooden doors above the steps.

Mary Beth hushed her. "Shh! You shouldn't say that so loudly. Besides, maybe it's their own fault. Maybe they got involved in something they shouldn't, and it serves them right."

"Like what?" Hannah leaned in, eager to hear her friend's theory.

Catherine stiffened. "Shouldn't we be more careful with how we talk about them? Those people had families somewhere, loved ones who just lost them and may not ever know what happened. Imagine hearing someone whispering about your missing kin like this."

The group fell silent. The usual knowing glances between them stalled, replaced by something uneasy. Mary Beth looked at the ground. Hannah toyed with the ribbon tied at her wrist. But Rosalind... Rosalind studied her.

For the first time, Catherine didn't see coldness in her gaze. There was something else—something searching.

Then, just as quickly, Rosalind blinked and looked away.

The church doors opened, and Brother Whitmore appeared, his boots thudding as he descended the steps.

The girls greeted him, even Ellen. Catherine did not.

His gaze swept over the group, his smile widening when he reached Rosalind and the others. "Hello, young ladies. It's certainly nice to see you gather at the church. There's no better place to be, right? It's always good to gather with fellow believers." His smile dimmed when his gaze landed on Catherine.

"Hello, Miss Porter."

Catherine dipped her head. "Brother Whitmore."

"I hope to see you at service tomorrow."

"I always attend service," she said evenly. "With my pa."

"Yes." His smile cooled. "Of course."

She knew he didn't care for her. He never said it outright, but she could see it in his eyes, hear it in the careful way he spoke her name.

Not quite an outsider, but never fully one of them.

Ellen shifted beside her, her expression thoughtful. "We should be going," she said quickly. "Your pa is expecting us."

Brother Whitmore nodded approvingly. "Best not keep a man waiting. Good evening, Miss Hollis."

Ignoring Catherine, he turned back to the other girls. "Now, how about helping us set up for the vigil? The others are inside."

The group ascended the steps, their soft laughter trailing behind them as they disappeared through the doors.

Ellen exhaled. "Well. That was something."

Catherine's lips pressed into a thin line. "Welcome to Meridian."

Ellen frowned. "They weren't rude, exactly. But they weren't very nice."

Catherine shrugged. "They don't have to be. They already belong."

Ellen shook her head. "Shouldn't church be a place where everyone belongs?"

Catherine didn't answer. She had asked herself that question too many times.

Ellen huffed, crossing her arms. "Well, I think somebody should say something. There should never be favorites in church. Besides, if anyone should belong, it's you, Catherine. I've never met anyone kinder or more loyal."

Catherine's lips twitched, a small, grateful smile forming despite the ache in her chest. "I could say the same about you. We may not belong in there"—she pointed back to the church—"but we belong here, together."

She looped her arm through Ellen's, and Ellen patted her hand. It was easy to forget the years between them. Ellen carried herself with a grace beyond her age, wise and steady.

Still, it hurt.

Catherine loved Ellen, but she might be leaving soon. And as much as she didn't want it to, belonging still mattered to her.

A breeze lifted her hair, carrying something with it—not a voice, not a whisper, but something else. Something like an answer, unspoken but felt.

You already belong, child. You are mine.

Her pulse stilled.

She would know His voice anywhere. It wrapped around her like the shawl on Ellen's shoulders, warm and certain.

The moment passed. Dust stirred along the street, rising in puffy clouds.

Ellen coughed.

Catherine exhaled. "Come on. Let's go see the pups."

Her friend hesitated, glancing toward the road that led home. "But... shouldn't we wait for your pa? He wanted us to ride with him."

Catherine sighed, shifting the weight of her basket. The ache in her chest deepened. As much as she tried to brush it off, she wanted to belong—in the church, in the town, in *someone's world*. Maybe that's why she couldn't leave those pups to fend for themselves. They didn't belong either. Not really. Not without their mother.

"I know, but he won't be done at the post office for a while, and I don't want to just stand around when those pups might be in danger."

Ellen bit her lip. "You think something could hurt them? Aren't they safe at Zeke's?"

Catherine exhaled, the memory of the mother coyote's brutalized body flashing in her mind. *It could be anyone we know.* Rosalind's statement echoed in her mind, closing in and threatening her sense of security. "I don't know, I guess so. But I'll feel better if we check on them."

Ellen glanced toward the road again, uncertainty flickering across her face. "What if whatever-or whomever- did that to their mother comes back?"

"All the more reason to check on them," Catherine said. "We'll be quick. We'll make sure they're safe, and then we'll come back and ride home with Pa."

Ellen still didn't look convinced, but after a pause, she nodded. "Alright. Just for a minute."

"Just for a minute," Catherine echoed, knowing full well that wasn't true.

As they made their way toward the riverbank, the afternoon light stretched long across the ground, the wind curling through the grass like something restless.

Zeke's place wasn't far from the bridge, tucked near the river's edge where the land sloped low. His setup was modest—a cabin with a simple lean-to for storing his hunting and trapping supplies, and a barn for his stock and animals. He lived alone, like several men.

Mr. Blythe, Matt, and several others. *It could be anyone we know.*

She swallowed, keeping her gaze forward.

They were only going to check on the pups for a minute.

But they were leaving behind the safety of many eyes and witnesses.

As they approached the bridge, Catherine couldn't ignore the way the river whispered beneath their feet, almost mocking her desire to escape the company of the town. She couldn't shake the feeling that indifference would be better company than the invisible force that warned her danger followed them out of town.

―――

They stepped into the barn, the heavy wooden door groaning like an old man rising from his chair. The scent of hay and earth mingled with the lingering musk of livestock, thick and warm in the cooling air. Dust motes hovered in the slanted light filtering through the rafters, caught in the hush of the settling evening.

Outside, the first whispers of autumn stirred the trees, their leaves rustling like dry paper, brittle against the fading light.

Catherine's shoes scuffed against the packed dirt as she followed Ellen to the crate, where soft whimpers drifted up to greet them. Ellen wasted no time, kneeling on the barn floor and reaching for one of the pups. The tiny creature wriggled in her grasp, nuzzling into her warmth with blind trust.

Catherine paused, watching as her friend stroked the animal with careful fingers, her expression tender, almost reverent. The girl had such an easy way with creatures, as if she understood their quiet language in a way most people never could.

She crouched beside Ellen and lifted another pup, cradling its fragile weight against her chest. It squirmed at first, then settled, its tiny heart hammering against her palm like a fluttering moth. The soft fur smelled of straw and warm earth, its breath sweet yet thick and curdling, like milk left too long in the sun. Not exactly pleasant, but comforting all the same.

She ran her fingers over its downy head, feeling the small rise and fall of its breath, the way it leaned into her touch without hesitation.

Trust.

Such a fragile, dangerous thing.

A gust of wind curled through the cracks in the barn walls, slipping between the wooden slats like fingers seeking purchase. The boards groaned as the wind rattled them, whispering in the stillness, stirring the dust. Somewhere beyond the trees, a branch cracked, sharp and abrupt, swallowed quickly by the hush.

Catherine's shoulders tensed.

She glanced toward the door, scanning the darkness creeping into the barn from the late afternoon light outside. A sudden unease prickled at the back of her neck.

She turned back to Ellen, swallowing against the feeling.

"Come on," she murmured. "Let's check their food before we get in trouble for sneaking out here."

Ellen grinned, rocking back on her heels. "I admit I didn't want to go against orders, but now that I'm here..." She looked down at the coyote pup nestled against her. "Well, I won't tell if you won't."

Before Catherine could respond, heavy footsteps scuffed against the dirt outside.

She froze.

The barn door swung open with a slow creak, and both girls flinched, eyes wide.

Zeke's silhouette filled the entrance, framed by the deepening twilight. The dim light caught in the wild mess of his dark hair, casting his face in sharp relief—all angles and planes, shadow and glinting green eyes. He let the moment linger, then smirked as he stepped inside.

"Well, what do we have here?" His voice was slow, easy, as if he hadn't just given them both a fright.

He crouched beside Catherine, reaching to scratch behind the pup's ears, his face too close, his presence pressing in. "Didn't expect to find two pretty ladies keeping these little fellas company this evening. Sure glad it was you, though."

Ellen beamed, but Catherine shifted slightly, glancing away from his closeness. "We wanted to check on them," she said. "That's all."

Zeke chuckled, rubbing the pup's head. "And you thought sneaking out here alone was a good idea? Does your pa even know you're out here?" He tilted his head, his grin widening. "I think I need to drive you both home."

Before Catherine could answer, another voice interjected.

"That won't be necessary, Zeke."

Her pa stood in the doorway, his frame rigid, his expression carved from shadow and stern angles. His voice—low and firm—left no room for argument.

Zeke straightened, stepping back slightly.

Catherine set the pup down as if that might soften her father's mood. It didn't.

His eyes swept over them, first to Ellen, then to his daughter. "I told you not to walk anywhere without a male escort you can trust, preferably me."

Catherine bristled. "Pa, I—"

"You what?" His voice sharpened like the edge of a whittling knife. "Forgot about the people who've gone missing? Forgot that someone—some person—killed that coyote in a way no animal would? That there are stock animals missing all over the county? What if whoever did that decided to do the same to a girl walking alone?"

Catherine swallowed hard. She knew he was right. And beneath his anger, fear lurked just beneath the surface.

Ellen shifted beside her. "Sir, I—"

He held up a hand. "Ellen, you both know better. I'm sure Thatcher will have a few things to say to you, too."

Catherine cast a glance at Zeke, who had the nerve to smirk, clearly enjoying her reprimand, but he made it worse by speaking. "It's true neither of you should be walking anywhere alone these days."

Part of her wanted to argue, to say she wasn't a child needing constant watching. But another part—the one she didn't like admitting existed—knew the air felt different now. Heavy. Watching. And from Zeke's expression, she wondered if he felt it, too.

Her father sighed, rubbing a rough hand over his face before motioning toward the door. "Come on, the wagon's outside. Ellen, you and your grandpa are eating supper with us again. I'm glad you girls are enjoying each other's company, but no more sneaking around. You hear?"

Ellen nodded, cutting her eyes at Catherine, who sighed, knowing there was no use arguing.

"Yes, sir."

She shot Zeke a glare, but he only chuckled, rubbing one of the pup's heads.

"See you later, ladies," he said, winking at Catherine. She bristled with indignation. Why did her pa have to reprimand her in front of *him* of all people?

Zeke stepped closer, voice low. "Be careful, Cat."

His breath brushed her ear, and chills rippled down her spine.

As they stepped outside, the sharp night air wrapped around her, heavy with the scent of honeysuckle turned bitter by the cold. The trees groaned above them as the wind stirred their limbs.

But Catherine knew it wasn't the cold or her pa's displeasure that made her shiver.

As they climbed into the wagon, she couldn't shake the feeling that someone—something—was watching. Hidden just beyond the trees, breathing with the wind, waiting in the dark.

Waiting for her.

Dead Men Have No Names

Reese

Reese scrubbed the countertop harder than necessary, the sponge dragging in harsh circles against the worn laminate. Dylan had been here. In her house.

She couldn't shake the feeling he'd left something behind—not physically, but a stain, a presence. Even days later, the weight of his arrogance lingered in the air like a bad perfume that refused to fade. His smug grin, the way he leaned against her kitchen counter as if he still owned it, still owned her.

She hadn't missed the way his eyes roamed, scanning the boxes, the photographs, the letters—things that didn't belong to him. Had that been his real reason for showing up? What did he want? Hadn't he taken enough from her already?

Reese gritted her teeth and tossed the sponge into the sink. She didn't want to believe Dylan had any real stake in her life anymore. He had his perfect little family now, a pregnant wife, a whole new existence. But then why had he been so comfortable in her space, walking through her house like a man taking inventory?

She wouldn't let him get to her. This house belonged to her. This life belonged to her.

And this life might include another man. James.

Unease twisted in her stomach. She needed air.

Reese grabbed her cardigan and stepped onto the porch, letting the cool night push against her skin. The wind had picked up, sending the trees swaying against the darkness. The branches creaked, whispering among themselves in voices just too low to make out. She shivered and listened for the sound of Addie's dog barking, the occasional hum of a truck in the distance, anything to root her in something normal. Instead, she heard the river. Low, steady, whispering. Calling.

The bridge.

The thought pulled at her, subtle but insistent, strong like a magnet's force. Go.

Dylan's betrayal burned. That much was clear. But under the anger, something else stirred. Something older. Something she hadn't dared name.

Was it fear?

Or was it grief?

Before she could untangle it, her feet were already moving toward the bridge. Gravel crunched beneath her hurried steps, the wind pressing insistently at her back, as if guiding her forward.

The wooden planks groaned beneath her feet as she stepped onto the bridge. The wind carried the scent of the river upward, thick and damp, tinged with something else—something old. A smell like earth left too long in the dark.

The decayed structure felt like a threshold—between the past and the present, between the seen and unseen. Even in daylight, the old bridge carried a quiet menace. At night, it felt like a place outside of time. The river moved sluggishly beneath her, its surface rippling in the moonlight. Somewhere beyond the tree line, a bullfrog croaked, breaking the silence for only a moment before settling into stillness. Despite her unease, the sounds rested against her ear, like a balm to a wound.

Reese leaned against the railing, inhaling the damp scent of the water, her mind still tangled in thoughts of Dylan. Was he really gone? Or was he waiting, lurking in the shadows of her life, looking for a way to hold on to the chains in her mind.

A shuffling sound pulled her attention away from her thoughts.

Reese stiffened. Someone stood at the far end of the bridge.

A man.

She couldn't see his face, only his silhouette against the tree line, motionless, watching.

"James? Is that you?"

Her pulse pounded in her throat. It wasn't James. He would greet her.

"Dylan?" Surely he wouldn't come back this soon.

And it wasn't Stuckey, or a ghostly spirit. This man was flesh and blood. Real.

He shifted on his feet, and the light hit his face. A strange, sick feeling twisted in her gut. She couldn't explain why, but—she felt like she knew him.

Not by name. Not by memory. By something deeper, something unspoken, and she didn't want to hear it.

The man didn't move but stood as if he belonged to the shadows.

She could barely breathe.

A truck rumbled in the distance, its headlights flashing through the trees. For a split second, the beam illuminated his face—

And Reese's breath caught in her throat.

It wasn't a stranger.

It was—

Darkness swallowed the light, and he was gone.

Just like that.

Reese stumbled backward, her heartbeat slamming against her ribs.

It couldn't be. Her uncle had died. Maybe James was right, and imagination manifested itself.

The wind kicked up, rattling the bridge, sending a shiver up her spine.

But what if it was? Reese rushed back to her house-Uncle Art's house- wondering if she should have come here to this place, a place where reality altered itself. Or maybe something else altered it.

"Oh, him. Of course, I remember him. I played cards with him one evening."

"What? When?"

James barely had time to process Addie's words before she snatched the photograph from his hand and tapped a finger against it, her expression twisting in an unreadable mix of exasperation and unease. It was the unease that unsettled Reese the most. Addie, who faced near-death accidents and spoke of ghosts with casual disdain, looked afraid.

And that wasn't normal for her.

"Who do you think took this picture, detective? Did you two even consider who sat behind the camera?"

The question knocked around in Reese's skull, ricocheting against every logical thought. It was such an obvious thing. Too obvious. And yet she and James—James—hadn't even asked it.

James was stone-still beside her, staring at the photograph like it had betrayed him.

"I know what you're thinking," Addie said. "You're wondering' how you missed something' so big. Especially you, James." She gave him a pointed look. "But do you know why you missed it?"

"No," James said flatly, "but I'm sure you'll tell us."

"That's right; I will." Addie sank into her recliner, patting Cash's head as he climbed onto her lap like a much smaller lapdog. The Rottweiler, content, rested his chin on his paws, eyes flicking between them, silent and possessive. "Young folks today miss so much because your heads are so filled up with 'Instabook' and the like."

Reese and James shared an amused grin at the misnomer, while Addie scratched behind Cash's ears, her eyes going distant, like she was rifling through old memories. "I can't tell you his name because he only went by a nickname, although it sounded like a regular name. Would've thought it was his name, if Art hadn't told me otherwise."

James straightened. "What was it?"

Addie exhaled hard, as if the name itself tasted bad in her mouth. "Knox."

Something tightened in Reese's chest, cinching like a rope being yanked hard and fast. The room swayed, just a little. She hardly registered James grabbing her arm.

"Reese? You okay?"

"She's white as a ghost," Addie muttered. "Jamie, get her some water."

Reese barely heard them. That name—it roared in her ears like an oncoming train, drowning out everything else. A name she hadn't heard spoken in decades, a name buried beneath years of silence and unanswered questions.

It couldn't be.

James crouched beside her, handing her a glass of water. She took a sip, barely registering her motions.

"Reese, talk to us. What is it?"

She forced herself to swallow, forced her throat to work. "That nickname... I've heard it before. It belonged to my father."

James's brows furrowed. "Wait. You're telling' me your uncle was hanging around with a man named Knox, and your father—his own brother—was also called Knox? That's a strange coincidence, unless your father--."

Reese's lips parted, but no words came out. The truth clawed its way up her throat, rough and raw. The man at the bridge...no. No way it was...When she finally spoke, her voice barely carried past the roaring in her ears.

"It's not a coincidence, but it should be impossible."

Addie frowned, leaning forward and squinting her eyes.

James studied her, his sharp mind already working the problem. "What do you mean, Reese? Why?"

Reese forced herself to meet his gaze. She had to say it aloud. Had to break the seal, let the words escape into the air where they couldn't be taken back.

"Because my father's been dead for over thirty years."

The Vanishing and the Vigil

Catherine

Catherine stepped into the clearing, her pulse drumming in her ears. The air smelled of dewy earth and river mist, tinged with the fading scent of last night's fire. But the fire itself was dead—just a pile of ashen remains that hadn't seen flame that morning.

Something wasn't right. The space filled with a quiet that echoed the emptiness of the cold campsite.

Her father stepped beside her, arms crossed as he surveyed the camp. The stillness didn't comfort. The quiet was louder than it should have been. The morning had been noisy on the ride over—birds calling, the wind stirring through the trees—but here, there was only silence.

Catherine's skin prickled.

"Now, where could they have gone?" Her father's voice was low, cautious.

She hugged her arms, staring at the empty tent, the undisturbed bedrolls still tucked along the canvas wall, as if Ellen and her grandfather had intended to return. "They wouldn't just leave. Not when they knew we were coming to take them into town this morning."

Her father's gaze sharpened as he swept the camp, taking in every detail. He didn't speak at first, but then he took a slow step toward the fire pit and crouched, sifting his fingers through the ashes. "Fire's cold. That means they didn't eat here this morning. These ashes are from last night."

Catherine swallowed, her stomach knotting. She bent, pushing back the tent flap, half-expecting Ellen to pop out laughing, teasing her for looking so worried. But the inside was undisturbed. Their belongings were stacked neatly against the side, everything in its place—except for them.

"Pa, I don't like this."

Her father exhaled through his nose, his jaw tightening. "Let's check the water. Maybe they took the boat out early."

Catherine followed him, her skirts rustling against the tall grass as she scanned the ground for footprints. If Ellen and her grandpa had left on foot, surely there would be some sign of it. But the damp earth was undisturbed—no clear prints leading away, no dragged trail from a hastily packed camp.

Thatcher's boat sat just where he left it, with the oars at the bottom, dry, and lying one on top of the other. Her father squatted near the bank, studying the water. The river moved lazily beneath the slanted morning light, carrying leaves and broken twigs along its surface. He pressed a palm to the wet soil, testing it. "No sign of the boat being pulled in or out," he muttered.

Catherine's breath hitched. "Pa... do you think—?"

He stood, brushing his hands against his trousers. "I think we don't need to start worrying just yet."

She frowned. "But if they'd left, wouldn't they have taken their things? And why is their fire cold? That means no one's been here, not even last night."

Her father nodded, his jaw tightening. "I gotta admit, that part don't sit right with me, either." He turned slowly, scanning the campsite again, taking it in as though looking at it with fresh eyes. "But Thatcher knows how to take care of himself. He scouted in the war. Told me himself he sleeps with his pistol at his side. No one would sneak up on him easy."

Catherine glanced at the tent again, the unease in her stomach knotting tighter. "Unless they were already inside the camp when he went to sleep."

Her father didn't answer.

Catherine turned slowly, her boots pressing into the damp ground, sinking slightly with each step. She moved without thinking, drawn toward the overgrown path leading along the riverbank.

Then—something caught her eye.

A hat.

She stumbled slightly, her breath catching as she crouched down. The worn brim of Thatcher's hat lay on its side, a damp stain along the fabric. The morning dew had settled on it, but beneath that, the fabric was dry. Catherine smelled a hint of tobacco, Thatcher's scent still lingering in the air.

It had been here overnight.

Her father stepped behind her, his shadow falling over her as he reached down, taking the hat from her hands.

Her throat worked against the words she didn't want to say. "He never goes anywhere without it."

Her father exhaled through his nose, his jaw flexing as he turned the hat over, brushing his fingers along the brim.

Then his expression shifted, and his fingers stilled.

Catherine's stomach tightened. "Pa... what is it?"

He turned the hat slightly, angling it toward the sunlight.

A smear of something dark clung to the fabric.

Not just dirt.

Not just damp.

Blood.

Faded, dried—but still there.

Catherine's breath shallowed. Her gaze darted back toward the tent, toward the untouched belongings, the cold fire, the eerie and quiet clearing.

Then her eyes landed on the fire pit.

Something glinted among the ashes.

Not wood. Not coal.

A chain.

Partially buried, Catherine pulled it up, examining the tiny links of silver. She'd seen this chain before, around her friend's neck. Ellen wouldn't go anywhere without it. Looking closer, she noticed it had been snapped, broken, as if it had been yanked off. The locket was no longer attached. Where was it? Where was Ellen?

She took a step back, then handed it to her pa, her eyes filling with tears that forced her to suspect the truth.

Her father picked it up, turning it in his hands. His mouth was set in a grim line, his fingers wrapping around the chain like it might tell him what had happened here.

But her father turned toward her, handing her the chain, his voice low and final. "Get to the wagon, Cat."

Her feet refused to move. "Pa—"

"Now."

His tone left no room for argument.

She turned and ran, her pulse thrumming in her ears. The clearing blurred around her, the trees bending, the river murmuring like a warning that danger approached. She climbed onto the wagon seat just as her father emerged. He reached into the back of the wagon and retrieved his rifle, before joining her on the seat.

He flicked the reins harder than usual, sending the horses into a brisk trot.

Catherine twisted in her seat, watching the campsite shrink behind them. The empty tent. The untouched belongings. Blood on Thatcher's hat and Ellen's broken chain and missing locket.

Her father's hands were white against the reins, his breath controlled in that way that meant he was holding something back.

She swallowed. "Pa... we're going to the sheriff, right?"

His jaw flexed. Then, finally—

"No. I'll go to the sheriff. You are staying out of this. No arguments, Cat, and you'll stay in town today, too."

Her stomach knotted. "But—"

"I don't want you out at that cabin alone. And I don't want you to look for them. You'll help Zeke at the post office until I figure out what's going on."

She opened her mouth to argue, but the words died in her throat.

Her father's grip on the reins didn't loosen.

Catherine stared ahead, gripping the chain tighter in her hands.

And somewhere, deep in the back of her mind, a single thought pushed through the fear.

Ellen's gone.

And I'm so afraid we're not going to find her alive.

———

Stuckey sat in the dimness of his cabin, rolling the empty whiskey glass between his fingers, his jaw tight with self-loathing.

He shouldn't have done it.

He swore—swore—he'd only take those who wouldn't be missed, those drifting through town like leaves on the current, who could vanish without a ripple.

But he'd let the hunger take control.

He couldn't tolerate the light surrounding her.

Light that begged to be snuffed out.

He dragged a hand down his face, cursing himself. He'd been careful all this time. How had he let this happen?

A flicker of movement caught his eye.

A shadow stretched long against the cabin wall, twisting unnaturally in the candlelight.

It slithered.

Laughed.

Not with sound—but with something deeper, something Stuckey felt in his bones.

They had been watching him.

Guiding him. Taunting his lack of self-control.

He gritted his teeth, gripping the glass until it nearly cracked. "I know what I'm doing," he muttered.

But did he?

Because now, he had to cover his tracks.

That girl and her grandfather weren't nobodies.

People would notice.

The thought sent a sharp thrill through him—a rush of fear and excitement, tangling together until he couldn't tell where one ended and the other began.

Would they figure it out?

Would they suspect?

The risk should unnerve him, but his pulse quickened at the thought, and beneath it all, something darker stirred.

The hunger claimed him again.

Already, the last kill faded, dissolving into the past like a dream slipping from memory.

And that meant he needed more.

Soon.

The shadow slinked across the floor, long and thin in the flickering light. Stuckey watched it, mesmerized, his breath shallow as it curled and shifted like a living thing. It twisted in ways that didn't match his own movements, bending unnaturally, refusing to obey the rules of light and form. A slow grin curled his lips.

He knew better than to question what was right in front of him.

Something burned in his chest, a raw, itching fire that wouldn't settle. His fingers twitched, his nails digging into his palm until they left little crescent moons in his skin. The blood in his veins pulsed, hot and insistent, demanding something he couldn't name.

He licked his lips, the motion slow, deliberate.

The room smelled of sweat and damp wood; the staleness hung thick in the air. The weight of it pressed against his lungs, making each breath feel like it carried something unseen, something waiting. He rolled his shoulders, the tension there creeping up his neck, slithering beneath his skin like a thing with teeth.

He had done well. He knew that. The world shifted as it should. But there was still unfinished business, still a wrongness that scraped against his bones. It was never enough.

He stood abruptly, the chair legs scraping against the wooden floor, the sound splitting the quiet like a knife. His head snapped toward the doorway, eyes narrowing at the empty space beyond it. The air felt thick, almost humming, as if something waited just beyond the edge of his sight.

He swallowed against the dryness in his throat. Her.

She didn't know he posed a threat. The whole town thought they could ignore it. Pretend he was a whisper in the dark, a bad memory that could be buried beneath time and silence. But shadows didn't stay buried. They stretched. They crept. They disobeyed light and form.

And soon, they would see.

His gaze flicked back to the wall, watching the shadow ripple as he moved. His fingers itched again—not with nerves, but with something deeper, something that slithered just beneath the surface of his skin.

Slowly, he pinched them over the flame of the candle, holding there, longer than he should have. The burn licked up his nerves like a promise, sharp and quiet.

And when he finally let go, when the pain should have overwhelmed him, all he felt was the shadow curling tighter around him.

Smiling, Stuckey whispered into the thick, stale air, "Soon."

The gravelly voice that came out of his mouth startled him, but only for a moment before the darkness cloaked him in willful euphoria.

———

Uneasy bodies filled the church, stiff-backed men and pale-faced women clutching handkerchiefs and prayer books as if they could ward off the unseen. Their fear thickened the air, and the demons moved through it like fish through water, their presence unnoticed but suffocating all the same.

Sleim drifted like a snake sliding between them, listening to their shallow prayers, tasting the doubt in every whispered plea. Faith was fragile here. Fractured by fear, by uncertainty, by the knowledge that evil had already slipped into their town and taken root in their midst.

At the pulpit, the man they followed had no strength to stand against it.

Brother Whitmore lifted his hands, his voice calling for the Lord's guidance, but the words rang hollow. He didn't believe in the war waging around him, didn't see the forces at work beneath his own roof. The demons barely paid him any mind. They knew dead faith when they heard it. Surfaced intentions couldn't replace sincerity. All it took to disarm him was a little pride, just a little sprinkled here and there within the cracks of his certainty. Pride dressed itself as confidence, as wisdom, but in the end, it only left him exposed—open to manipulation, blind to the battle already being lost around him. Worse still, his love for the flock was not whole. It was selective, measured, granted only to those he deemed worthy—those who upheld the image of the church he wished to present. The others? They were merely bodies in pews, tolerated but not truly tended to. And so, where love should have built a fortress, indifference had left an open gate. Surfaced intentions never reached deep enough to fight what lay beneath the surface.

Sleim turned his gaze toward the storekeeper, watching as he stepped forward. No nervous glances, no shifting on his feet like the other men who were uncertain of their own words. Mr. White was steady, his voice carrying through the church with practiced ease.

"The Lord calls us to be vigilant," he said, his tone calm but firm, sweeping his gaze over the congregation, letting his words settle in. "To be wise as serpents, yet harmless as doves. And wisdom means knowing when to act and when to wait."

The murmurs stirred. The shift in the air was immediate. They were listening.

Sleim grinned, his jagged teeth glinting in the candlelight only his kind could see. They should listen. They should doubt. They should turn on one another.

Mr. White continued, his voice measured, as if reluctant to speak but compelled by duty. "Now, I don't mean to stir fear where there should be faith, but I wonder if we've been too trusting. Evil does not always announce itself—it moves in quiet places, in the corners where no one looks."

Pastor Whitmore straightened slightly, clearing his throat. "Brother White, fear is the enemy's tool. We must be cautious not to let it divide us." Sleim choked with laughter. The fool shouldn't talk about division. He loved how blind these believers were to their own flaws.

Mr. White nodded slowly, his expression unreadable. "Of course, Pastor. And yet, caution is not fear. It is wisdom, is it not?"

Sleim felt the demons curl in anticipation, feeding off the tension. They moved closer to Stuckey, their prized tool in the game they played. Among the believers, he passed unnoticed, his disguise carefully fixed. It wasn't hard—most of them wore their faith like a well-pressed Sunday suit, something to be put on for appearances, but never lived in long enough to wrinkle.

A man let out a sharp breath, his hands clenched into fists at his sides. "So what are you saying, Mr. White? Should we be looking at each other instead of looking for this girl and her grandpa?"

"I'm saying we must be careful," Mr. White said smoothly, voice low and controlled. "We must not let our familiarity with each other blind us."

The pastor's jaw tensed, but he said nothing more. He had enough sense to know the tide had turned. The people wanted some answers, and the storekeeper gave them something to consider. The more they feared, the more they'd fracture. And fractured flocks were easy to devour.

Mr. White sat down, apparently satisfied that he spoke what he thought.

The demons feasted on the murmurs twisting through the crowd, doubt thickening the air like gathering storm clouds. But then, another sound rose—not a wavering voice of uncertainty, but something different. A prayer from the prayer warrior. It did not cower. It did not waver. It pressed through the heavy air like a candle flame refusing to be snuffed out.

The sight of it sent a ripple of displeasure through the demons. Prayers weren't meant to be whispered during doubt and suspicion. Prayers were supposed to be choked by fear, not strengthened by it.

A demon crept close, curling its blackened talons along the pew where the man sat. "We should break him," it murmured. "He's only a man."

Belias appeared at Sleim's side. "Call them off, Sleim. He is not alone."

Sleim turned and saw him. Raphael.

The warrior angel stood like a sentinel, his golden armor glinting, his massive wings tucked tight but ready. He did not move. Did not speak. But his presence alone was enough to keep the darkness from seeping into the man beneath his charge. Raphael bore the light of the Christ. Light that couldn't be overcome by shadow, no matter how thick it pressed in. It flickered, unwavering, a steady force against the tide of corruption that slithered through the church walls, unseen by mortal eyes. The demons raged against it, clawing at the edges, seeking a crack, a weakness—but there was none.

Raphael stood firm. His presence alone was a wall, a shield, a declaration that no matter how deep the darkness reached, the light would always push back. His eyes, like burning gold, met Sleim's without blinking.

Sleim bared his teeth, disgust curling through him. The fool had protection. That meant breaking him wouldn't be easy.

No matter.

They didn't need him.

They had Stuckey. He sat quietly among the believers, blending like he always did, unnoticed even by the men who knew his name.

And if Stuckey remained among them, doing their bidding, shaping the church's fears, bending their thoughts, it was only a matter of time before the church—the town—devoured itself.

———

Catherine sat stiffly on the bench outside the church, the night air cool against her skin. She barely noticed the voices inside anymore. It was all just noise now, pressing and meaningless. She had to get out of there.

A shadow shifted beside her, and she glanced up. Rosalind hesitated before lowering herself onto the bench, smoothing her skirts. "I'm sorry about Ellen, Catherine," she said, her voice quiet but not forced. "You two seemed close. I really hope they find her."

Catherine swallowed, her throat tight. "Thank you."

The words felt small, but Rosalind nodded as if she understood. The other girls nearby cast subtle glances her way, offering no words but letting their quiet presence speak instead. It was enough. It was more than she had expected.

Rosalind studied the church doors, then sighed. "My pa says they'll turn on each other before long."

Catherine exhaled slowly, watching the stars flicker above. "It certainly sounds like it."

For a moment, neither spoke. The silence was a rare kind—one without judgment, without expectation.

Then Rosalind rose, brushing her hands over her skirts. "I'd better go before Ma and Pa start looking for me."

Catherine nodded but she didn't move, her hands folded in her lap.

Rosalind hesitated just a moment longer before stepping away, her figure vanishing back into the light of the church doors.

A lone tear slipped down Catherine's cheek. The sorrow remained, but Rosalind's quiet kindness left something behind.

An ember of resolve.

A reason to hope.

Catherine had prayed before—at least, she thought she had. She had whispered desperate pleas in the darkness, had thrown words heavenward when fear clutched her ribs like a vice. But those prayers had always been reactions —not conversations. Not surrender.

This felt different.

The weight pressing against her chest wasn't just fear. It wasn't just exhaustion. It was the realization that she had been holding on too tightly—to her pain and loneliness, to her doubts, to her own ability to control what was never meant to be controlled.

She inhaled, closing her eyes. And for the first time in longer than she could remember, she prayed—not to demand, not to bargain, but to release.

"God, I don't know what comes next. I don't know how to stop being afraid, to stop hurting. But I know I can't do this alone. I don't want to hold onto this fear anymore. I don't want to keep You at arm's length just because I don't understand everything. I trust You—even when I don't know how. Help me trust You more."

She exhaled, the words settling between her ribs like something solid, something unshakable. Something shifted inside her, and the cold pressing against her heart eased. The fear was still there, but it didn't own her anymore. And for the first time, she wasn't fighting for clarity, or for a place to belong anymore.

She was choosing to trust the One who had already given her both.

WHAT THE RIVER BURIED

Reese

The house creaked, wind whispering through the eaves as Reese sifted through the box on the floor. She and James decided to do a full inventory search of everything in her uncle's house, hoping to find some answers to the questions about her dad. Her fingers skimmed across old envelopes, faded receipts, and yellowed newspaper clippings before landing on something different.

A book.

Leather-bound, cracked at the edges, the spine creased with time.

James crouched beside her as she pulled it out. "What is it?"

She turned it over in her hands, her pulse steady but deep. "I think it's a journal."

James leaned closer. "Your uncle's?"

Reese exhaled. "Looks like it."

She opened the cover, her uncle's handwriting slanting across the first page. It hadn't changed. The slight tilt, the way he pressed too hard on the downstrokes—it was all the same as the birthday cards he used to send, back when he still sent them. The last card she'd received from him came at her high school graduation. Then, nothing.

She read the entry aloud.

April 5, 1992

I bought the house today.

I stood on the back porch and looked out at the river, and for the first time in years, I could breathe.

Brenda might not understand why I want this place, but I do.

He and I were kids the last time we came here. Mama and Daddy rented a cabin on the water one summer, and it was the last time I remember us being happy. Before Knox changed. Before everything else started falling apart. Something happened to him here, but we didn't notice until it was too late.

Back then, the water didn't feel cursed. It felt like a place of safety. I want that back. I believe I can find it here at last.

Reese inhaled, her own breath catching on his words.

James sat beside her on the floor, flipping through the other papers in the box as he listened, but every few seconds, his eyes flicked to her, gauging her reaction.

She didn't know if she wanted to keep reading.

"This isn't just any memory. This is the last time his family felt normal." Her words echoed louder than they should have. She wasn't just reading about his family—she was reading about hers. A family she barely knew beyond the gaps and silences. She turned the page, the ink darker, the handwriting messier. She looked at the different date with a different entry, and it chilled her.

It's strange, the way memory works.

I stood on the bank today, feet in the same water I once swam in as a boy, and for a moment, I almost felt like that boy again. But the moment passed too quickly.

Because I remember the way that summer ended.

Knox was different when we went home. More than rebellious—angry. Cold. Mean in a way I had never seen before. Mama cried a lot. Daddy stopped talking to him unless he had to.

I told myself it was just growing pains. That people change. That it was just a phase.

I was a fool. Ignorant to what lie just beneath the surface. Holding on to what I thought I knew, instead of what showed up right in front of me.

I didn't know, back then, that sometimes change means something much worse.

Reese dropped the journal like it burned. The chill wasn't just from the drafty old house — it came from inside. From the words. From the realization that she might not want the answers after all. She didn't want to read anymore. What kind of man was her father, and why did her mother tell her he was dead?

James reached for the journal, flipping ahead. His jaw tightened. "It gets worse, I'm afraid." He handed the journal back to her. She didn't recognize the smudged ink that sprawled across the page now, as if his pen had written in desperate prose. As if his hand trembled.

June 2022

I was wrong.

Knox didn't change, but he's gotten worse.

He let something in.

Patricia thinks I'm crazy for even entertaining the thought, but I see it in her eyes—she believes it too.

She's been reading the books I bought years ago when I, too, wanted to understand. Studying. Trying to find explanations. I don't know if I can believe the things she's saying, but I know what I've seen.

I always thought a man couldn't just wake up one day and become evil. It usually takes time. But it seemed like Knox found a way to do it overnight.

I think it started that summer. After we left here.

I don't know what happened to him that year, but I know it wasn't natural.

And now Patricia thinks it's happening again. Since he's come back. Or maybe it never left him. Prison either makes or breaks redemption. Patricia wants to intervene before he hurts someone again.

Reese's hands clenched into fists. "Patricia was trying to stop him."

James frowned, flipping to the next page. "And I bet that's why she disappeared. The question is, what did he mean by again? Who else has he hurt?"

Reese read the next entry; this one had been written in frantic, uneven strokes.

She went to him.

I told her not to. Oh, Patricia, why didn't you heed my warning?

I told her she didn't know what she was messing with.

But Patricia cared too much and wanted to help.

And now she's gone. Just like my parents.

Reese gasped. Her father killed his parents? Her grandparents? Her stomach recoiled, and she put the journal down, covering her mouth. James put his hand on her shoulder, and she handed him the journal for him to continue reading.

The police don't have answers. They don't even care. A grown woman disappearing without a trace, and they just assumed she left of her own will. But I know better. Or maybe they just didn't want to look anymore. Her daughter knows something happened. Yet, she suspects me to be the monster.

But I know that's what he is.

I saw it in his eyes when I asked about her. He smiled, but his eyes were dead. He didn't even try to lie.

She's gone.

And I can't prove a thing. Truth is, I could be next. I should have never come back here. I thought he'd stay in prison. I had no idea they'd let him out after they found out what he'd done.

Reese's breath came fast now, her heartbeat pounding in her ears.

James set the journal down between them. "Your uncle knew he killed Patricia." His voice was low, steady. "And he was terrified."

She swallowed. "But why didn't he say anything? Why didn't he—"

"He probably didn't think he could." James picked up the book again, flipping ahead, and when he found another entry, his expression darkened.

I was careful.

I was so careful.

But he knows.

Somehow, he knows about Reese, my beautiful niece.

I never should have let him be near me. I never should have answered the phone when he called. But he wore me down, like he always does. Told me he had changed. That he wanted to fix things between us.

I wanted to believe him because I missed my brother.

I should have known better.

Now he hurt my love, Patricia.

And now he knows about Reese.

I don't know how much time I have. But if something happens to me, someone must protect her. Dear God, please protect her. I promised Brenda I'd never let him near her.

Someone must keep her safe.

I've made up my mind. I'll sell the house. Move somewhere quieter. Somewhere farther away. I should've done it sooner. Brenda would've told me to. But something keeps me here—maybe fear, maybe foolish hope. No more. I'll contact a realtor tomorrow. Before something happens to me. I should have changed the will long ago, should have known better to risk it. I just wanted to leave her this place I love. But now I must leave it for good.

Reese's pulse stilled.

James finished the entry, reading in low tones.

I have no choice. I see him in my dreams, watching me through the trees.

I see him standing on the bridge, waiting.

He wants me to be afraid, but I'm not afraid for myself.

I fear for her.

If anyone finds this, if anyone is reading these words, please— Keep her away from him.

Silence stretched between them. A thick, suffocating silence.

Reese's throat felt tight. "So, it's true. My father's alive and my mother lied to me."

James exhaled. "It looks that way. But to keep you safe. And your uncle died trying to keep you safe. You were loved, Reese."

The wind howled outside, rattling the windows. The river, deep and dark beyond the house, seemed to churn harder, a restless force that had seen it all, hidden it all, buried it all.

And now, it was giving up its secrets.

Reese traced her fingers over the worn leather cover, its surface cool beneath her touch. The journal sat heavy in her lap, as if the weight of its contents pressed down on her.

The truth had been here, waiting, all along.

James shifted beside her. "Reese?"

She swallowed, forcing the lump in her throat down. "I— I need a minute."

She didn't look up, couldn't tear her gaze from the journal in her hands.

The room suddenly felt too small, too suffocating.

Her father was not who she thought he was. And this book had just rewritten everything.

———

A wind swept through the trees, rustling the leaves in a way that wasn't natural. It wasn't the sound of a summer breeze or the shifting of storm clouds. It was something else entirely—something unseen but deeply felt. The air hummed with a presence, the fabric of the unseen world tightening like a bowstring.

A figure stood at the edge of the river, watching the house with protective eyes. His form flickered, the light within him a radiance not meant for mortal eyes. Beside him, Uriel, Tyrius, and Lior appeared like reflections of the stars themselves, their faces solemn as they gazed upon the home where Reese sifted through the past.

"It's begun," Uriel murmured, his voice a quiet storm.

"The veil between past and present is thinner here," Tyrius answered. "She stands at the crossroads of what was and what is, but the enemy will not let her pass without a fight."

Lior, ever silent, placed a hand over the hilt of a sword bound in celestial fire. "They have worked long to twist the truth, to bury it beneath years of deception. The lies are unraveling, but what will she do with the truth when it finds her?"

Raphael, the one standing closest to the water's edge, watched Reese through the unseen plane. "That is what the enemy fears. That she will see beyond what they've told her, beyond the wounds they have inflicted. That she will understand who she is meant to be."

Tyrius stepped forward, his wings shifting with an unseen breeze. "She has been marked for destruction since before she took her first breath. They succeeded with her father. They will not risk failing with her."

"They have already lost," Raphael said. "But they will not stop clawing at the illusion of victory. And that is why we are here."

Across the river, just beyond the glow of the angels' presence, the shadows pulsed with something darker, more insidious. Sulfur and rot filled the air as unseen figures coiled at the tree line, their glowing eyes locked on the house.

"She is unraveling," Sleim hissed, its voice a caustic whisper.

Their commander Sonnellion loomed behind them, seething. "Doubt is not enough. It must consume her. If she sees too much—if she finds what was hidden—our hold weakens."

"The hold will not weaken." The words slithered through the night, cold and sharp, dripping with ancient malice. Belias stepped forward, his voice like iron grinding against bone. "We have worked too long, too deep. She will not escape what we have built in this place."

Ravoth, his form slinking in the shadows, snarled, his claws digging into the earth. "We have stripped her of trust. We have fed her isolation. All she needs is one final push to send her over the edge with him. The generational curse is strong, and it's time to push."

The demons crouched in the darkness, watching, waiting.

Inside the house, Reese turned another page, tensing as she stared at the empty page—but unaware of what filled the air just beyond the bridge.

And the war demons prepared for battle.

Of Mud and Mystery

Catherine

Catherine pulled her shawl tighter against the autumn chill, the Mississippi dampness settling into her skin as she stepped off the wooden planks onto the muddy road. The sun had barely begun its descent, and already the sky deepened into rich purples and blues, streaked with gold. A few lanterns flickered along the street, their glow feeble against the stretching shadows.

Beside her, Zeke walked with an easy stride, his boots scuffing against the damp earth. But there was something different about him tonight, a tension in the set of his shoulders, a quiet watchfulness in the way his eyes flickered to every shadow. He had been like this since Ellen and her grandfather vanished—more guarded, more deliberate.

"We'll check the bridge first," he said. "If they were out that way, maybe we missed something in the dark."

Catherine hesitated. Her father wouldn't like her going there, not with everything happening. She was about to speak when movement from across the street caught her eye. Mr. White stood outside his shop, speaking in low tones to Mr. Blythe. Their conversation seemed calm enough—until she noticed the way Mr. White's fingers tapped against his arm. A quick, twitchy movement, like a man holding back something he wasn't ready to say. Or something he wasn't ready to do.

Mr. Blythe, on the other hand, nodded slowly, rubbing his jaw. Then his gaze flickered up and met hers.

Catherine stiffened, startled by the intensity of his eyes. There was something watchful about him, something restrained, but she couldn't tell if it was caution or something darker.

"Something's going on there," Zeke muttered beside her, following her gaze.

"You don't think..." She hesitated, lowering her voice.

"I think a lot of things," Zeke murmured. "But none of 'em I'd say out loud yet."

Mr. Blythe nodded at Mr. White before crossing the street, disappearing into the livery. The storekeeper hesitated a second longer before stepping back into his store, shutting the door behind him.

Catherine exhaled, suddenly uneasy. Her gut told her something hovered, like an evil that waited for its moment to pounce.

Zeke patted her shoulder lightly, his touch warm despite the cold creeping into her bones. "Come on, let's check the bridge before it gets too dark."

"I don't think my pa wants me out there, Zeke."

His eyes softened, the moonlight catching the blue in them. "I won't let anything happen to you. Besides, your pa trusts me to protect you." He reached out, tucking her chin with his knuckles, the touch light but steady.

"Can you trust me, Cat?"

She wanted to, but something about the way he asked made her wonder—was he just reassuring her, or did he have a motive for asking?

"C'mon. You can ride behind me on my horse, Gunner."

Minutes later, they rode down the path leading to the bridge, the sounds of town fading behind them. The wooden beams loomed ahead, half-shrouded in creeping mist that swirled in ribbons around them. The bridge stretched across the water like a relic of something long forgotten, and Catherine felt like her time at the bridge with Ellen drifted away with the waters below.

Zeke stepped ahead, his boots thudding against the wood. "There must be a clue somewhere. People don't just up and disappear."

Catherine didn't respond, her throat tightening. The dampness clung to the air, thick with the scent of river mud and something colder beneath it.

She stepped carefully, her gaze sweeping the bridge. Then she saw it.

A glint of something caught between the planks.

Her pulse quickened as she knelt, her fingers reaching through the narrow gap. She pulled it free, her breath catching in her throat.

The locket. But only half of it. The part with the picture of Ellen's mother broke off, just like the chain. Where was the other half?

Her stomach twisted violently as she brushed away the clinging wet dirt.

"Please, no," she whispered, her grip tightening, tears flowing with the realization of what this find indicated. A lost chain is one thing, but both the chain and the locket are broken.

Zeke crouched beside her, his face darkening as he saw what she held.

"She never took it off," Catherine choked out. "She told me that herself."

Zeke's breath shuddered as he ran a finger over the locket piece in her palm, his hand shaking. "Someone yanked it off her."

Catherine trembled as his hand hovered over hers, but then he dropped his next to his side. She turned the piece over in her palm, observing the dampness along the edge, but something still clung to the surface. Holding it in the light, she gasped.

A red smear. Just like the one on Mr. Hollis' hat.

Zeke cursed under his breath, then with wide eyes, shook his head. "I'm sorry, Catherine. I shouldn't have said that. But Lord help me, whoever did this has a reckoning coming."

Catherine swallowed hard, fighting back the surge of panic rising in her chest. She forced herself to breathe, to stay steady.

Then something rustled beyond the bridge.

Zeke stilled, his body shifting just slightly in front of her, shielding her with the movement. "Stay close," he murmured, his voice a thread lower than before.

Catherine's fingers curled around the locket, her pulse hammering. It wasn't the sound of an animal. Something heavy and deliberate moved just beyond the woods. The air shifted, colder somehow, thick with something unseen but pressing.

Zeke's hand brushed against his belt, where a knife was tucked, and the sight of his fingers tensing around the handle sent uneasiness through her. She hadn't seen that knife before.

And for some reason, that unsettled her more than it should have. How well did she really know Zeke? She trusted him. She did. But trust didn't mean certainty. And tonight, certainty felt like something slipping through her fingers—just like Ellen had.

A low creak sounded from beneath the bridge, as if something—or someone—lurked in the darkness below.

Catherine fought the instinct to run, forcing herself to remember the feel of the earth beneath her boots, the weight of her own breath. She wasn't weak. But she wasn't sure if she could leave Zeke's side. Or if she should leave his side.

Zeke's whole body tensed, and he turned his head slightly, his voice barely above a whisper. "When I say, we move. Fast."

She nodded once, gripping the locket so tightly the edge bit into her palm.

The wind shifted, stirring the mist that hovered just above the water. For a moment, it was quiet. Almost peaceful. And then—

Something moved. A dark blur, fast and low beneath the bridge.

Zeke grabbed her wrist, yanking her back just as something rushed past them, too fast to be seen, but strong enough to be felt. A rush of air, the heavy scent of decay, and the distinct sense that they weren't alone.

The silence that followed was unnatural. Listening. Watching.

Zeke pulled her close, his breath steady, but she could feel the tension surging through him. His expression was unreadable—tight, something deeper flashing in his eyes before he blinked it away. His body tensed, shook even, but he pushed her toward the horse, his tone almost angry.

"We're leaving," he said, no longer asking for her trust, but demanding it.

Catherine swallowed hard but nodded. She wouldn't argue with him this time. Whatever they just encountered still waited for any sign of vulnerability.

They moved quickly, climbing onto Gunner's saddle and headed back toward town. The further they got, the more the air shifted as if the shadow decided to let them go.

She didn't even know if it was a thing.

She stared at the locket piece in her hand. What happened to the other half? Had it fallen into the river below, lost forever beneath the current? Or was it buried somewhere, waiting to be unearthed—just like the truth?

Would Ellen and her grandfather ever resurface? So many unknowns still lay buried, like the unmarked graves of those still missing.

But someone knew.

Someone knew what happened to them. Someone knew what happened to the locket.

And maybe... they still had the missing piece.

———

Matt stood on the steps of the post office, arms crossed. "Maybe this has nothing to do with the other missing people. Maybe they got tired of the camp and left without saying anything."

Catherine turned to him, frowning. "Then why would they leave their tent with all their things?"

Matt shrugged. "I don't know, Catherine. Did you really know them all that well? Besides, if something did happen to them, I don't think we should get mixed up in it. It's not really our problem. I mean, don't get me wrong, I understand you're concerned, but you shouldn't be, not at the expense of your safety."

Catherine felt something cold settle in her stomach. Not because of what Matt had said, but because of how easily he said it—like it was just another inconvenience, not a real concern.

"Not our problem?" she repeated, incredulous. "Matt, we don't just forget people. What if something bad happened to them?"

Matt let out a long sigh, rubbing the back of his neck. "What do you want me to do? Go look for them in the woods? If something bad is out there, how can we really help? We don't even know where to start."

"We start by caring," a voice cut in.

Catherine turned. Zeke approached, as a look of disdain crossed his features.

Unlike Matt, he had been vigilant in the search efforts. "We know they didn't just leave the camp. Something happened. It's obvious if you survey the site."

Matt let out a short, humorless laugh. "Alright, detective. What do you suggest?"

Zeke rose to his feet, leveling Matt with a steady gaze. "That we do something."

Matt held his hands up in mock surrender. "Look. I just don't think it's a good idea for her to go searching for answers. If you want to endanger yourself, fine. Just leave Catherine out of it."

"He can't leave me out if he wanted to. I'm already in it, Matt. Ellen's my friend, and I don't abandon my friends." She gave him a pointed look. It hit its mark.

"Suit yourself, Catherine."

Catherine's stomach churned as he walked away without another word. She had expected Matt to take charge, to care—but he hadn't. He had dismissed it, like it wasn't worth his time. Like Ellen and her grandpa's welfare didn't matter.

Zeke, on the other hand...

She looked at him, really looked at him. The set of his shoulders, the way his hands curled into fists like he was already planning his next move to find her friends.

He was already looking for Ellen, but Matt walked away.

Zeke stepped forward. Zeke cared.

Catherine swallowed hard. That difference meant everything, and she didn't know how she'd missed it before.

She had missed so much before.

A Road of Reckoning

Reese

Reese sat stiffly on the second-to-last pew, the familiar discomfort already setting in. The hymns, the announcements, even the rustle of bulletins—all of it felt like a life she had once known but no longer belonged to. Why did she let them talk her into coming back?

Addie sat beside her, singing in full, off-key southern gusto, while James sat on Reese's other side, quiet, but present. Reese noticed his hand resting on the back of the pew behind her shoulder, close—but not touching.

When the music faded, and people began settling in, Reese spotted two familiar faces a few rows ahead—Sharon and Tiffany. Sharon's gaze caught hers briefly, giving a soft acknowledgement with a nod and an uncomfortable smile.

The pastor's voice rose gently from the pulpit, preaching about the story of the prodigal son. It wasn't the usual spin—he didn't focus on the son's return, but on the father watching the road, waiting. Always waiting. The father's love wasn't hesitant. It wasn't suspicious. It wasn't indifferent. It was ready.

Reese shifted in her seat, arms crossed, but her throat burned. What if God was like that? Watching the road for her—not with crossed arms, but with open ones. Not demanding explanations, just wanting her home.

Yet even if she could believe that, how was she supposed to trust the people sitting in the pews, when those who sat with her before left her on the seat alone? The ones who had looked away when it mattered most?

I'm not asking you to trust them first.

The thought pressed gently, as if whispered. She closed her eyes.

Just trust Me—and I'll show you how to love them again. Because all the love you need is mine, and I've shown you my love, daughter. You just need to open your eyes.

The words slipped under her defenses like water through a crack. It didn't remove the ache, but it softened it.

Maybe Addie wasn't just stubborn. Maybe James wasn't just patient. Maybe even Sharon, broken as she was, was here for a reason.

Reese stared down at the worn Bible in her lap, and she clutched it, inviting the warm leather to remind her what she'd missed.

After the service, Sharon and Tiffany approached her on their way out. Tiffany lifted her shoulder in a shrug of explanation. "Mom wanted us to come to church, but we didn't want to go to Nana's old church, so we came here instead."

Sharon, draping an arm across Tiffany's shoulders, looked at Reese directly. "We had no idea this is where you attended. Small world in these parts. Mom loved the Lord, even when life didn't make sense. She wasn't perfect, but she knew where to turn, and she always wanted us to turn to him, too." She glanced around the sanctuary. "It feels strange, but right to be back in a church."

Addie jumped in, with all the tact of a bulldog in a China shop. "We've all got things that keep us away sometimes, honey. Pride. Fear. Anger. But you find your way back when you're ready. Ain't no shame in takin' the long way around."

Sharon nodded. "I guess that's true." She looked at James and Reese. "Any new information on my Mom?"

Reese slid her eyes to James, unsure what to say. "Not yet. We're still checking some things out."

"You'll be the first to know," James said.

Sharon's sad smile mirrored Tiffany's. "Well, I guess if one needs to hope, this is where to find it." She glanced around the sanctuary.

"You've got that right, honey," Addie said. "No better place to look."

James' gaze flicked to Reese, and though he said nothing, the understanding in his eyes said plenty. Her throat tightened. Maybe it was the way Sharon smiled at her as Tiffany clung to her side, or Addie's relentless honesty, or maybe it was James' steady silence—but for the first time in a long while, she didn't feel like she was standing outside the circle.

———

Despite the turmoil she'd experienced the past week, Reese felt peaceful as her cheek pressed into her pillow that night. Just as she drifted off to sleep, footsteps creaked down the hallway, snapping Reese awake. Sitting up to listen, with fright sending her heart into overdrive, she reached for her robe next to her bed, slipping it around her shoulders as she edged over to drop her legs to the floor. Holding her breath and willing her heart to stop beating so hard it shook her, she turned the knob to her bedroom door like it might explode any minute.

Peering out of her door into the darkness of the hall, she gasped as a dark figure stood looking at the clock on the wall. He turned, so she ducked back, praying she wouldn't cause any sound that might alert him to her presence. She locked the door and pressed her back to it, whispering frantic prayers as her heartbeat rattled in her chest.

The creaking of his steps moved closer to her door, then stopped. Tightening her hands around her mouth, she watched the doorknob and backed up as whoever stood on the other side turned it without success.

Reese looked at the window in her bedroom, contemplating how far she could drop without hurting herself. While the house only had one floor, it had been built up on stilts to prevent any flooding from the river, and this side didn't have a deck, so crawling out the window might not end any better for her than encountering whoever stood outside her door.

Was this Stuckey? No, that was a real person. It was him.

Her phone! She had her phone! But if she tried calling 911, he'd hear her.

The footsteps moved away from her door, but she could hear him opening and closing drawers in the room where Uncle Art's rolltop desk held so many answers and questions alike. Was he looking for the journal? The one that implicated him in his brother's death and Patricia's disappearance.

She tiptoed to her nightstand and picked up her phone, turning the volume down before texting James, who surely slept with his phone on. Maybe as a police officer, he was a light sleeper. She knew she was grasping at straws, but she had to try.

Someone is in my house. If you're awake, could you please come? And bring your gun! James, please be awake.

She waited, but no reply appeared on her screen, so she placed it in her robe pocket and focused on an escape plan.

Outside, the crickets chirped as if they knew danger approached and wanted to warn her. She could hear him rummaging through something, and she hoped he only cared about whatever he wanted to find, and that she didn't factor into his reasons for entering the house that night.

She moved with the grace of a ballet dancer as she picked up a chair that belonged to a lift desk in her room and placed it underneath the window, but after stepping onto it and staring down below, she discarded her idea that she might risk jumping to the ground and rolling. She'd likely break her neck and not her fall.

Images of TV characters tying sheets together flashed through her mind—but reality wasn't so forgiving. Even if she had time, the rickety iron headboard she'd bought online wouldn't hold. No sturdy bedposts, just a rounded frame and thin bars. Trusting it meant trusting she wouldn't drop to her death.

The slamming of a drawer urged her to move in panic. If he decided to look for whatever he wanted in her room, he wouldn't have to work too hard to break that doorknob. Stepping down from the chair, she looked around for a weapon. Her closet only held plastic hangers. Why couldn't she be like her mother, who refused to use anything but old wire hangers? She could do some damage with one of those things.

She scanned her dresser and makeup vanity for anything worth wielding against her intruder, but all she could see were her picture frames, some makeup, perfume bottles, and a few hair scrunchies. Why didn't she unpack those large candlesticks, which still lay buried in one of the few boxes still piled in her living room?

The steps moved closer to her door again, and the doorknob turned. Reese moved toward the closet, grabbing a perfume bottle and a picture frame before stepping into the narrow space where her clothes hung from their useless plastic hangers, and she edged her way to the back before sliding the door shut without clicking it into place.

She didn't know why, but it made her feel better to have something in her hands, and it did the same when she shut the door to the closet, although it would be the first place he looked. Maybe he'd think she didn't sleep there that night? Had he been watching the house? She knew the answer as soon as she thought of the question. Of course, he knew she was in that room.

The knob moved back and forth in an angry motion, and a heavy force pushed against the door. She dropped the picture frame from her hand but didn't bother to retrieve it because she heard the door break open and his footsteps approach the closet. Reese watched as the door slid open, and light filled the small space from his flashlight, covering her eyes as he turned it in her direction.

"Hello, Reese. It's nice to finally meet you. Come on out, and let's get acquainted."

He reached in and yanked her out by her wrist, but she held the perfume bottle in her other hand, so she sprayed the mist into his eyes, pressing the nozzle several times as he yelped and dropped the flashlight. Pushing him down, she ran into the living room and darted for the sliding glass doors on the deck, closing them behind her, and hoping he'd think she ran out the front door instead. Her bare feet skipped down the stairs, almost slipping beneath her, but she managed to reach the solid ground at the bottom.

Hearing the doors slide open above her, she broke into a run, not even recognizing where she ran, but knowing she couldn't stop until she found a safe place to hide.

Her pursuer gained ground behind her, and she panicked when she realized where she was headed. The bridge loomed ahead, with its ominous silhouette and haunted history that seemed to cry out from its beams. She stepped onto the bridge with a careful step, hearing the water rush beneath her after the hard rain provided a generous downpour that filled its depths.

Where could she go? Nothing but blackness awaited her on the other side, and the worst sort of darkness pursued her from behind. Why didn't she run toward James and Addie? Too late to change her direction, she pressed forward on the fragile boards, feeling the planks shift beneath her toes.

The wind howled through the trees, whipping around Reese as she stumbled forward. The bridge loomed ahead, its wooden beams stretching into darkness. Her pulse hammered against her ribs. She wasn't sure if the rushing sound in her ears was the river below or her own blood pounding.

Behind her, footsteps crunched over brittle leaves. Slow. Measured.

"You can't outrun this," the voice called, low and taunting. "You think running changes what is?"

The words crawled under her skin. They weren't just words, and it wasn't just the chase. It wasn't just fear.

It was history circling back. Addie had been right—evil did leave its mark.

The bridge groaned under her weight as she reached the center, her hands gripping the worn railing. A gust of wind sent a rope swinging below, its frayed end twisting in the dark. She squeezed her eyes shut, shaking her head. Not now. Don't think about that now.

The footsteps stopped. Silence stretched between them like a blade.

Her stomach twisted, like a noose tightening deep in her gut, cinching tighter with every breath.

Like a past that refused to stay buried.

Reese turned, forcing herself to meet the darkness head-on. "I'm not afraid of you."

But her shaking hands betrayed her.

And somewhere nearby the shadows—those terrible, shifting shadows—knew the truth.

"There's nowhere to go, Reese. Your mother poisoned you against me, didn't she? Your mother, bless her, always thought she could outsmart me. She thought she could hide you from me forever. My brother helped her hide you from me, too. He tried to pretend he didn't, but I knew he helped her escape with you. I looked everywhere for her when I got out. Art tried to hide, too, but I found him. He shouldn't have come back here. Sentimental fool."

"You're my father." She didn't pose it as a question, but as something she'd known—deep down—since Addie mentioned the nickname. Yet hearing it confirmed tore through her like splintered wood.

His eyes darkened, and she moved backward, watching the backs of her heels as she stepped, but being careful not to lose sight of his position as he edged toward her.

"What did she tell you about me, Reese?"

"Not much. She told me you died."

"I'm sure she wished I had, but as you can see, I'm very much alive. How did she say I died?"

"She said you ran off and left us, and that she'd learned from Uncle Art that you'd died in an accident."

"Well, at least I can count on your mother to almost tell the truth, since that's how your uncle has seen me for years now. Dead to him. Except here I am, and he's not. Neither is your mother. I guess we know what happens to liars."

"My mother was the most honest person I knew."

He stepped closer and she backed up, wondering if the wind around the bridge would carry a scream away with the water or if it could jerk James and Addie awake in their house down the bank.

"Brenda lied when it suited her when it meant she could protect herself. Or *our* daughter."

He lunged forward and she reacted, stumbling on the bridge and tumbling to the side, screaming as she felt her foot slip through one of the planks, trapping her as she held on. Pain shot through her ankle as her father stared at her.

A figure emerged behind him. A face, evil and menacing, reveling in her fear, feeding off it.

Stuckey.

Judgement is Coming

Catherine

A ripple of hushed murmurs passed through the crowd gathered outside the sheriff's office. Lanterns swung from posts, their flickering light throwing long, twisting shadows over faces pinched with

worry. No one spoke above a whisper, but suspicion thickened the air like a coming storm, pressing down on their shoulders, turning neighbors into suspects.

Catherine stood among them, her hands clenched into fists at her sides as she listened to the growing unease.

"They still haven't found them."

"Two people gone without a trace, just like the others. Who's to say it won't be one of us next?"

"It's someone here. It has to be."

The words spread like fire licking dry leaves.

"Mr. Blythe is always out late. Never says where he's been."

"What about the Sanderson fella? Didn't he just move to the river? No one knows much about him."

"And Zeke Tolliver—we don't know much about him, either, do we?"

Catherine's head snapped toward the voice. Mary Tuttle stood near the back of the group, arms folded tight, her lips pursed. Mary had set her cap for Zeke, and her words were laced with the sting of rejection.

"That's ridiculous," Catherine said before she could stop herself.

Mary's gaze settled on her, calculating. "Is it? Everyone's so certain that the guilty man is lurking somewhere in the dark, but sometimes evil walks in the daylight. In plain sight. Smiling, shaking hands." She lifted her chin. "Besides, someone saw Zeke buy another shovel days ago."

"So?" She asked like that didn't matter, but even her pa had wondered about it, and now she must admit she wondered, too.

"So—why did he need another shovel when he already had one?"

"Maybe because he's a farmer, and farmers often have many tools."

Someone else spoke—it was Zeke's voice, calm but cutting. Heads turned. "I am a farmer, and I do have many tools. But I bought another shovel because mine disappeared from my barn."

Mary's cheeks reddened at being caught talking about her crush.

Catherine scoffed. "And just so you know, Matt Sanderson has an alibi for the night Ellen and her grandfather disappeared."

Mary narrowed her eyes. "How do you know that?"

"Because he stayed at the boarding house that night. His place has a wasp problem, and he had to smoke it. Mrs. Webb can vouch for him."

"People must sleep sometime. How do we know he stayed there all night?"

The weight of the crowd's eyes turned to Catherine. She stepped back, and fought to keep her breath steady, but inside, unease twisted through her. The truth is, she didn't know. She also didn't know Zeke well enough to be so defensive of him, either.

"Well," Mary said. "Do you trust him?"

"Yes," she said. "I do." She didn't know if Mary asked about Matt or Zeke.

The sheriff stepped forward, his expression weary. "I understand everyone's afraid, but wild accusations won't solve this. Whoever's responsible for Thatcher Hollis and his granddaughter, we'll find them. We'll get to the bottom of it."

Someone in the crowd huffed. "That's what you said about the others."

Silence stretched thin.

Catherine glanced around, her stomach twisting. Eyes everywhere glared, narrowed, as they assessed one another. They weren't just looking for justice anymore. They were looking for someone to blame.

And she wasn't sure how long it would be before someone turned on the wrong person.

———

The celestial warriors stood at the edges of the riverbank, their presence unseen by human eyes but felt in the tremors of the air. The night pressed down, thick with something unspoken, something festering beneath the surface of this town, woven into its streets, its homes, its church.

Raphael stood like a fortress, his golden armor catching light not of this world, his presence unmoving beside the man he was bound to guard. The prayers surrounding him were tired, but persistent, a flickering flame against the encroaching tide of darkness. Uriel stood to his right, ever watchful, ever ready, his countenance shadowed with unspoken grief.

"This town is breaking," Uriel murmured, his voice barely more than a sigh in the wind. "The fear feeds them. It gives the darkness its roots."

Beside them, Tyrius clenched his fists, his massive frame tense with restrained energy. "This place is drowning in rot—the air reeks with it. These people are devouring each other with doubt and suspicion. Even their prayers carry the weight of their fear." He exhaled sharply, his wings shifting with agitation. "It is working against us."

"It is working because the heart of this town is already poisoned," Lior added, his silver eyes narrowing as he gazed toward the church in the distance. "They gather there tonight to pray again, but even in their unity, they are divided. They suspect each other. They turn their eyes to men instead of the One who can protect them."

Uriel's gaze flickered to where the demons slithered unseen through the streets, feeding on the cracks forming in the foundation of the town's faith. "They have been waiting for this," he said darkly. "They are not the ones breaking the people. They are merely guiding them to do it themselves."

Raphael turned, his eyes steady, unmoved. "We are not sent to stop them from falling into their own blindness. But we are here to fight for the ones who can still see."

Tyrius's wings twitched. "And what of the one who does not resist?" His voice was a low growl, barely containing his fury. His gaze shifted toward the man wrapped in darkness, his soul bleeding its poison. The man who had been lost long before the killings began. "He makes no effort to fight them. There is nothing left of him to resist."

"He hasn't resisted for some time," Uriel admitted. "He's embraced the hunger inside him. What remains of his humanity is only a hollow mask."

Lior's wings curled slightly, his voice heavy with understanding. "His master has fully claimed him. The deception is complete. And yet, the Father still waits, still offers grace."

"Not for much longer," Raphael said, his gaze sharpening. "Judgment is coming."

Uriel watched as the demons slithered closer, emboldened by the wickedness fermenting in their chosen vessel. "He has fed them well. But they do not yet see that their own pride will be their downfall."

"The Almighty will not allow us to intervene directly yet," Raphael reminded them, his voice steady but edged with something unspoken.

Tyrius clenched his jaw. "Then when?"

"When it is time," Raphael said simply. "When he takes the final step. When his fate is sealed."

The angels stood in silence, their presence like pillars of light against the deepening dark. And as the night stretched over Meridian, they waited.

For soon, the devil's work would be complete.

And judgment would descend.

———

The blade slid through flesh with ease, parting skin like the rippling of a river. Stuckey exhaled slowly, steadying the trembling in his hands, though it wasn't from effort.

It was anticipation.

The man beneath him gurgled, hands clawing weakly at the wound gaping at his throat. His eyes were still wide, still registering confusion, like he hadn't quite processed what had happened yet. Time wouldn't give him the chance.

Stuckey leaned in close, whispering against the man's ear as the light faded. "You were nothing, friend. No one will miss you."

The body shuddered once more before going still.

Stuckey let out a slow breath, wiping his blade against the man's coat before standing. The night around him hummed with the sound of cicadas, of the river chattering in the distance. The world didn't pause for death—it carried on as if it had never happened.

He rolled his shoulders, waiting for the usual rush to hit him. The pulse of satisfaction, the sense of power.

But it wasn't there. It wasn't like the others.

He glanced down at the man again, the stillness, the silence.

No challenge. No thrill.

Just another body.

His jaw clenched. Killing was a need, a hunger—but it wasn't supposed to be empty. It wasn't supposed to feel like this.

The last one had been better. The fear in their eyes. The struggle. That moment when they recognized him.

That was what he wanted.

Not nameless drifters. No more nobodies.

The thought burned through him, hot and consuming. He had been careful for too long. Playing his part. Keeping his mask in place. Stealing animals. Slaughtering strangers.

He stepped back from the body, dragging it toward the river's edge where he'd bury the corpse deep in the earth, packing down the mud and washing the topsoil with the water from the shallow bank. Everyone expected mud along the riverbank.

He had chosen his victim well this time. No ties, no connections. No one to come looking.

Disgust coiled in his gut. Churning, raw disgust.

Coward.

He refused to play this game anymore. He hated hiding more than he feared the noose.

It was time to test destiny's patience.

A slow, wide grin crept across his face as he thought of his next victim.

Oh, yes. This one would be missed.

This one wouldn't just be a kill. This one would be the kill.

And it just might set him free.

A Confrontation to Cross

Reese

Reese's breath came in sharp, panicked gasps as she clutched her injured ankle, staring up at the man who had the power to end her. The man who had a part in her existence. For a moment, just a moment, the malice in his eyes wavered, something breaking through the inky void—recognition.

His lips parted, his brow furrowed, and in that instant, he wasn't the monster who had chased her onto this cursed bridge. He was her father.

His gaze flickered down to her ankle, and a flash of concern crossed his features. His hands, which had clenched in anger or trembling with something far darker only moments before, flexed at his sides as if he was debating reaching for her, helping her.

Reese saw it—saw him.

A father torn between what he had become and what he should be, maybe wanted to be.

"Dad..." Her voice cracked, raw with pain and something more fragile—hope.

He took half a step forward, struggling with an unmet decision. The wind howled through the trees, whispering around them. For a heartbeat, Reese thought he would drop to his knees, take her hands in his, and pull her to safety. He would help her. He would—

A dark cloud slithered through the air, creeping like smoke from the trees, curling around his legs, his arms, his throat. His entire body went rigid. A shadow deepened behind him, stretching impossibly long against the wooden planks. A figure—Stuckey—emerged from the darkness, a sick grin twisting his already inhuman face.

―

The bridge trembled under the unseen force, an ominous energy crackling through the air. Shadows twisted, writhing like living things as grotesque figures emerged—demons, hunched and snarling, their clawed hands stretching toward Reese's father. Their guttural growls resonated through both realms, their forms barely clinging to existence in the mortal plane.

A golden light cut through the darkness, and a warrior strode forward, armored in celestial fire, his face hard with unshaken resolve.

Raphael's blue-tinged sword burned as he lifted it, its blade pulsing with divine energy. Behind him, Uriel and Tyrius moved into place, their own weapons shimmering, forming a barrier between the demons and Reese. Lior stood slightly apart, his piercing gaze locked onto the enemy, his spear crackling with divine fire.

Across from them, the darkness shifted, forming something more monstrous. Sonnellion stepped forward first, his presence twisting the air around him. Beside him, Belias sneered, his claws flexing as he prowled forward. Ravoth's hulking form loomed behind them, his eyes burning like embers, and at their side, Sleim hissed through jagged teeth, his elongated fingers twitching with anticipation.

The demons hissed, their distorted forms slithering across the bridge's beams like oil spreading through water. Stuckey's spirit, looming behind Reese's father, turned slowly, his form flickering in and out of sight.

"She is not yours," Raphael declared. "Her heavenly father protects her where her earthly father cannot."

A demon lunged, shrieking, its talons slicing through the misty air. Raphael swung his sword in a clean arc, the blade severing the creature in half. A wail split the night as the demon's form disintegrated into nothingness.

***

"No." Her father's voice was strangled, strained. His fingers dug into his palms. "We can't. I don't want this. Leave her alone. This has nothing to do with her."

Reese barely registered her father's words. His tone was firm, but pleading—and directed at someone else. He wasn't speaking to her.

Stuckey's image loomed before him, flickering like a mirage over the warped planks of the bridge. But the spirit didn't taunt Reese. It taunted him.

Her father's body tensed. "Not now. Not again," he muttered, his voice lower. Desperate. "I never wanted to hurt them. I don't want to hurt you."

For just a heartbeat, she saw him—not the monster, but the possibility of a father. The man he might have been. The man she'd only imagined as a child. But the moment shattered as the shadow wrapped tighter, swallowing what little humanity was left.

Then, he staggered. His head lolled back, his chest heaving. A battle waged where she couldn't see—inside his mind, his soul. He jerked forward, his fists clenched at his sides.

"I told you—not now!"

Reese recoiled as Stuckey's spirit seemed to meld into her father, wrapping around him like a living shadow. His face twisted, his features contorting into something wild, grotesque. A scream rose in her throat, but she swallowed it back.

Her father shuddered. Then the struggle stopped.

And the man who faced her now wasn't her father. It was a demon.

Reese did the only thing she knew to do. She prayed.

———

Raphael drove his blade into another demon, its agonized screech piercing the veil between realms. Shadows twisted violently as they recoiled from the light. Uriel clashed with Sleim, their weapons sparking in the unseen realm as divine steel met corrupted claws. Tyrius struck at Ravoth, forcing the beast-like demon backward. Lior's spear shot through the air, impaling one of the lesser demons before it could slip past their ranks.

Sonnellion turned to Belias, his lips curling into a smirk. "You think they'll last this time?"

Belias' claws flexed, his eyes glowing. "No. Our power is stronger."

Tyrius' silver armor gleamed beneath the darkened sky as he stepped onto the battlefield, his flaming crown casting eerie shadows over his face. "Not this time. This time, we have the prayer cover."

"Finish it," Raphael commanded, his voice calm but weighted with authority.

Tyrius' gaze locked onto Stuckey's spirit, still anchored to Reese's father. He raised his sword, the tip glowing with raw power.

———

The cold, expressionless smile sent ice straight through her veins.

"Generations return to this bridge, and they do our bidding here." His voice was wrong—his, but not his. "And you won't be the last to carry out this curse."

Reese's breath came in short, ragged gasps. He stepped closer, and she stumbled back, the old planks creaking underfoot. Could this really be happening?

"Dad." Her voice trembled. "I know you're in there."

Something flickered in his eyes. A hesitation. But it was gone in an instant.

"You can't escape the legacy of those who came before you," he sneered.

Reese's heartbeat pounded against her ribs, but she pulled her ankle free from the gap in the bridge floor, wincing with pain. Her father had killed Art. He had killed Patricia. This—this thing—wasn't just her father anymore. But her father made choices that let it in. She needed him to remember who he was outside this evil, or who he should be.

"Uncle Art loved you," she whispered. "Mom loved you, too. She ran to protect me... and I think—I know—deep down you want to protect me, too. You don't have to do this."

His face twisted, but then he laughed—a horrible, guttural sound that sent her heart skittering.

"He can't hear you," the thing inside him rasped. "Like many before him, he's listening to another voice—one that won't be beaten by weak pleas and empty prayers."

Reese's heart jumped, but she didn't have time to react.

"Prayers aren't weak." A new voice rang from behind them. Strong. Resolute.

"Addie!" Reese wanted to run to her, but he blocked her path.

The older woman stood at the edge of the bridge, her Bible clutched in one hand, her face fierce as the wind tugged her blouse loose from her waist. The thing inside Reese's father hissed.

"Your prayers can't stop what happens here." His voice grated like a rusty iron. "They thought they stopped me with prayers before. They thought they stopped us with a noose. But I remain. And I will remain, for generations to come."

Addie's eyes burned like embers. "This generational curse ends with Reese, and you know it."

The laughter that followed was worse than before. "Does it?" The red haze in his eyes deepened. "She suffers as he does. And while she may not kill like me, she will be like me—feeding suffering into the world with her own hands."

Reese's blood turned cold. "I'll never be like you. I know Jesus, so you can't control me like you do my father."

"Lies," the thing hissed. "You believers lie to yourself. You justify your own behavior, thinking evil has different measures of impact. Even apathy serves Lucifer in magnitudes. There's more than murder at our bidding." His grin widened, inhuman. "Go ahead and keep lying to yourselves. Your lies serve us."

Reese shook her head. "No. There's a difference between falling into sin before repenting, and willfully practicing it. I refuse to believe that a surrendered heart serves what you fight for."

"Reese, stop talking to it!" Addie's voice was sharp now. "That's not what's needed now! Speak truth!"

Reese's heart slammed into her ribs as the air shifted around her. Her own words wouldn't save her, but God's Word could.

Her father—or what wore his face—recoiled, his body lurching, his hands clamping over his ears.

Addie opened her Bible, her voice rising—not loud, but sure—as she began to read, and the words rolled like thunder across the bridge, each verse laced with power, wrapping around Reese like an unseen shield. The air crackled. The shadows twisted in agony.

Reese clenched the railing and whispered, "God, please..." Then, she repeated the scripture Addie recited. "The light shines in the darkness, and the darkness has not overcome it."

The demon shrieked, and the bridge trembled beneath their feet.

———

Raphael's eyes burned as he lifted his blade toward the heavens. He did not hesitate.

"Now."

Uriel's sword plunged downward, piercing through the last of the demons gripping Reese's father. A wail tore through the night as Stuckey's spirit convulsed, its form flickering and unraveling. The shrieking shadows clawed at the air before dissolving into nothing..

———

Her father crumpled to the bridge, writhing as the last of the evil inside him fought against the light. For a heartbeat, Reese thought he might reach for her—not to harm, but to surrender.

But instead, he staggered upright, his body jerking with unnatural, broken movements. His gaze met hers—haunted, torn—and then he ran. He bolted into the trees, limbs twisting as if something still inside him refused to let go.

Silence fell across the bridge.

Reese's knees gave out, and she collapsed onto the rough planks, barely feeling them beneath her. "Addie," she rasped, swallowing hard. "Where's James?"

"Right here."

Reese turned. James stood at the edge of the bridge, gun in hand, breath coming fast. His eyes scanned the trees, before dropping to hers with a look of concern.

"Are you alright?"

She let out a sharp laugh, rubbing her hands over her face. "Where were you?"

"I went to your house. Thought he took you. I called for backup—cops will be here any minute. Where is he?"

Reese's stomach twisted as she looked at the place in the trees where her father disappeared.

Addie let out a dry chuckle, shaking her head. "Jamie, police detective or not, you have no idea what's goin' on."

James shot her a look. "What are you talking about? It was him, wasn't it? Your father?"

Reese exhaled, long and slow.

"It was him," she said, voice hollow. "But I don't know if there's anything left of him anymore."

James frowned as he reached for her, and she allowed him to pull her into a hug. The trusses groaned above them, and Reese wished she'd never laid eyes on Stuckey's bridge.

The Devil's Crossing

Catherine

Catherine hadn't planned to stop at the general store, but she had no choice.

They were out of flour, and she and her pa would need some supper when they got home. He hadn't liked the idea of her going alone, not this close to dark, but he had allowed it—so long as Zeke met her to walk her back to the post office.

She tugged Ellen's shawl tighter around her shoulders as she stepped toward the store, the familiar weight of it a comfort. The fabric was worn, fraying at the edges, but she hadn't been able to let it go.

As she reached for the door, a voice stopped her.

"Miss Porter."

She turned. Mr. Blythe stood a few steps away, looking behind her at the store, then back at her. He hesitated, as if deciding whether to speak.

"You needing something from White's this late?"

She nodded. "Just flour."

His gaze flicked toward the store again, his expression un-readable.

"I see." He gave a small nod, stepping back. "Well. Best not linger long." He hesitated, before turning to walk back to the livery, glancing back at her.

Something about his tone gave her pause, but before she could question it, he turned away. She shook off the unease and stepped inside.

The bell overhead jingled.

Silence.

The store was too quiet.

Usually, this time of evening, there were at least a few folks finishing up last-minute business. But tonight, the only sound was the faint tick of the clock behind the counter.

She hesitated. Something felt off.

"Mr. White?" she called.

No answer.

Her pulse quickened. Maybe he had already closed up shop. But the lamps still burned low, their flickering glow stretching long shadows across the floorboards.

A slow creak broke the silence.

The door to the back room edged open.

"Miss Porter."

She startled, hand pressing to her heart, but relieved to see Mr. White where he should be, and not missing like the others.

Mr. White stepped through, wiping his hands on a rag. His smile flickered into place, but it didn't quite reach his eyes.

"Didn't mean to spook you," he said. "You caught me just before closing."

She swallowed, nodding. "I just need flour. I won't keep you long."

For a moment, he didn't move. His gaze flickered—as if he struggled with a decision.

Then he gestured toward the storeroom. "Flour's in the back. Why don't you fetch it while I finish up here?"

That was strange.

He usually fetched it himself. Or asked what quantity she wanted.

A prickle ran up her spine, but she forced herself to nod. She was being foolish. Jumping at shadows.

She stepped past him into the storeroom. He moved to the front door. Probably to flip the open sign to "closed"

The air, thick with the scent of burlap, was dry and stale. The storeroom smelled like sawdust, and the wooden shelves towered over her, stacked with tins, sacks, and crates. She reached for the flour, fingers brushing the rough burlap when a flash of silver caught her eye.

Something small, and tucked between a stack of folded cloth and a tin of nails.

She stilled.

It couldn't be.

But as she stepped closer, her pulse slammed in her ears.

A locket. Or half of one.

Her stomach twisted as she reached for it, turning it over in her palm.

Ellen's mother. The beautiful face, so like her beautiful daughter's, smiled back at her.

Catherine's breath caught. The other half had been found on the bridge, and it sat inside the purse hanging on her wrist.

She swallowed hard. This wasn't misplaced. It had been taken and kept here at Mr. White's store.

She took a step back, blood roaring in her ears. Why would he have it? She couldn't allow her mind to answer.

A floorboard creaked behind her.

She spun. Mr. White stood in the doorway of the storeroom. She hadn't even heard him move.

His eyes flicked to her hand as she slung it behind her back. "You found something," he murmured.

Her fingers curled around the locket, while her mind screamed at her to stay calm. Act normal. Keep him talking. She brought her hand back to her front, holding the locket out in her palm.

"It—it looks like Ellen's," she said, keeping her voice steady.

His smile didn't falter. "Does it?"

Too smooth. Too easy.

She forced herself to nod. "Maybe she lost it here when we came in together." Her voice shook, and she tried to make it steady. "The chain was thin, so that's probably what happened."

A pause. The silence stretched between them, and Catherine wondered if he could hear her heart pounding.

He finally broke the silence. "I suppose that must be it," he murmured, his eyes not leaving hers.

The locket burned the inside of her palm, branding her with a warning.

She had to get out of here. Now.

She took a step forward, but he moved too fast. Before she could react, his hand snapped around her wrist.

She gasped, jerking back, but his grip tightened, twisting her arm behind her.

She struggled, thrashing against him, but he shoved her forward, slamming her against the support beam.

Her breath came in ragged bursts as he reached for the coil of rope beside him.

"This isn't how I wanted it," he muttered, almost to himself. "Not like this. But now, I don't have a choice. I must improvise."

The ropes bit into her wrists, pinning her tight. Her thoughts reeled in shock. It was him the whole time. He talked to Ellen. She introduced him to Ellen. Her head spun and she swayed on her feet.

Gripping the rope that tethered her to him, he turned toward the front of the store.

"It's a good thing I locked up."

Her heartbeat thundered inside her chest, her blood rushing to her temples.

She couldn't let him take her from here, not without leaving a clue.

She still held the locket piece in her fist.

As he pulled her from the storeroom to the back of the store, she tossed Ellen's locket onto the floor of the main store.

Someone would find it. Mr. Blythe knew she went into Mr. White's. Was he still watching? Would he see she hadn't exited the store?

He hadn't been guilty, but suspicious of the man who was. Somehow he had known.

And Zeke. He would come. He was supposed to meet her there.

He'd come and find the clue she left behind.

He had to.

Catherine stumbled as Mr. White dragged her through the trees, the roots and thick underbrush clawing at her skirts, as if the very earth resisted his path. The river's murmur grew louder with every forced step, a cold wind slicing through the branches and stirring the leaves into a whispering chorus. She struggled against his iron grip, her breath sharp and ragged.

"You shouldn't have gone looking," he murmured, his voice eerily calm, almost disappointed. "I told myself I wouldn't rush this. Wouldn't take you too soon. But you just couldn't leave well enough alone, could you?"

Catherine clenched her jaw, her mind racing, searching for anything—anything—to slow him down. "People will know," she said, her voice steadier than she felt. "They'll find out it's you."

He laughed, a low, guttural sound. "Will they? Do you know how many travelers have vanished by my hand, and no one so much as blinked?" He wrenched her forward, forcing her to stumble. "No one will find you, Catherine. And if they do… they'll only find what I leave of you."

Her stomach lurched, but she forced herself to focus.

Think. No, Pray.

As soon as she uttered her words in her mind and spirit, she heard his voice.

Do not be afraid. My angels have charge over thee.

Though her blood still rushed with fear, Catherine felt an immediate assurance that no matter what, even if Mr. White killed her, she'd be in good hands. She knew Jesus wouldn't leave her alone with this monster. Somehow, she knew Ellen hadn't been alone, either.

They reached the edge of the riverbank, the moon casting a sickly glow on the rushing water. The bridge loomed in the distance, its silhouette dark and foreboding against the sky.

He turned her toward him then, his fingers digging into her arm. "You should be honored, you know. It's rare I get to savor this. But you—" He exhaled sharply, his eyes gleaming with something feral. "You're different. I've waited for this. For you."

"You killed Ellen." Tears blurred her vision and fear pounded against her chest.

"Yes, and she gave me a thrill, too, but you'll be a greater ecstasy." When her eyes widened, he chuckled. "Oh, don't worry. My interests no longer seek sexual fulfillment. No, what I have planned for your body is far better than that."

"I don't understand. Why?"

He sighed. "I had hoped you'd be different, sweet Cat. Why'd you have to ask why?" His disappointment accompanied something else in his expression. "There is no why."

She must keep him talking.

"But you seemed so...so..."

"Insignificant?"

She said nothing, afraid to set him off more. But, he didn't look unsettled or enraged. In fact, he looked the opposite—poised, controlled, pleased. As if time itself belonged to him, and no one could cross it to stop what he wanted to happen.

When she said nothing, he continued. "Isn't it funny how the insignificant go unnoticed unless they force others to notice? I think you know what I mean, don't you, Catherine?"

"So you kill because people ignore you?"

"There you go again, wanting the why." His voice was smooth, almost amused. "Everyone always wants the why. I told you, there is no why. It just is. Accept it. Embrace it, Catherine. Own your destiny."

Her stomach twisted, but she held his gaze. "Who are you? Is your name even Mr. White?"

He took a slow step closer, lifting the knife until the tip traced the curve of her jaw, his touch deliberate. A single, sharp sting.

"Poor Mr. White," he murmured. "Ole Daniel White didn't know who he invited to share a warm fire and a meal at his campsite." His lips curled, but his eyes remained cold. Dead.

He tilted his head.

"No, I'm not Daniel White." He turned the blade, letting it catch the faint glimmer of light. "Name's Stuckey."

Her breath stalled, and he smiled at her silence, twisting the knife in his fingers for emphasis.

"Please." Her voice was barely a whisper. "Where did you bury them?"

His expression didn't shift, but something dark flickered in his gaze.

"I don't need to ask who you mean, do I?" His voice was almost playful. "Why do you need to know?"

He leaned in, breath warm against her cheek.

"Would you like to lie next to her for eternity?"

The knife slid along her throat, slower this time. The pressure deliberate, as if savoring the moment. A small slice. A shallow sting.

She gasped, the pain flashing white-hot, but she bit back a cry.

He smiled. But it wasn't real.

"No," he whispered, shaking his head. "I won't bury you near her. But you and I?" His voice dropped lower, almost tender. "We'll be linked for eternity now. There's no greater bond than the one between the killer and the victim."

She fought to keep her breath steady, to push past the suffocating fear, but his sick ramblings didn't distract her from the shift beyond the trees.

Something moved.

A ripple in the shadows.

A presence she couldn't see—but felt. Something dark approached them, a shifting shape just beyond her vision, barely distinguishable from the night itself.

She stiffened as the wind died and the forest held its breath.

The thing in the trees—it moved. Not like a man. Not like anything she'd ever seen before. It glided closer, the darkness around it deepening, pulling the very shadows toward itself.

Her chest tightened.

Stuckey didn't seem to notice.

She opened her mouth—whether to scream, to pray, she wasn't sure—

A great light exploded through the trees. It didn't burn so much as consume.

The darkness recoiled, shrieking.

Catherine gasped, throwing an arm over her eyes. The sudden radiance bathed the forest in blinding brilliance, illuminating the trees, the river, even the bridge in a way the moon never could.

For a single heartbeat, the world held still. The air crackled, charged with something far beyond human comprehension.

Catherine staggered backward. She couldn't see it—whatever it was—but she could feel it. A war unseen, raging just beyond the veil of her understanding.

Stuckey stiffened beside her, looking around the space where they stood.

For the first time, he faltered. His breathing hitched, and his gaze shifted. Uneasy, he loosened his fingers around her arm, his grip loosening just slightly.

Catherine seized the moment. With all her strength, she drove her knee up, striking Stuckey hard in the groin. He doubled over with a sharp grunt, his grip loosening just enough. She tore free, scrambling backward, her boots slipping in the mud. Her heart pounded, her breath wild in her throat.

She ran off the bridge and into the brush, the shadows inviting her to hide.

Behind her, Stuckey let out a curse, his footsteps crashing after her.

She darted through the trees, limbs whipping at her face. She had no sense of direction, only the desperate need to flee. But then—then she felt it.

A shift in the air.

Not just the wind. Something more. Something vast. The shadows thickened. The temperature dropped unnaturally fast. A suffocating pressure pressed against the earth itself, the trees groaning as if burdened. The night pulsed—not just with the sounds of the chase, but with something unseen.

Catherine stumbled to a halt, instinctively turning toward the sky after hearing the crack of thunder without a storm. And then—deep within the pulse of the forest—she knew.

She wasn't alone.

———

The darkness struck first.

The forest shuddered, the trees groaning as the wind shifted—unnatural and wrong. The shadows at the edge of human vision deepened, coiling like something alive.

Then—they came.

Figures emerged from the gloom, their bodies twisting, shifting, writhing between shapes both monstrous and human. Their eyes burned with a hatred older than time itself.

Three of them.

Belias. Ravoth. Sleim.

But they were not alone. The lesser ones came too—murder, lust, fear, pride—swarming and skittering in the darkness like carrion feeders awaiting the slaughter. Names whispered in nightmares.

For years, they had watched, manipulated, whispered death into willing ears. They had guided Stuckey's hands. They had rejoiced in every soul lost.

And now—they moved to claim another.

A tremor rippled through the air. Then—light. It tore through the sky, shattering the thick blackness like a blade through silk. They descended.

Uriel. Tyrius. Lior.

Wings of fire and storm and weapons gleaming with the brilliance of eternity. The warriors of Heaven met the legions of Hell.

Belias shrieked in rage. "You're too late," he hissed, his form twisting and writhing, the darkness roiling like smoke. "He's mine. Victory will be ours this time."

Uriel did not flinch. "Not tonight."

He struck first. A warrior of the Most High, his form blazed like molten fire, his sword a burning arc as he cleaved through the air toward Belias. The demon met him head-on, claws dark as ink, jagged and pulsing with curses that had drowned civilizations.

Their impact sent a shockwave through the forest—a blast of gold and shadow, a force so great the river itself recoiled, its waters thrashing violently as if aware of the war that had come to its banks.

Belias counter-attacked. The deceiver. The serpent-tongued. The whisperer of doubts. Uriel's blade shattered his first strike, sending a hiss of white flame racing up the demon's form. He shrieked, but he did not fall. Instead, he lunged, twisting like mist, reforming in an instant.

"You think you can win?" he spat. "He doesn't resist us. He hasn't in a long time."

Uriel's gaze did not waver. "But she does."

Belias hissed, recoiling at the truth in those words.

The girl.

Her prayers. Her faith. Even in fear, even in this moment—she reached beyond the darkness.

She had called for Heaven's aid, and it had come. A power greater than the swords clashing. Greater than the flames burning through the darkness.

It was unseen, but its presence was undeniable.

Prayer.

Not just hers, but the man named Blythe, the one the others suspected. He was the strongest warrior in town, stronger than the man who should have led them. But even he prayed now, too, like the others.

Somewhere—perhaps kneeling in their homes, perhaps gathered, perhaps only whispering His name in their hearts—believers cried out to Jesus for their town.

And He heard them. Their prayers strengthened the warriors of Heaven.

Tyrius roared as he struck Ravoth, his sword flashing in the darkness. The demon reeled, snarling, his form rippling in and out of solidity.

Then, Lior lunged at Sleim, who sought refuge behind Belias.

"You feel it, don't you?" Lior murmured, his voice like the roll of distant thunder. "Their prayers weaken you."

Sleim snapped his fanged mouth, his eyes narrowing.

"Prayers." He spat the word like venom. "Useless words. Begging for mercy from a King who does not come."

Lior smiled—a knowing, unshaken smile.

"Oh, but Christ has already come. He's coming again. And you can't stop the earth from receiving His presence, though your master will try. But the best part?"

Lior's wings unfurled, light radiating from his form, his sword lifted high. His voice was thunder and fire.

"Jesus wins."

The name tore through the air like a storm unleashed.

At that same moment, a few voices rose in prayer. Some whispering in quiet strength and confidence. Some pleading on their knees in fear. But they all said the same name.

Jesus.

The name ripped through the battlefield, carried by the prayers of saints, woven into the very light itself.

Sleim reeled back, his form convulsing, his screams splitting the night. The sound shattered the lesser demons. They shrieked and scattered, fleeing into the abyss like smoke caught in a violent wind.

Ravoth staggered, his form flickering, faltering.

Belias, too, shrank back, snarling in agony. Disbelief crossed his features, as he writhed in anguish. "No! Not again!"

Lior's sword thrust forward, searing through Sleim's chest, twisting deep into the very core of his being. The demon's body cracked apart, not into nothingness, but into shadow—fracturing, splintering, dissolving into the unseen.

A final, gasping hiss. A snarl of hatred and defeat.

Then—nothing.

The name of Jesus thundered through the forest, shaking the earth with its power.

The demons fled.

———

Catherine ducked behind a tree, her chest heaving. The damp air pressed around her, thick and suffocating, filled with the scent of rain-soaked earth and dying leaves. Her pulse pounded in her ears, loud enough that she feared he could hear it too.

Somewhere behind her, Stuckey moved through the brush. His boots slipped in the slick mud, but he didn't curse or stumble. He was patient. Confident.

"You can't run forever, Catherine." His voice slithered through the trees, deceptively calm. "You know that, don't you?"

She clenched her fists, nails biting into her palms. Running would only delay the inevitable. He was faster. Stronger. He had hunted before.

Something in the trees flickered, a shadow that did not belong.

She swallowed hard, forcing her breath through her nose.

The moment she ran again, he'd be on her. But if she stayed, if she fought—

She didn't need to fight alone. She could feel it.

Even now, even here, she was not abandoned.

Stuckey lunged.

At the last moment, she dropped low, fingers closing around a heavy branch slick with rain. With every ounce of strength in her body, she swung, the wood cracking hard against his leg.

A sharp, guttural snarl tore from his throat as he staggered, his balance momentarily lost. For a fleeting second, she caught a glimpse of his face—not contorted in pain, not even twisted in anger. He was amused.

Then she ran, but not blindly.

The light at the bridge called her, its instant glow pulling her forward through the darkness. Every step sent a fresh burst of pain through her limbs, but she did not stop. She could not stop. The wind howled around her, whipping her hair into her face as her lungs burned with each frantic breath.

Behind her, Stuckey laughed. Not a mindless roar of rage, but something lower, more deliberate. A slow, wicked chuckle that curled through the trees, slithering up her spine.

"Oh, Cat," he purred, his voice carrying through the night, thick with amusement. "You should know better."

His footsteps crashed through the underbrush, steady, unhurried. He was gaining on her.

"You think you're different?" His voice came closer, threading through the night like a noose tightening around her throat. "That you can get away?"

She pushed harder, her legs screaming with the effort, but he was too fast.

"Run, little girl," he taunted, his tone dripping with cruel pleasure. "Make this fun for me."

Her breath came in ragged gasps, her muscles burning, threatening to give out beneath her. She wanted to collapse. She wanted to scream. Instead, she prayed, forcing the words past her trembling lips.

"Jesus, please help me."

Her feet pounded against the earth, her heartbeat hammering in her ears, and still, Stuckey pursued.

Zeke's horse pounded against the ground, the lantern in his hand swinging wildly with each stride. He had known—felt it deep in his gut—something was wrong.

The locket Catherine had left behind in the store had sent his blood running cold. Ellen's locket. A silent warning, a desperate clue.

Thank God for Mr. Blythe, who had been watching the store and realized Catherine never came out. The moment Zeke heard, he hadn't hesitated. He and Blythe had gone straight to her father first, then the sheriff. Matt, who had been at the post office, had joined the posse without hesitation.

Now they all rode hard toward the river, their urgency driving the horses to their limits. The bridge loomed ahead, the night closing in around them.

They had to reach her in time. How he had not seen it? How had he missed the evil right in front of them?

Zeke gritted his teeth and kicked Gunner harder.

They weren't too late.

They couldn't be too late.

Catherine reached the bridge, but so did Stuckey.

A hand wrenched her back, yanking her so hard she lost her footing. She hit the wet earth hard, the impact knocking the air from her lungs.

"You shouldn't have run." His voice was quiet. Matter-of-fact.

She gasped, thrashing beneath his grip, but he was too strong.

Stuckey didn't react, didn't lash out. He simply reached into his coat, withdrawing the knife with slow, deliberate precision, as if he had all the time in the world.

He rolled it between his fingers, the blade catching the faint moonlight.

Catherine froze, watching him hold the knife like a treasured friend.

No rush. No theatrics. Only certainty.

"See what you made me do?" he murmured, turning the knife idly in his hand. "I didn't want to rush this. I wanted to take my time." His gaze flicked to her, sharp and unreadable. "You ruined that."

The cold press of steel returned to her throat, deliberate this time, the tip biting—not deep, not yet. Just a warning. Catherine's breath shuddered as he watched, not expecting her to scream or beg. Just waiting. Like he had done this a hundred times before. Her nails clawed at his wrist, her vision tunneling, just as she heard the whisper.

It's over, child. You're safe.

Then—a gunshot.

Stuckey jerked. His grip loosened, just enough for her to twist away, gasping for breath, but Stuckey grabbed her around the neck again, holding the knife to her throat.

"Let her go."

A voice—Zeke's.

Another shot, and Stuckey dropped to the ground. Catherine collapsed onto her hands and knees, coughing, dragging air into her lungs.

Footsteps pounded against the bridge. A hand touched her shoulder, steadying her. She blinked up.

Zeke and her pa. Matt and Mr. Blythe.

They stood over her, weapons drawn, eyes hard.

The sheriff kept his rifle trained on Stuckey, who clutched his bleeding shoulder, but his face remained eerily blank. No rage. No panic. Just the slow calculation of a man adjusting his odds.

His chest rose and fell in even, measured breaths. His fingers twitched toward his belt.

Catherine's stomach turned.

A second knife. He wasn't done.

His eyes flicked over them, weighing his chances, and then he smiled.

"You think you can take me?" His voice was quiet. Calm. "You think this is how it ends?"

He exhaled a soft chuckle, almost as if amused by their naïveté.

"You can't end this. You'll see."

Then—he moved.

A final, reckless attempt.

His hand shot for the knife, but the sheriff fired his gun in a flash, hitting Stuckey in the thigh.

Stuckey staggered, knees buckling in pain.

Zeke lunged, slamming into him before he could recover. They hit the ground hard, Stuckey grunting as he thrashed against Zeke's grip. But Zeke held fast, his teeth clenched, pinning him down as the others closed in.

Mr. Blythe kicked the knife aside as the sheriff wrenched Stuckey's arms back, binding them with iron cuffs.

Catherine was still gasping for breath when her father dropped beside her, wrapping her in his arms.

For a moment, she didn't move. Then she clung to him, her fingers twisting into his coat as a sob shuddered from her chest.

Stuckey, face-down in the dirt, turned his head, snarling through blood-stained teeth. Then—his mouth twisted into something that wasn't a smile. His voice slithered through the air, low and guttural, echoing as if more than one voice spoke at once. "You think you've won. You've won nothing."

He stared into the sky, as if not speaking to them at all, his voice unnatural, shocking them all.

Even the temperature reacted, cooling, and the night pressed tighter. The hairs on Catherine's arms rose, a sick chill creeping down her spine.

The sheriff tightened the cuffs, his voice cold. "There's no winning here. But I do know you've lost. You'll hang right here on this bridge, noose 'round your neck, rotting for all to see. They'll be telling stories about your rotting corpse for decades to come."

She saw something different in Stuckey's eyes, as he flinched.

Fear and horror.

Catherine exhaled, long and unsteady.

It was over.

The hunter had become the prey.

———

The crowd gathered at the foot of the bridge, murmuring like the restless current beneath them. The scent of damp wood and churned earth hung in the humid air, mixing with the distant smoke of torches flickering against the night. Somewhere in the trees, a crow let out a sharp caw, the sound tearing through the stillness like a warning

At the center of it all stood Stuckey.

His hands were bound. The noose hung loose around his neck, tied to the thick wooden beam that stretched over the water. He had been dragged here like a rabid dog, yet he didn't fight. Didn't plead. He merely stood there, staring ahead, his expression unreadable, as if none of this mattered.

Catherine stood near the front, her father beside her. His presence was solid, steady, but the tension in his stance mirrored her own.

The sheriff stepped forward, clearing his throat. "For your heinous crimes, you are sentenced to hang. And here your corpse will hang and rot, for all to witness your filthy demise."

Bro. Whitmore, standing a few feet away, clasped his hands together. "There is still mercy, even now, if you seek it," he said, his voice steady. "Tell us where the bodies are. Confess, repent, and call upon the Lord."

Stuckey's lips twitched. His head tilted, slow and deliberate, his gaze shifting toward the pastor.

And then he laughed.

Low. Amused.

But when he spoke, it wasn't his voice.

The sound slithered through the air, thick and unnatural. Twisting. Layered. The same voice that had whispered through the night before—the one they had heard at this very bridge where he'd been captured.

"You think this is the end of me?"

A hush fell over the crowd. The torchlight flickered, the wind shifting, carrying the scent of the river up through the boards beneath their feet.

Stuckey turned his head, his gaze sweeping over them, as if memorizing each face, before landing on Catherine's.

"You think you've won?" His voice rippled through the air, twisting and deepening. "I have worn a thousand faces. And I will wear a thousand more. There is more to be done here, and I'll be back."

A crow cawed again, abrupt and jarring in the silence. Catherine's father tensed beside her, and she clenched her fists at her sides, willing herself not to shudder.

The sheriff's hesitation was brief. He gave a short nod, and two men moved forward, grabbing Stuckey's arms. The sheriff stepped back.

But then—

Stuckey flinched.

His smirk faltered, just for a second. His head snapped down as if he saw something no one else did—something below him, something waiting.

His chest rose sharply, a breath pulled in fast. The bravado bled from his expression, his sneer weakening at the edges. His eyes darted to the trees, the water, the sky—frantic, searching.

"No," he rasped, the voice no longer layered—no longer inhuman. Just his own, raw and frightened.

The crowd stirred. People felt it, even if they couldn't see it. The air had changed. The night felt heavier, thick with something unseen.

He tried to take a step back.

But the sheriff gave the order, and the men shoved him.

Stuckey plummeted. The rope snapped taut, and his body jerked violently, legs kicking for a moment before they stilled. His head lolled unnaturally, and his limp corpse swung beneath the bridge while the river churned, black and endless.

No one spoke for a few moments. Then the chatter began as the crowd dispersed, voices hushed, heavy with the shock that the town's storekeeper had murdered people right under their noses, and no one had seen it coming.

They left him there for three days.

Catherine never went back to look at him, but she heard the whispers. The crows had already begun their work, picking at his flesh. His body swayed like a rag doll in the breeze.

It should have satisfied her. It should have given her peace. But it didn't.

Hanging him hadn't changed what she lost. It hadn't erased the fear or the emptiness he left behind.

And worst of all, he had ruined this place for her. The bridge had once been her refuge, where she could escape the noise of the world and think. Where she had stood alone with only the wind and water for company.

Now, it felt different. Stained.

She and Ellen had met here, if only for a few short visits. It was the first place she had let someone in. And now, it was where she had to let go.

On the third day, the town gathered again. It was time to cut him down.

The sheriff and a few men climbed onto the bridge, knives in hand. The rope gave way, and Stuckey's body tumbled, crashing into the water below with an unceremonious splash. The river took him. The town offered no grave for men like him.

A flicker of movement caught her eye.

Away from the others, Mr. Blythe knelt in the grass, his head bowed, lips moving soundlessly. His hands rested on his thighs, fingers curled, steady even as the wind shifted around him. He wasn't watching the river. He wasn't watching Stuckey's body at all.

He was praying.

Catherine's breath caught in her throat. And a chill ran through her, but not from fear.

Slowly, she stepped closer. The others were too busy to notice—pulling their hats lower, muttering amongst themselves, but she did.

And for the first time, she saw him clearly. The man she once suspected.

"Mr. Blythe?" Her voice was quiet, almost hesitant.

He didn't startle. He simply lifted his head, his eyes calm—not surprised to see her. As if he had expected her all along.

"You were praying," she said, the words more of a statement than a question.

Mr. Blythe nodded once, slow and deliberate. "Ain't the first time."

Her pulse pounded in her ears. "Was it you? I felt it at the bridge? When he—" She stopped, unable to finish the sentence. "I felt someone praying, and it gave me the strength to pray, too."

Blythe's gaze didn't waver. "It was me then. And before that. It'll be me long after this day."

Catherine swallowed. "Why?"

He exhaled, staring past her toward the water, as if he saw something she couldn't. "Because there's a bigger battle than what we see," he said quietly. "And it don't end with a hanging rope."

His words settled deep, filling the spaces of her mind that she had been too afraid to acknowledge.

It had never been about an evil man, a murderer.

The darkness had been here long before any of them. And Mr. Blythe... he had been standing in the gap all along. Catherine took a slow breath, her fingers curling around Ellen's locket.

"You fought back," she murmured. "But it didn't save her."

Blythe's lips twitched, a sadness tinging his features. "Make no mistake, Miss Catherine. Evil can only win the temporary battles, and even then, they're still losing. But sometimes the grief of those wins can hide the eternal victory from us, but we must look. It's there."

She glanced around at the others, still murmuring, still pulling their coats tight against the wind. They had no idea.

No idea that the real battle hadn't been fought with a rope and the law.

It had been fought on seasoned knees.

For a long moment, Catherine simply stood there, watching the man who had been protecting this town in ways no one had ever seen. They had all missed it.

And for the first time, she understood.

Prayer wasn't just words.

It was a weapon of war.

Later, Catherine stood at the edge of the bridge, watching the ripples glide across the water—calm, indifferent, as if they hadn't just swallowed a corpse. Her pa had fixed Ellen's locket, and she had washed out the blood on Thatcher's hat. He wore it every day now. A reminder. A mark of the friends they lost, just as they had grown to love them.

She turned the locket over in her fingers, the hinges restored, the two halves no longer apart. Inside, Ellen's mother's face stared back at her, frozen in time. So much like Ellen's.

A movement at her side drew her attention.

Rosalind Greer stood a few feet away. She hesitated, the same guarded look in her eyes, but it wasn't sharp. It wasn't smug. Instead, there was something Catherine hadn't seen before—uncertainty, maybe even regret.

For a long moment, neither spoke.

Then, Rosalind exhaled, shifting awkwardly before reaching into her pocket. She pulled something out—a small, pressed wildflower, the same kind Ellen wore in her hair the day Rosalind met her at the church on the steps.

She held it out, hesitating.

Catherine hesitated too before reaching out and accepting it.

Their fingers brushed, and Rosalind spoke, her voice softer than Catherine had ever heard it. "I should have been kinder to you both."

Catherine swallowed hard, her fingers curling around the delicate bloom. "Me, too. I think I isolated myself, and that just made it easier to feel alone around everyone else. Until Ellen."

A quiet nod. Then, after a beat, a small, tentative smile.

"See you at church?"

Catherine nodded, a smile breaking through. "See you then."

Rosalind turned and walked away, joining her friends in the crowd.

Catherine stood there for a long moment, staring down at the flower. Then she turned and let it slip from her fingers, watching as it drifted down, disappearing into the river below.

Rosalind had given her a way to say goodbye.

A warm hand slid into hers. She looked up, eyes misted with tears.

Zeke.

She squeezed his hand, letting him know she welcomed his touch. Across the way, she caught Matt's eye. He tipped his hat, nodding, as if he understood what she had just realized herself. Catherine watched as he sidled over to Rosalind, and the group of girls around her blushed as he approached.

Zeke's grip tightened, steady and certain. His eyes searched hers, then he reached up, brushing away a tear with the pad of his thumb.

This time, she didn't flinch or pull away.

Her father stepped beside her, laying a firm, calloused hand on her shoulder—and another on Zeke's. No words, just presence. Both men knew exactly what she needed. God had given her their support all along, and she had been blind to it. Maybe even blind to His.

Catherine let out a breath she didn't know she'd been holding.

Turning the locket over in her palm one last time, she lifted it to her neck and fastened the chain.

"I'll make sure you're remembered, Ellen," she whispered. "Your legacy of friendship won't be forgotten."

The river softened, its murmurs gentle now, carrying away the past in soft rippling waves.

She wasn't sure what came next, but for the first time in a long time, she wasn't afraid to find out.

Because now she wouldn't need to find out alone.

A Bridge of Hope

Reese

The morning mist unraveled over the river, stretching low along the banks in thick ribbons of silver. Reese stood near the water's edge, her arms wrapped around herself against the damp chill. Somewhere beneath the earth, buried under two years of silence, Patricia Langton waited to be found.

James stood a few feet away, speaking with two uniform officers, gesturing toward the tree line that bordered the property. "Start here," he instructed. "This is the most likely place. We know the soil was disturbed, and if she was buried in haste, the rains could've loosened it further."

Reese barely heard him. The world had narrowed to the slow, steady rush of the river and the feeling that something long hidden was about to come to light.

Then Cash whined, his tail stiff as he sniffed at the wind. He paced at Addie's side, restless, his nose working the air in quick, sharp motions.

"What's the matter, boy?" Addie murmured, giving his head a scratch. "Smell somethin', do you?"

The black Lab gave a short, urgent bark, then lunged toward the trees.

"Cash!" Addie yelped, nearly losing her grip on the leash as he tugged hard, dragging her a step forward.

James turned sharply at the sound, his hand instinctively resting on his holster. "Something's over there."

Reese's pulse quickened. "He smells something," she said, her voice barely above a whisper.

Cash whined again, pawing at the damp earth beneath the thick branches of a cypress tree. He lowered his head, sniffed deep, then started digging. Dirt flew behind him in frantic bursts.

"Whoa, now," Addie said, trying to steady him. But the dog wouldn't stop. "He's never done anything like this before."

James moved toward the spot, kneeling as Cash's paws scraped against something solid. The moment James reached into the disturbed soil, a glint of gold flickered through the dirt.

Reese's breath caught.

Addie crouched down, brushing aside the remaining soil with careful fingers. Slowly, she lifted a delicate chain, pulling free a small, round locket, its once-polished surface dulled with time. She turned it over, rubbing her thumb over the engraving.

Then she froze. "Land sakes," she whispered.

"Is that a locket?" Reese asked, stepping closer, her heart thudding.

Addie swallowed hard and nodded. "I've seen this before."

Before Reese could say anything, the sound of footsteps crunching through leaves made her turn. A familiar figure approached, her face pale, her eyes wide with something between hope and dread.

Sharon's steps faltered as she approached, her eyes darting from the soil to the faces around her. "I heard the police were searching near Art's house," she said, her voice uneven. "Is this about my mother's disappearance?"

No one spoke. But when Sharon's gaze dropped to the locket in Addie's hands, she gasped, covering her mouth in shock. She moved toward it slowly, as if afraid it might vanish. Addie hesitated, then placed it into her waiting palm.

Sharon closed her fingers around the locket, pressing it to her chest. For a long moment, she just stood there, eyes closed and releasing quiet tears.

Reese couldn't look away. The weight of generations hung heavy in the air, pressing down like the mist itself.

Sharon exhaled unsteadily. "My mother never took this off. She's here."

Reese felt a strange pang in her chest. "You're certain it's hers?" She already knew the answer. It was the same locket she'd seen Patricia wearing in the photo.

Sharon nodded. "And my grandmother's before her. And my great-grandmother's before that." She lifted her eyes, meeting Reese's with something unreadable. "It's been passed down through the women in my family for generations."

A chill swept over Reese's skin, but she didn't understand why. The breeze whispered against her ear, as if trying to tell her a secret.

James exhaled. "If she never took it off, then we should look nearby."

Before the words fully settled, one of the officers called from several yards away.

"We've got something."

The breath left Reese's lungs. James moved first, heading toward the spot with purpose. Addie kept a firm grip on Cash's leash, whispering quiet reassurances to the dog.

Sharon didn't move. She stood clutching the locket, her lips parted slightly, her face a mask of grief and something deeper—an understanding that this wasn't just the end of her mother's story. It was the closing of something much older, and something that had crossed the bridge of time to bring them all here.

As the officers worked carefully to uncover the truth, Reese let her gaze drift back to the river. The water rolled on, silent and steady, a keeper of secrets long buried.

But secrets never stayed buried forever.

———

Sharon sat on the worn-out porch swing, staring straight ahead. Tiffany sat next to her, her head on her mom's shoulder.

Addie had called her church friends, and they brought food, hugs, and goodie baskets to Sharon's house. Reese, standing off to the side, had never seen so many casseroles at one place. For some, grief made them hungry to fill the emptiness; for others, grief filled them with so much pain, they had no room for anything else. Either way, those who showed up brought more than casserole dishes. They brought their support.

Sharon exhaled, her voice quiet. "I've been meaning to show you this."

Reese turned, her brow furrowing as Sharon held out a letter.

"It's old," Sharon murmured, running her fingers over the inked words. "Written by my great, great grandmother. Her name was Catherine, and she lived here about the time Stuckey killed those people. Our family has often speculated if she knew him."

Reese hesitated before stepping closer. "Really?"

Sharon nodded, her throat working against emotion. "She wrote this after her friend Ellen disappeared. That's why we think she might have known Stuckey. That maybe he had something to do with her disappearance. This letter has been in my mother's trunk for as long as I can remember. I think you should read it."

She handed Reese the letter. The aged paper had yellowed, its edges brittle with time, as if it had been waiting all these years for this moment. The parchment crackled as Reese unfolded it carefully, her eyes scanning the faded ink.

June 23, 1892

Dear daughters and granddaughters to come,

I do not want my friend Ellen to be forgotten. She disappeared, but a piece of her remains, not only with her locket, but in my heart forever.

I know the world moves on too quickly, that people will whisper about what happened and then let time steal her name from their lips. But I won't.

I want her to be remembered, the way she remembered her mother. She wore her locket every day, a small token of love that she carried close to her heart. And now I wear it, not because I believe it holds power, but because I believe love and loyalty does, and that should be honored.

She was my first real friend. The first person who saw me, truly saw me, and did not turn away. She wanted to know me, just as I wanted to know her.

People will say that we shouldn't dwell on the past, that we must move forward and let the dead rest. But I believe remembering is a kind of love. And love does not die just because a person is gone.

So I will wear her locket. And I will pass it down to you, not because it is valuable in the way men count value—but because it is proof that she lived.

It is proof that she mattered. Just like you do.

Wear this locket to remind you of that. And wear it to remind you how important it is to see others.

To love others, and to value them as Jesus does.

Always.

Catherine Porter Tolliver

Reese's fingers tightened around the paper, her vision blurring at the edges.

The weight of the words settled into her chest, pressing against old wounds she hadn't even realized were still open.

She had spent so much time running from the past, trying to forget.

But maybe forgetting wasn't the answer.

Maybe remembering was.

She swallowed, blinking away the sting in her eyes as she looked at Sharon. "She didn't want her friend to be lost to time."

Tiffany spoke up. "And she wasn't. Because someone cared enough to remember."

Reese smiled at the girl. A silence stretched between the three, but it wasn't empty. It was full—of grief, of love, of something deeper than both.

Catherine had worn it for Ellen.

Now Sharon wore it for Patricia.

A quiet breath escaped her lips. "She was right. Love doesn't die just because a person is gone."

Sharon offered a small smile. "No, it doesn't."

Reese knew that remembering the past wasn't just about remembering loved ones. It was about learning from those you've loved and lost. Maybe remembering wasn't the chain holding her back. Maybe it was the bridge forward.

And for the first time, Reese didn't just carry the past.

She honored it.

The house groaned under the weight of what lingered. Even in the stillness of the late afternoon, a heaviness clung to the walls, pressing against Reese as she stepped inside. Shadows slithered across the corners of the room, stretching unnaturally long in the dim light filtering through the curtains. The air held the damp, metallic scent of something old and restless.

Addie followed close behind, her Bible clutched tightly in her hand. James had wanted to come too, but Reese insisted she needed to do this—whatever this was—without him.

The moment she crossed the threshold, the change was palpable. It wasn't like before, when the house had hummed with unseen eyes watching her, when the very walls had breathed unease. No, this was different. A hollowed-out silence. An absence that felt almost worse.

The spirits that had tormented her weren't here.

Not anymore.

Addie sniffed, cocking her head like she could hear something Reese couldn't. "It's like a graveyard in here."

Reese swallowed hard, nodding. "They're gone, though, aren't they?"

Addie took a step forward, slow and measured, her boots tapping lightly against the wooden floor. "Not all of them."

A breeze passed through the room, though the windows were shut. Something unseen. Something watching.

Addie turned toward the hallway leading to the back of the house, to Art's study—the room where so many questions had unraveled into something more sinister. Reese followed, feeling a tightness crawl up her spine, the kind that made her want to turn back but knowing she had to press forward.

The desk drawer was ajar.

She hadn't left it that way.

A single envelope rested on top of the scattered papers, the name "Reese" written in a sharp, jagged scrawl.

She hesitated before reaching for it, fingers trembling as she tore it open. The scent of cigarettes and something damp—river water, maybe—clung to the paper.

Reese,

I should have stayed away. I should have fought harder. But I didn't.

Because I see her in your eyes. I see Brenda. And I see Art.

I don't know when I stopped being myself. It happens slowly—like a whisper in the dark, like something crawling under your skin, waiting for the right moment to take hold. I don't even know when I stopped trying to fight it.

But I know this: you don't belong here.

You think it's over, but you don't understand. You never will. That place—this place—it doesn't let go. And if you stay, it will sink its teeth into you the same way it did me years ago.

I won't be here when you come looking. Maybe I never really was.

You should leave this place. You should run. But we both know you won't.

I hope you're stronger than I was.

The signature was nothing more than an ink-stained smear. Unreadable.

Reese exhaled, long and slow, forcing her fingers to unclench the letter before it crumpled in her grasp.

Addie took the letter from her hands, reading over it before pursing her lips. She shook her head, but instead of the sharp-edged judgment Reese expected, her voice was steady, firm. "What plagued him doesn't have to plague you. This place has no power over Jesus, and you belong to him."

Reese looked at her, something hollow in her chest filling ever so slightly.

Addie's gaze didn't waver. "You hear me, girl? I don't care what kind of evil ran through his veins, or what kind of evil has worked around this bridge for over a century. It stops with you. You ain't him. He allowed the darkness to take him, while you embraced the light."

"But I didn't. I allowed the darkness to swallow me, too, Addie. I allowed what Dylan and the others did to me to taint my view of Him. I realize that now."

"You came back, didn't you? The difference between you and him is clear to me." Addie's voice softened, but her words held steady. "We all walk through darkness, Reese. Some let it drown them. Others reach for the One who can pull them out—even when they're too weak to climb on their own. And that reach? That's what makes all the difference."

Reese swallowed, nodding, her throat too tight for words, and the words settled into the cracks in Reese's heart, planting something there, something small but real. She let out a breath she hadn't realized she was holding. For the first time, she understood—truly understood—what it meant to surrender. She had spent so long gripping the pain, the fear, the distrust, thinking she could handle it alone. But she couldn't. She was never meant to.

A silent prayer formed in her heart, not of desperation, but of release. Lord, I trust You. I don't know where this path leads, but I know I don't have to walk it alone.

A gust of wind rattled the old house, but Reese didn't shiver this time.

She was done being afraid. She was reaching, and this time, she wouldn't let go.

———

Outside, the late evening sky hung low and bruised with the weight of an impending storm. Reese pulled her jacket tighter around herself as she stepped out the door. Addie stayed behind, giving her space, her presence still a solid weight in the background.

She didn't see him at first. Dylan.

He leaned against the railing near the bottom of the steps, hands shoved into his pockets, his expression unreadable. She wondered at the distinct impression he gave her. Regret.

"You look good," he said, and there was something almost rueful in his voice.

She let out a small breath, steadying herself. "Why are you here again, Dylan?"

He shrugged, but there was something restless in his stance. "Heard about what happened with your dad and how they found that missing woman. It was all over the news, social media, too. Thought you might need—" Seeing her expression, he trailed off, shaking his head with a short, humorless chuckle. "I don't know what I thought."

Reese studied him, seeing him clearer than she ever had before. The man who had chosen another. The man who had betrayed her. And yet, she wasn't angry anymore. She wasn't even hurt.

She was free.

"I don't need anything from you, Dylan," she said simply. "Not anymore."

Dylan nodded slowly, shifting his weight. "I guess I deserve that."

She tilted her head, considering. "Maybe. But I'm not retaliating here; it's just a fact. I don't carry it anymore."

Something flickered across his face, like he understood what she wasn't saying. He exhaled, glancing past her, toward the house, the river beyond it. "You're staying, then?"

"Yes." No hesitation. It surprised them both, but then he nodded again, slower this time.

Dylan looked behind her as a presence moved close to her side, quiet and steady.

James. Where did he come from? Didn't matter. She was just glad he was there.

He didn't say anything. He didn't have to. His fingers brushed against hers, tentative, like a question. Reese answered by slipping her hand into his. He squeezed and she squeezed back.

A promise. A beginning.

But no words. No declarations. Not even kisses. Yet.

They weren't necessary. Just something steady, something real that they both allowed to take hold in their life.

Dylan dropped his gaze to their clasped hands, before staring hard at James' challenging stare. Then, he nodded at Reese, before slipping away from her life for good.

She had finally crossed the bridge, and she didn't stand on the other side alone.

Epilogue

Reese smoothed her palms over the fabric of her dress as she faced the auditorium. Rows of expectant faces stretched before her, where women gathered for healing, for hope—for truth. She had already told them her story—the bridge, the demonic hauntings, the truth about her father. The scars she bore, and the journey that led her here. It was the same story she told in her bestselling memoir. Reese still reeled from the work God allowed her to do, despite the wounds she allowed to stifle it before.

The air held a quiet hush, the weight of past burdens filling the space like an unspoken prayer. She had been here once—seated among them, lost in grief, haunted by her own past, and disconnected from the body of Christ.

But now?

Now, she stood, connected to His plan, a part of the church in ways she'd never imagined in the days of isolation and abandonment.

She took a sip from the water bottle provided, then set it aside. Gripping the edges of the podium, she took a steady breath, silently praying for the right words to come.

"I never wanted to talk about my story," she began, her voice steady. "For a while, I thought that if I ignored the past, I could move on from it. But that's the thing about wounds. Ignoring them doesn't heal them. It just lets the infection fester until it defines us."

A murmur of quiet agreement rippled through the crowd.

She exhaled. "I grew up with a mother who protected me from the truth. She kept me from the darkness that nearly consumed my father. I never really knew him, not the way a daughter should. And when the truth finally caught up with me, it nearly destroyed me, too."

Her fingers tightened around the microphone.

"For generations, the bridge in my town carried secrets. Darkness clung to it like a sickness, spreading grief, loss, and fear. When I arrived here, I found myself haunted—both literally and spiritually—by things seen and unseen. But the tragedy?" She let the silence stretch. "That was in how quickly I let it take hold. I let betrayal distort my view of God, even before I understood what I was doing. I let pain speak louder than His voice. And I convinced myself that if I shut Him out—if I shut others out—I wouldn't have to feel the ache of abandonment. I wouldn't have to face the wounds left by people who were battling their own darkness."

A lump formed in her throat, but she pressed forward.

"But here's the truth." She looked out into the audience, meeting the eyes of women who had walked their own roads of suffering. "You can run from Him all you want. You can try to shut Him out, shut others out. But He doesn't stop calling. He doesn't stop reaching. And when you turn back—even if all you have left is a whisper of faith—He is there."

A hush fell over the crowd.

She let the words settle before continuing. "Sometimes we try to shift our hurt onto people who had nothing to do with it. The past tried to own me. It tried to own my father, and it's owned others before us. But here's what I've learned in my story. The enemy doesn't get the final say, and darkness doesn't get the final word. Christ does. I don't even know where my father is now. But I do know where my Heavenly Father is, and He's never left me. He won't leave you, either."

She let out a breath, glancing toward the front row. Sharon sat there, hands clasped in her lap, watching her with quiet encouragement. Their friendship had been unlikely, unexpected—but real. And it had grown into something she never could have imagined.

Just two years ago, they had stood on opposite sides of a family's grief. Now? They stood together.

And James...her strong, steady love, who stood by her when she wasn't sure if she could stand herself.

Her eyes flickered to where he sat, her husband now. He gave her the smallest smile, but the warmth in his gaze said everything.

Addie stayed home, and Reese couldn't be more thankful. She and James had adopted their first baby, a girl named Ellen Catherine. Sharon was thrilled.

Reese turned her attention back to the crowd.

"My father lost himself," she said softly. "But I didn't have to. And neither do you."

She hesitated for a moment, then glanced down at the small locket resting against her collarbone. "I'm wearing my friend's locket today, just as another woman before me did. I read a letter from her once, a woman who lived long before my time. She spoke of how important it is to remember the people we love, how even when they're gone, their stories live on. And she was right. Our stories matter. And that's why I write. I've spent the past year putting my story onto pages. I realize now that God gave me a voice, so I'm going to use it. I write because I know what it's like to feel unseen, unheard, unwanted. And I want others to know that no matter how deep their wounds, no matter how far they've strayed, they are never too lost to be found."

A few heads bowed, some nodding in quiet agreement, others wiping away tears. Reese took a breath.

"And if there's anything I've learned through all this, it's that we don't fight our battles alone. We never have to." She smiled, letting her voice lift with quiet conviction. "And that's what I stand on today."

She let the final words settle, scanning the faces before her. So many carried their own battles, their own wounds.

"We were never meant to stand alone," she said, her voice steady. "Not in our grief, and not in our fear. The enemy thrives in isolation, in keeping us convinced that no one understands, that no one will stand with us. But that's a lie. A lie meant to keep us weak, to keep us from reaching for the strength found in Christ—and in each other."

She let the truth settle in the room, pressing it deep.

"We fight together," she continued. "We stand together. Because without Christ, and without His people, we are vulnerable. But with Him? With each other? The darkness doesn't stand a chance."

A quiet breath escaped her lips.

The past no longer had a grip on her.

And for the first time, she wasn't just free—she was surrounded.

———

A warmth filled the auditorium, though no one could see its source.

High above the stage, where light shimmered between the rafters, two figures stood in quiet observation. Their forms were woven of radiance and fire, their presence ancient yet ever watchful.

Raphael inclined his head, his gaze resting on the woman below. "She speaks the truth now."

Beside him, Uriel watched as Reese took her seat, the echoes of her words still lingering in the air. "It was never about the evil at the bridge," he murmured. "Not really. It was about what bound them to it."

"A binding that has been broken."

Tyrius stood nearby, his golden-hilted sword resting against his back. "The light was always greater. She only had to reach for it."

Lior, silent as ever, studied the gathering of women below. "She is not the same as she was." His voice carried the weight of something unseen. "The wounds remain, but she stands. And in standing, she leads."

Raphael's gaze flickered toward the front row, where Sharon sat. "They were never meant to walk alone."

Uriel nodded. "Few are."

Far below, Reese lifted her head, her eyes catching Sharon's for a brief moment, an unspoken understanding passing between them.

The angels observed, unseen but ever present.

"The mark of light remains," one whispered as they began to fade from view, their presence slipping beyond time itself.

A bridge had been crossed.

And on the other side, the angels rejoice.

A Note from the Author

Dear Reader,

Thank you for joining me on this journey through *A Bridge to Die On*. This story, though fictional, is rooted in the deep and often unseen battles we all face—spiritual and emotional. Reese and Catherine, though separated by time, each experience what many of us know too well: isolation.

Sometimes we isolate ourselves out of shame, fear, rejection, or the belief that no one would understand our burdens—or want to. Yet, we were never meant to stand alone. God designed us for community—to bear one another's burdens, to encourage, and to walk alongside each other in both joy and suffering. The body of Christ is meant to be a refuge, though at times, broken people within the church can unintentionally push others further into isolation. Still, God calls us to seek fellowship, knowing that through His people, we often experience His love most tangibly. And, in ways we don't always recognize at first, there are seasons when God Himself calls us into isolation, not to harm us, but to draw us closer, to refine us, and to reveal His presence when all else seems lost.

This theme is woven into every part of this story because it's a truth I've experienced, and one I believe many readers carry silently.

You may also notice that the story draws inspiration from the real-life legend of Stuckey's Bridge, a well-known piece of Mississippi folklore from Meridan, Mississippi. Over the years, the bridge has been surrounded by ghost stories and local legends, most of which paint Stuckey as a ruthless innkeeper who preyed on travelers. I took some liberties with the legend, but what drew me to it wasn't the ghost story as much as what the bridge itself represented — how the past and present often meet in ways we don't expect.

And how redemption often waits on the other side when we're willing to face the past with His grace.

I hope you found within these pages not just suspense or intrigue, but also a quiet reminder that no matter how distant God may feel, or how isolated you may become, His grace is never far. Even when we cannot see it, He is building a bridge of hope beneath our feet.

Thank you for reading. May this story linger with you and, perhaps, offer you hope the next time you feel alone.

Soli Deo Gloria,

Fayla Ott

About the Author

Fayla Ott is the author of historical and supernatural suspense novels that aren't afraid to face the dark — and still point to the light. She writes stories where broken people wrestle with deep questions of faith, family, and redemption. Whether grounded in history or tinged with the supernatural, Fayla's books explore how grace meets us even in the loneliest and most haunted places.

When not writing, Fayla juggles life on a small farm with her husband and youngest son, teaching college English, homeschooling, and keeping the coffee pot warm. She loves hiking, traveling, quiet mornings, and the kind of storytelling that lingers long after the last page.

You can connect with her online at www.faylaott.com.

Acknowledgements

I want to thank my husband, who not only encouraged me through every step of this story but who also stood beside me — on the very bridge that inspired it. That trip meant more to me than he knows, and I'll always be grateful for the way he walks with me, both in life and in story.

Also by Fayla Ott

- *The Golden Hour* (Arledge Hall Book One)

- *The Longest Day* (Arledge Hall Book Two)

- *Afflicted*

- *Seventy Times Seven*

- *A Bridge to Die On*

For updates on upcoming releases visit my website at www.faylaott.com

A Small Favor

If this story meant something to you, I'd be so grateful if you'd consider leaving a review.

Your words help other readers find the book and encourage me more than you know.

You can leave a review on my website, or feel free to leave it at the book retailer of your choice. I also welcome and appreciate book reviews on Goodreads!

Thank you for taking this journey with me.

~Fayla

You can scan the QR code to leave a review on Fayla's site:

Newsletter Signup

Stay Connected!

Want to hear about new books, behind-the-scenes details, and exclusive offers?

I'd love for you to join my newsletter.

You can sign up anytime at:

www.faylaott.com

Or Scan the QR code: